Bones
&
Bloodlines

LAURIE ALBERSWERTH

BONES & BLOODLINES

A Jude and Audie West Mystery

Bear Write Media

St. Louis

This book is a work of fiction. Names, characters, places, and incidents are products of the author's imagination or are used fictitiously. Any resemblance to actual events, locales, organizations, or persons, living or dead, is entirely coincidental. (Also, the author is aware that, as of the publishing date, no Jeep is rated to tow the Wests' travel trailer. She has hopes for the future.)

Cover design by Laurie Alberswerth

Cover illustrations by Michael Alberswerth and Laurie Alberswerth

Title font, Odachi, used gratefully with permission from creator Mehmet Tugcu

ISBN (paperback): 978-1-960550-00-2
ISBN (ebook): 978-1-960550-01-9

Published by Bear Write Media, St. Louis, Missouri, USA

Want a sneak peek at Audie's notes as she and Jude begin this adventure?
Head over to **www.LaurieAlberswerth.com** for a FREE download!

Dedication

To my amazing husband, artist extraordinaire, and partner in every exploit, Michael. We're not the Wests, but we'd get along with them great in real life. And you'll always be the Jude to my Audie. Only a spouse knows the crazy that lies within a writer—I can't thank you enough for living with it so well.

This book is also dedicated to all the family and friends (most especially my long-suffering parents, Bill and Charlene Wilman) who have asked 7.9 million times if the book is finished yet. Guess what—it's finished! Well, this one is, anyway. See, Book 2 is coming soon, but my characters are staging a protest, and my laptop is impersonating a brick, and no, I can't name a launch date quite yet so please stop asking, and look! Something shiny!

My love and thanks to you all.

"And each separate dying ember

wrought its ghost upon the floor."

-*The Raven*, Edgar Allan Poe

CHAPTER 1

The jagged stone sliced through the vellum—and Audie's palm—with precision to rival a chef's knife. As red droplets bloomed across the wax rubbing and blotted out all the pertinent details, Audie remembered why she left the cooking to her husband.

"Lovely." She sat back onto the leaf-covered ground for a whole three seconds before the earlier rain added insult to injury. Jeans soaked, wax swallowed by the weeds, she scrambled to her feet. "Oh for Pete's sake."

"Did you say something?" Jude materialized from the cornfield that bordered three sides of the tiny graveyard, carrying an armload of pale yellow, unshucked ears. His black hair fluttered over his left eye, and he swung his head to shift it. As usual, it didn't help.

"Just that Elise Durand continues to be a problem a hundred and sixty years after her death." She held out the ripped parchment as he neared.

"Sweetheart, if she's still bleeding, we have bigger problems than we knew."

Audie examined her skin where the gravestone had lodged its grievances. "No worries. It's not the specter who's bleeding."

He piled the corn at the base of a rotting tree, swatted dust off his jacket, and lifted her hand. "In my non-professional opinion, it doesn't appear life-threatening."

"We're in the right spot if it is."

"Don't say that. This plot was like trying to track down lost Aztec gold. I'll never find my way, alone, on the anniversary of your demise." He drew her close, his free arm pointing toward a vision of his bereaved future. "Picture me, all weepy, bearing flowers…"

She gave him the damaged rubbing and a peck on the cheek, then wriggled away from his personal stage play. Heading for the backpack beside Philippe Durand's older obelisk, she said, "Guess I'd better live. I'd hate to be the cause of all that drama." She pulled a tissue from the bag's front pocket, closing her fist around it. "New topic: why do you have corn?"

"Peace offering to the skunk. If we feed him tonight, maybe he won't circle so close to the fire."

"I'd say get enough for the raccoons too, but it's a state park campground, Jude. Feeding the wildlife is frowned upon."

"I'm not giving out Budweiser and Pringles. I just don't want him near the camper. Or us."

"The Pringles might work better."

"That's not sustenance, woman. Have I taught you nothing?"

She checked her hand, plucked a bandage from behind the tissues, and covered the cut. Tearing another sheet of paper off the roll, she returned to Elise. "Is the plan to roast those ears, basted in butter, rosemary, and garlic?"

He paused. "That's an idea. Maybe you have been listening."

In front of the stone again, she stepped into her footprints and peered down at the fallen foliage.

"If you're waiting for Madame Durand to rise and say hello," Jude said, "this ends our genealogical partnership."

"I dropped the wax."

"Ah." He turned to the corn. "Fortunately, I have a hawk for a wife. I give you three seconds to find—"

"Got it!" She reached to where the small, dark disk peeked from under a sycamore leaf the size of a beagle.

"Small rodents should be wary, Eagle Eye."

"I thought I was a hawk." She reclaimed her spot on the memorial's base and smoothed the new paper over the lettering. "Help me hold this, will you? We're low on tape."

He once more abandoned his ill-gotten grains and pinched the top of the sheet. Nearby, leaves rattled along the edge of the short, wrought iron fence, unable to escape the cemetery. "I can't believe where we found her."

As the black wax brought the engraving into focus, a blast of October wind cut through Audie's coat and she shivered. Four plots—four marked plots, anyway—made up the entire local population. Children Emile and Eliot were both dead before their second birthdays, a year apart. Six months after Eliot, beloved husband Philippe was gone too. The image of a woman bowed beneath that much grief frosted Audie's sight as Elise's own mortal end—September 9, 1861—took shape.

Then the paper tore again.

"You've got to be kidding me. I knew we should've used interfacing instead of vellum."

"We don't do enough rubbings to perfect the technique."

"They're falling out of favor because some folks aren't as careful as they should be." The jagged spot mocked her. "I don't want us to get a reputation like that."

Jude leaned forward for a better view. "We can fix the tear from the back. Bob will be elated we found her after all the searching he'd done. This was one tough mother. Or great-great-great-grandmother."

Audie sighed but finished the transfer. "Locating a grave doesn't solve the whole mystery."

"Nothing ever solves the whole mystery. There's always more to find, or we'd be unemployed. At least we have a date of death and a final resting place."

"And a half-dozen new questions." She ran over the inscription one more time, surveyed her work, and stood. She took the sheet from Jude and rolled it, tapping the ends to even them. "I don't think Elise wanted to be found."

"What do you mean?"

"We're on the far edge of a cornfield, hidden in the woods. A narrow dirt path—"

"Mud path."

"—a narrow mud path is the single means of access to a postage-stamp-sized burial plot. We spent three months hunting through records and satellite images, and the homestead is still hiding. No other relations are buried here—only Elise and her first of four families."

Jude nodded. "We can't find the husband who gave us our client, and her marker goes after a pound of your flesh. Yeah, okay, maybe she didn't want to be found." He studied the name carved generations ago. "Good reminder that not every old story is a romantic one. We don't know what might've been going on in the life of Madame Durand."

He reached for Audie's hand, but she snatched it away. "Sorry. Filleted flesh, remember?"

"Whoops."

"Blame Elise." As Audie packed her supplies and slid the

parchment into a plastic sleeve, Jude frowned at the rutted road they needed to walk to their ride.

"We should've gone ahead and driven that last bit."

"No, you were right to stop. Better to have muddy shoes than get stuck miles from town."

"The Jeep could've made it." His look of consternation shifted to the dead tree.

"Ah—the corn. Well, I can bring the backpack, and you take the vermin offering."

"We put that bag on you and you'll wind up tipped over like an inverted turtle."

"I'm not an invalid."

"No, inverted. Or a penguin with no sense of its own center of gravity. Either way, the bag weighs a ton and you do not." He ran a hand through the bangs once more flopping across his eye. "I saw an old sheet or something caught on stalks between the field and the woods. I can use that as a sack for the corn."

Those long legs carried his lean frame over the fence and into the world beyond. She grinned. In the midst of a job, rooting out the fundamentals of people who lived centuries ago, her other half worried about distracting skunks. Gourmet skunks.

Elise had gone through four spouses. Audie prayed she'd never have need of a Number Three.

A yelp rose from beyond the trees.

"Jude?" *Please be him and not an angry corn monster.*

"Hey, Aud." Okay, not a corn monster. But his voice… "Could I borrow you for a second?"

Her stomach sank. She dropped the rubbing and darted through the fence gate, a thousand likely scenarios and several unlikely ones racing with her. He was hurt. He fell into a cistern. He tripped on an abandoned piece of farm equipment—wouldn't be the first time for that one—and now intestines were spilling onto the soil.

Rough corn leaves smacked at her face as she tried and failed to stay on the wooded side of the line. "Jude? Hon, where are you?" The wind through the stalks and her feet trampling downed husks drowned out everything else. "Jude!"

He emerged from the woods and grabbed her before she could take another step. She scanned him up and down. "You're okay? You're not hurt?"

"No, no, I'm fine." Keeping one hand on her arm, he moved aside. "But I don't think he is."

Audie's panting breath caught in her throat as the hollow sockets of a human skull stared up at her from the muck. Beside it lay a filthy, water-logged blanket, rolled like a burrito, with more dingy yellow bones protruding from the top. Her hand shot to her mouth. "Oh dear Lord."

Near the cemetery, a car door slammed.

CHAPTER 2

"Stay behind me," Jude whispered.

She gripped his jacket sleeve, almost stepping on his heels, as he crept toward the clearing and the low fence. "Didn't plan otherwise."

Tension seemed to bleed from the leather coat. An isolated graveyard, a dried-out crop, an extra skeleton where it shouldn't have been…

Maybe those were her nerves she felt, not his.

The front bumper of a vehicle peeked from the stalks by the farm road, but the cemetery was empty. Where was he? Or she? Or they? Jude neared the dead tree.

A figure loomed from behind the black trunk, titanic and shadowed. Audie's heart shot straight from of her chest and landed somewhere in eastern Wisconsin.

"Care to explain what you're doing on private land?" the baritone voice boomed. Of course it did. Demon corn monsters had to speak with authority.

Gradually, the beast transfigured, solidifying into a broad-shouldered man—human—wearing a tan police uniform and an olive green coat. One hand held their backpack, the other rested near his hip holster. As Audie wondered who to contact in Sheboygan to retrieve her runaway organ, Jude pulled himself up to his full height. *That'll help.* He was still at least three inches shorter than the officer and outweighed by a time and a half.

"We needed access to this cemetery for family-tree research," Jude said. "That's allowed under Missouri state law."

"These are your relatives? I didn't even know there was a plot in these parts."

"You're not the only one. But they're not ours. We're genealogy researchers. Someone hired us to find a couple of missing ancestors for them."

The man cocked his head, trying to guess which planet they'd beamed in from. "That's a job?"

"For us, yes. Check the bag. We were doing rubbings of the Durands' gravestones." He reached out. "Jude West. This is my wife, Audra."

"Audie." She slipped around Jude, offering what she hoped was one of her more charming smiles.

He hesitated, then took the bait. "Sheriff Owen Carmichael. I saw the fresh ruts off the road, then your car back there." He opened their pack, gave a cursory inspection of the vellum, notebooks, and maps tucked inside, and zipped it again. "This path doesn't get much use unless they're harvesting, and your tracks didn't look like Kirby's Deere. Figured it was kids in the cornfield getting set to do something stupid, but the Jeep was too nice."

Jude chuckled. "If you knew how many miles were on it, you wouldn't think so."

The moment's relief blew away with another stiff gust, and Audie nudged her husband's ribs. "Shouldn't we, uh—"

"Right. Sheriff, just came across something you need to see."

Carmichael hooked a thumb over his shoulder at the tombstones. "Bodies in the middle of a cornfield? Not too surprising, really. Small family graveyards can be found all over the county."

"Those bodies aren't the ones we're worried about. You want to walk on down this line between the field and the woods?"

The lawman's forehead furrowed, and Audie watched his fingers touch the grip of his gun. Two strangers in farm country, near dusk, hanging in a cemetery well off the beaten path—sure, that doesn't seem murdery. "Jude, it may be better if we go first."

Carmichael nodded. "Lead the way."

Jude took to the trail, slowing as he neared the grisly find. Yet, it wasn't grisly. As he skirted to the side, she searched for a speck of flesh or hair or gore anywhere nearby. Nothing. Merely bones and the dirty blanket, lying a full row inside of the corn stalks. At the corner of the blanket was an embroidered insignia, sewn in what must've once been red thread. The anemic pink seemed to be the outline of a building with letters below it.

Audie joined Jude at the side of the trail, giving the big man his first clear view. With a torrent of expletives, he stumbled to a flailing stop, at last catching himself enough to end the sequence with a plea to Jesus, Mary, and Joseph.

After a moment, the sheriff squared up his shoulders, cleared his throat, and bent down for a closer examination. How the body was shrouded—it seemed snug around the bones. Did someone use the blanket to carry this person into the field? Or were they shielding them from the elements?

Oddly sentimental, considering.

Carmichael clambered onto his hands and knees in the thick leaves, twisting his head almost upside-down to peek into the wrapping. "Better wait for the crime scene folks before I touch anything. Wish I could see a little more, though." The wind rose to remind them it was late October. "And it's going to be after dark before anyone can get here. Not how I thought I'd be spending the evening."

With much effort, he regained his feet. His brawn wasn't fat, though the vegan option lost to burgers most nights. He was probably as good at reassuring his citizens as he was intimidating those brewing up mischief. He studied the mud on his palms and trousers with a frown. "Are you two staying at the hotel out by the interstate?"

"No, we're over at the state park. Fillion. Got a camper there we travel in while we're working." Which was always, not that he needed to know that. Homeless by choice sounds like homeless-homeless to certain people.

An eyebrow rose, but the instinct to reach for the gun passed. Progress. "You do much of your work in Missouri?"

"About three-quarters of it," Jude nodded. "The state has genealogical goldmines. We have so many old-country communities—some French like here in Renarde, some German, Italian. Endless immigrant stories."

"The parks make great bases," Audie added. "Clients who hire us aren't searching for info from the metro areas like St. Louis or Kansas City. We go into the field and do the legwork they can't do."

"The field isn't always this literal, though."

Three gazes returned to the corpse at their feet.

"Right. I better call this in pronto. I'm afraid you two are going to have to talk to my deputy in town, give him your story, and leave your contact information."

"Of course." Was she beaming her most virtuous, law-abiding

expression at the officer? Based on Jude's poorly hidden smirk in her peripheral vision, yes.

Together, the trio started along the path to the cemetery, tromping through the undergrowth. Jude broke the gloomy silence. "I've got to ask, Sheriff. Do you have any idea who that body could be?"

The man didn't answer right away. He plodded toward his SUV without pause. At the graveyard, Jude hustled to grab the backpack and Elise's rubbing, and they hurried to catch up. Carmichael had the door open and was already climbing in.

"Sheriff?"

Behind the wheel, he deflated more than sat in the seat. After his tough-guy introduction, the shock at their find, and the subdued manner that had kicked in as they communed over a misplaced skeleton, he added another to the many faces of Owen Carmichael. The tense jawline of this one told her what he'd say before he said it. "A body decomposed that long? Yeah, I'm afraid I might."

Chapter 3

In contrast to the husky sheriff who was close to Audie's age, the deputy sitting across the desk from her might need his mother's consent to be absent from school. *When did twenty-two become so young?*

When did forty-three become so old?

"We don't get a lot of bodies around here," Officer Pelton almost giggled. During the fifteen-minute interview, he'd vacillated between giddiness and nausea. His cheeks turned chartreuse at their description of the skeleton, but otherwise, he teetered on the edge of excitement. Such a thing happening in his small, southeast Missouri town—who would've thought? Audie half-expected him to pull out his phone and ask for a selfie with them for his girlfriend.

Assuming he was allowed to date yet.

"That's often seen as a good thing," Jude said. She cringed as he gave the officer one of those classic Jude looks. Her trim husband, with those gorgeous cheek bones and the bit of flopping black fringe, could play the tough guy as well as Carmichael. As God had not blessed him with brawn, he simply had to do it with words and demeanor. Deputy James Barrett Pelton—"JB!" according to the piece of printer paper taped to his desk as a nameplate—cleared his throat and straightened his posture, adopting a more serious visage.

"Right." He scoured his chicken-scratched notes—the notes he'd already typed and could read easily if he'd check the computer screen inches from his face. Audie exhaled a deliberate, steady breath, and searched her memory for the patron saint of patience. "Okay, you were searching for a dead woman—"

"Yes and no. The one we were hoping for would've been underground for a century and a half."

"But you ended up finding a skeleton. What were you doing that far into the corn?"

"Hunting for children." Jude didn't miss a beat. "I'd heard voices."

JB's horrified face was more than Audie could bear. "He was picking a few ears of corn. He thought he saw a scrap of loose material—maybe a sheet or a leftover seed bag—and wanted to use it to carry them to the car."

"You were picking corn? You know that stuff's not for eating, right?" The horror had now morphed from worrying about their sanity to realizing they were something worse than crazy. They were city people.

"We know. It was for the skunk."

JB opened his mouth, but decided against questioning the statement. "Sure. The skunk." The keys clicked beneath his fingers. Audie feared what he might be typing. "You guys go around digging up family trees, huh? My aunt does that from her laptop."

Jude began to answer; Audie cut him off. They would never escape at this rate. Night had long fallen, dinner was but a dream, and a furry, black-and-white battalion probably surrounded their camper even as they sat. "Much has been digitized, yes. But there are still places, like the little Durand plot, where you can find information not documented anywhere else. As it is, our client is looking for a married couple, and we haven't found the mister yet, the woman's second husband. He disappears from the records, and suddenly a relative is raising their only child. No paper trails for any of them, so no computer data. That's why we're here."

"You visit a lot of cemeteries?"

"Yes. And libraries, courthouses, newspaper archives, local hangouts and restaurants…"

"Speaking of which, Deputy, are we almost done?" Jude's stomach growled on cue. "Lunch was a long time and an unidentified body ago."

The youngster scanned his monitor. "Yeah, I think I've got everything for now. Owen—um, the Sheriff—can get in touch with you if he has any more questions."

"We'll be working around town for at least a few days while we fill in the blanks on our case. Just call."

"Will do." They stood, and JB remembered at the last second he was Officer Pelton and gave his best firm handshake to Jude. To Audie, it was a "questioning all the rules on handshakes" handshake. She smiled. He was cute.

She could've been his mother.

Good grief.

She led the way to the front of the old brick station, feeling Jude's fingertips on the small of her back. With Oliver, that had driven her crazy. But he'd been a physical therapist. She'd always felt like one of his stroke patients, ready to topple in a heartbeat. Since Oliver? That light touch held different meaning.

A lot of things did.

At the entrance, she reached for the knob, but the door burst inward on them, sending her stumbling into Jude as a khaki-and-olive-green cyclone stormed the building. Owen Carmichael pulled up short.

"Sorry!"

Audie righted herself, returning her hobo bag's strap to her shoulder. "No worries. Anything wrong, Sheriff?"

He stared at her, or maybe through her, then yanked his hat off his straw-colored hair. He kneaded the hat in his big hands. "The body." He exhaled all the strain in a single rush of air. "It's who I thought it was."

JB Pelton rounded his desk, tripping over his wastebasket. "You mean—"

"Yeah. It's Cassie Powers."

CHAPTER 4

Seating herself at the diner's last open table, Audie did her best to ignore the sixteen strangers appraising their every move. Small-town curiosity was nothing new. And outsiders didn't arrive for late dinners on Monday evenings where the population is less than eighteen hundred.

She and Jude had been surprised when the parking lot to Metcalfe & Son's Family Restaurant—both the first "e" and the ampersand flickering in the neon signage—was jammed with cars at 8:10 p.m. Other Main Street businesses were dark, the sidewalks rolled up and stowed away for the night. The resulting gloom seemed a set stage for Saturday's Halloween holiday. But the buzz that grew in pitch when the two passed through the swinging glass doors explained a lot. Word had already spread across Renarde and probably the whole county by now: the body of Cassie Powers had finally been found.

To avoid the stares and the greasy menus, Audie studied the dessert case. Beside the display of meringue pies taller than they were wide, last week's *Renarde Gazette* announced: "Vietnam vet to be repatriated. Local boy coming home." Busy time for recovered Renardians. The title font must've been two inches tall. *After that much time, it should be.* She could read the first paragraph listing the soldier's name and date of disappearance. Beyond that, the print dropped to a size illegible from eight feet away.

A teenage girl in jeans and a pink plaid shirt approached the table with an order book and pen poised. Polite, she asked what they'd have to drink, told them the decaf coffee would be ready in a few, and went on her way. Her way, though, was only as far as the window to the kitchen, from which she pointed out her new associates—the tired-looking foreigners—to the cook.

Bringing the coffees and taking their orders for two chef salads—which earned them renewed gawking from the chicken-fried chicken supporters around them—Ginny the waitress loitered longer than necessary. Endeavoring to sound as nonchalant as a sixteen-year-old can, she asked, "So, are you two here for Spark in the Park?"

"We're here on a research mission," Jude said, handing her the laminated menu with the twinkling half-smile that had ridiculous effects on the female gender.

Audie had never believed in that sort of twinkle before him. *I'll never doubt again.*

Before the girl melted into a puddle and they never got their salad orders, they needed a distraction. "What's Spark in the Park?"

Ginny had to pick up her eyeballs from Jude's paper placemat and schlepp them across the table to answer. "It's this big thing every Halloween. It's actually called Cinders and Cider, but mostly we just call it the Spark. There's a parade before sunset, then the little kids do their trick-or-treating. After that, we have a huge party at the city park."

"Sounds fun."

"There's food and games and music. But that's not the best part.

They light a gigantic bonfire, like that deal in Arizona."

"Nevada," Jude chimed in. And there goes her attention. "Burning Man."

"Yeah. That. Anyway, they've been doing the Spark since way before I was born."

"Wow." That long. Ah, youth.

"But it almost didn't make it past its first year." Ginny was on a roll now as she dropped her voice and leaned in. "Because that's the night when Cassie Powers disappeared."

Like a lid on a sarcophagus, the entire restaurant fell silent. The name hung in the air, a poltergeist. Their guileless server paled as she realized she'd spoken unspeakable words.

A tall, slim man in a denim shirt and a pocket name tag reading "Rick Metcalfe" appeared at their table and steered the girl toward the kitchen. "It's all right, Ginny. How about you go put these good folks' order in, okay? I think they'd like to eat before midnight." She nodded and scurried from sight.

The man returned to the two—Audie had to lean backward in her seat to make eye contact. "I'm sorry about that. She's kind of excitable in the best of circumstances, and we had some bad news here in town today."

Conversation around them resumed, but never rose above a murmur. Each table still had at least one ear to theirs.

Jude stood long enough to shake the restaurateur's hand. "Jude West. This is my wife, Audra. I'm afraid we're a too familiar with the bad news."

"You are?"

"We're the ones who found the body."

"Oh, I see. That couldn't have been a pleasant way to be welcomed to Renarde." He gave a glance around the room, and thirty-two peepers darted to their plates. "I heard you telling Ginny you're here for research? Are you writing a book?"

Audie answered. "We're genealogists. A client hired us to find ancestors who've fallen off his family tree."

"That's a job?"

Don't roll your eyes. Don't roll your eyes. "Yes, and a pretty interesting one. We'd found a plot we were searching for when we came across…" Heat rose in her cheeks. That was someone's daughter, someone's friend.

The tall man sighed. "It's still sad. The decades don't stop that."

Ginny arrived with two large salads—a pallid pile of iceberg lettuce crushed under the weight of cheddar cheese, ham cubes, egg crumbles, and a ladle's worth of thin ranch dressing. Even Rick winced at the plates.

"We're more about our fried foods here. Should've recommended the chicken."

Audie assured him it was fine, then prodded the mound with her fork for anything resembling a vegetable. Jude dug in with gusto. *Now I know he's hungry.*

"I should let you two eat in peace."

He started to move off, but Jude swiped at a dribble running down his chin and said, "Why don't you grab a seat, Mr. Metcalfe, and tell us about what happened? If you have a minute."

People seemed to decide the show was over for the night, and the restaurant's denizens dwindled. Those paying their bills at the counter still hovered close to their table. But once they got their receipts and had their doggy bags bundled against the chilly air outside, they lost their opportunity to eavesdrop without also losing their status as proper Christians. Rick dragged over a red, vinyl-covered chair.

"It's been thirty years." He shook his head. "I can't believe it myself. The Powers girl, Cassie, was Alice and Gordon Powers' daughter. She had two brothers, Tom and Brice. Tom was a bit older, Brice a bit younger. Cassie was a senior in high school when it happened—we were in the same class. Good student—not valedictorian, mind you, but decent grades. College bound. She ran track, worked over at the drugstore. The single bad choice she ever made was going around with that Kane boy."

"Kane boy?"

His jaw tensed. "Hunter Kane. The kind of boy you'd say was from the other side of the tracks if Renarde had a train running through it."

"Troublemaker?"

He grimaced. "Rough home life, chip on his shoulder. Stepfather was always drunk and beating the mother. Kid got caught stealing. He'd pick a fight with you as soon as look at you, especially if you were what they called the jocks. Held a grudge against the kids who were going to do something with their lives." He paused, anger settling into weariness. "When Cassie started keeping company with Kane, there were a lot of unhappy people."

"I guess her parents weren't thrilled."

"Her dad was the local accountant, a real nice guy but buried in his work. The mother was the fretting type. They tried to get her to steer clear of him."

"How do you know?"

Rick turned on Jude with a scoff. "Wouldn't you? If it was your daughter?"

"He's only asking a question, Mr. Metcalfe," Audie said.

His lips drew into a thin line. "Yeah. Sorry. It's just—all this stuff from a lifetime ago, getting stirred up now?" He took in a deep breath and exhaled. “And, please. It’s Rick. I’m actually the ‘and Son’ of Metcalfe and Son’s, though my father passed quite a while ago.”

“What a nice legacy, being able to serve your hometown.”

He chuckled. “Mostly, it’s nice. Some days, it’s like the place won’t let you go.”

Jude resumed stabbing at salad remnants. Audie surrendered in defeat. Rick plucked a sugar packet from the ceramic holder and started playing with it.

“When Kane and Cassie disappeared that night, everyone knew it was going to end badly.”

Audie’s breath caught, and Jude fumbled with his fork. “Wait—this Hunter kid disappeared too?”

“Nobody realized they were both gone right away, of course. Too much chaos from it happening during that first Cinders festival. Almost all of Renarde was involved in the parade or the food booths. I was helping set up the bonfire. Lots of distractions.”

Jude shifted in his seat, an uncomfortable expression falling across his face. “Why hasn’t anyone mentioned this boy yet?”

“What do you mean?”

“Two seventeen-year-olds disappear together and no one talks about one of them?”

That uneasiness was catching, but Rick shrugged to cover it. “I guess nobody cares much about a murderer.”

“Come again?”

He leaned back, his palms open wide. “It makes sense, doesn’t it? A massive search went on for weeks. With no leads, it lost momentum when we had a major snowstorm first of December. No trace of either of them turned up, so everybody figured Cassie had met a bad end and the boy was to blame.”

"Why couldn't they have run off? Ditched the town where no one liked seeing them together and started over?"

"Hey, now," Rick began to rise.

Audie grabbed his arm, keeping her voice level. "Seriously, Rick, what was the theory at the time?"

"They didn't run off together." He spoke the words holding Jude in a steady gaze, then he turned to Audie and resettled in his seat. "They didn't. On the afternoon of Halloween, Cassie had been working at the drugstore. She got off at five and had promised to walk a neighbor girl, Emma, over to the festival after Emma's mother took her trick-or-treating. She left the store at five o'clock, but she never made it to the house. Cassie was not one of your flighty, irresponsible teenage girls. If she said she was going to do a thing, she did it."

Ginny floated by the table, refilled coffee cups while spilling half, and flittered off, the tears of lost caffeine trailing her.

"More so than most," he continued. "Anyway, with Kane disappearing, too, the prevailing theory was he tried something with her and when she didn't go along with it, well…" His voice trailed off, and he scrutinized the wet splashes on the tabletop.

Audie took a sip from the mug, struggling not to make a face. She peered across at Jude, the worry lines growing deeper by the second beneath that fringe of black hair. "It's been a long day, Rick. I think we'd better pay our bill and let you start closing for the night."

He pushed away from the table, the chair's metal legs squeaking along the mustard-yellow linoleum. "Your meal's on the house. We've waited a lifetime to learn what happened to that girl."

"Thank you very much, but I'm afraid you still don't know what happened to her."

Jude frowned. "There's always another mystery."

* * *

As they rolled into the wooded campground, the Jeep's headlights passed over a telltale stripe waddling across the road.

"Well, shoot. I left the corn at the cemetery, didn't I?"

"So much for Dr. Evil's brilliant scheme."

Jude pulled the car around and backed into their space, placing them in front of the travel trailer like he'd done it once or twice, which he had. Among the electric sites, strings of miniature plastic pumpkins, lit by LEDs, surrounded a large RV several spots away. At another camper, similar in size to theirs, Audie watched lime-colored glow sticks bobbing manically. Too many s'mores, too close to bedtime. The grandparents traveling with the kiddos were going to regret that decision and soon.

Dropping down from the seat, she breathed in the familiar smell of camp smoke and peered into the night toward the primitive sites. One brave tent stood against the late October chill. Orange flames leapt from the fire pit, and she could see two silhouettes huddled near it. Their voices carried, as they always did across these grounds, but nothing was distinguishable. And nothing raucous for a change. Only true nature lovers slept in a nylon dome on a cold Monday—not like some of the louder, river-floating groups who drank their way down summer streams by day, napped, then shot straight into rowdy belligerence after sunset.

Audie was not a fan.

Their skunk friend made for the Halloween lights—a quieter locale than where the kids were, yet with snack food potential. Smart fellow. He wasn't getting anything from the Wests tonight. They'd skip their customary fire. She wanted nothing more than to get into the warm camper and sleep.

Or pretend to sleep.

Close enough.

Jude grabbed the backpack of notes and the day's rubbings, and caught up with her at the side of the trailer. "Home sweet home," he exhaled as she unlocked the door and climbed the two steps into the space.

Eighteen feet of heaven, Audie thought, plodding in and shedding her coat. Toasty. Quiet. Cozy as the womb. Their retro-style house on wheels with the hot-rod red detailing had all they needed, though the word "tiny" applied to everything but the queen-sized bed. The table-slash-desk had seating for two. The kitchen came equipped with a two-burner stove, microwave, and a stainless-steel sink large enough for a dinner plate. The gourmet with whom she shared life had mastered efficient loading of the fridge and freezer—no ash-encrusted frankfurters for these happy campers.

Yes, everything they needed, even if the bathroom shower was such a size and shape they called it the Jefferies tube.

Oh well. For space, they had the entire outdoors at their disposal. Besides, it's a built-in fitness incentive: gain weight at your own peril.

Jude had a secondary wellness initiative: wood chopping. Whether or not they wanted for fire fuel, she knew where to find him if he needed to think, burn off nervous energy, or beat the heck out of something that wasn't an imbecile offending his rock-solid grasp of right and wrong.

Excellent policy. Even better exercise program.

He deposited the bag on the bench behind the table as she dropped onto the edge of the bed. "Do you realize this is the first minute we've had to ourselves since the cemetery?" He glanced her way and cringed. "Yeah, you realize."

"That bad, huh? Well, it's a lot to take in."

"You can say that again." He reached into the fridge and retrieved a pair of water bottles.

She caught the one he tossed her. "We come here for one bygone mystery and end up in the middle of a second."

"The locals don't think it's much of a mystery." He ran his hand through his hair and leaned against the kitchen counter, slim legs stretched in front of him. "Metcalfe has that Hunter kid hanging from the gallows already, and I doubt he's alone."

"I wonder what happened. Since we didn't find two bodies in that cornfield, it does make him sound suspicious."

"But the field had been planted. And it's probably been planted and harvested for years. No way has the farmer not noticed a decaying corpse for three decades." He shook his head. "And I don't like the wrong-side-of-the-tracks bit. Where someone comes from isn't as telling as people think it is."

For a moment, Jude twisted and untwisted the cap of his bottle. Audie stared through the liquid in hers, watching the magnified floor beneath her feet. The rainbow colors of her striped socks danced.

"I guess we won't solve it tonight. Besides, it's the sheriff's problem, not ours." He took another drink and returned the bottle to the fridge. "What's the plan for tomorrow, boss?"

"We've found Elise. That was a big milestone."

"You mean headstone." He grinned at her sideways. That twinkle again. She smirked.

"Yes, a headstone milestone. At least we got that far. We still don't know what happened to Husband Number Two, Henri Laroque. How'd he die? Where'd he die? Where were they living? And how did their child end up in St. Louis as Elise moved on to Husbands Three and Four?"

Jude sat beside her on the bed and half-leaned, half-collapsed into her lap. "All great questions, Mrs. West. I'm impressed you still have any mental acuity." His lids closed. "I need a nap."

She laughed. "In a minute, then you can have an eight-hour one. With all these questions, I think we should start the morning at the library. Awhile back, the county provided copies of public domain vital stats to the individual towns. We ought to be able to learn something about the Renarde part of the story if we go hunting through the stacks."

"What, you mean it's not online?"

She smacked his shoulder, from which he feigned grievous injury. "No, it's not online. And yes, this is a job." She pushed him upright. "And now, Mr. West, kindly climb onto your side of the bed. You're due for a nap."

The owl hooted its seventh round of *who-cooks-for-you* before Audie surrendered and slipped from beneath the blankets. Pulling a fleece sweatshirt over her long-john-style top and flannel leggings, she slid onto the bench behind the desk. She bent the mini-light to face away from her snoozing hubby and checked the clock on the microwave—2:37 a.m.

Made it longer than usual. All it took was finding an extra corpse.

Not a sleep aid I'd recommend.

Inch by inch, she unzipped the backpack, then extracted a binder, notebook, and pen. Jude shifted, and she froze. He slept at the forward end of the bed so she could escape insomnia's prison without disturbing his need for a more robust night's rest. But he also grew antsy when she wasn't beside him. Even in REM, he wanted to be sure she was safe.

I'll never deserve him.

As he wasn't bothered by that, it worked out for everyone.

He rolled over, and his breathing found its previous rhythm. She flipped the notebook to a blank page and opened the binder to the section marked "Bob Laroque—Paternal Ancestry." Starting at their client, she traced the tree upward. Names and dates filled the lines for Bob's parents, grandparents, all the way to one set of third-great-grandparents.

The other set? The sole reason they knew names was because their son, Gareth, listed them on his marriage license in 1870. Elise Durand and Henri Laroque. No birth dates, wedding date, or homestead location. Audie penned "September 9, 1861," under Elise's entry, now that they'd discovered her final resting place. Yet there sat Henri, alone with his empty spaces.

What had happened? And why was Gareth living with his father's relatives in 1847 if his mother was still alive and well in Renarde?

Audie would've pondered this for hours, hoping to make a breakthrough before they got underway at dawn, if the heater in the camper hadn't chosen that exact moment to explode.

CHAPTER 5

The concussive ka-chunk and scream of metal had Jude off the bed before Audie could reach for the pile of things she'd knocked over.

"What in the world?"

"It came from outside." She grabbed for her jacket as he hopped on one foot, pulling on shoes. "I think it was the electric heater."

Through the door and down the stairs, she followed him into the freezing night. Frantic barking met them as the campground dogs sounded the alarm. At the forward end of the trailer, the environmental unit lay silent, a cloud of smoke carrying the acrid smell of burnt wiring.

"Aw, he—."

"Jude."

"Sorry." He unlocked the Jeep and fished a flashlight from the gear stashed in the cargo space.

"Bring a Phillips screwdriver, would you?"

Audie climbed onto the tow bar, perched herself where she wouldn't block the dusk-to-dawn lamp by the park's bathhouse, and unscrewed the face panel of the heater. Attached to the fan hub were four intact blades. Great. But there should've been five.

"Let me see the flashlight." She waved away the residual smoke and aimed the beam inside. At the end of a trail of shredded electric wires, the errant piece of metal rested mournfully in the corner. She brought the broken chunk close.

"Fatigue," Audie said, her breath visible as she sighed.

"The fan or us?"

"Both. The metal wore out. It chose now to do something about it." She peered up at him through the murkiness. "Thank God it didn't start a fire. You were sleeping directly above it."

"And you weren't sleeping at all."

She dropped her sights back to the failed heater. "No big surprise there."

"So what do we do?"

"I guess when stores open, we'll see what we can jerry-rig together until we can get to a dealer."

"Parts are going to be limited around here. Should we drive to Cape or St. Louis tomorrow?"

Delays. As usual. "I'd rather not break up our job. Let's talk to Sheriff Carmichael, ask if he can guide us in a direction for parts. Hopefully, we can repair it enough to get through this case."

"You're the mechanic."

Audie smiled despite the bitterly cold metal freezing its way through her leggings. *Those hours with Dad had been well spent.* So many widgets taken apart in that garage. Had they always worked afterward? Well, that wasn't important. What was important was she'd married a man—rather, two men—who had no ego problems regarding her being the handy one in the relationship.

Besides, she needed them to tighten nuts and lift heavy things.

At least they could say they contributed.

The wind picked up again, and the dogs quieted over time. Thank heavens the neighbors had refrained from making a "helpful" appearance. They'd satisfied themselves with bleary-eyed peeking from behind checkered curtains. The resident owl, on the other hand, was having none of it. His peaceful autumn kingdom had far too many disturbances this night. *Who-cooks-for-you-all* indeed.

"Before that bird swoops down and makes a snack of our ears, let's go inside, huh?" She set the heater's cover on the ground by the hitch, and Jude locked the Jeep. "It'll stay warm enough inside for now."

Behind her, he yawned. "What time is it?"

"Must be after four." She checked the clock as they entered the trailer—4:13. *One point to Audra West.*

Jude groaned. "Great. Too early to do anything productive, too late to try to sleep."

"You can't drift off? I'll be quiet."

"I know you will. You're so quiet, I worry you'll run off one night, and I won't realize it until my second cup of coffee. But, no, I think I'm done."

"Then let's start with the coffee. You can help me make a list of things to search for at the library later."

"Aye, aye, Captain."

On his way to the car, Jude examined the morning's tragic scene in the daylight. The broken heater looked sad. The fractured shard of fan blade waited where they'd left it inside the housing, but the front panel lay flat in the grass, knocked over by the wind or the not-yet-placated skunk. Usually, they had raccoons to contend with. Why couldn't it be raccoons? They're soft and stripey too, but without an odor best described as eau de landfill.

I'm actually missing the bandit-faced little jerks. Even after that fiasco last year. They had the gall to walk off with an entire foil packet of seasoned cheesy potatoes! What is wrong with me?

Sleep deprivation. It was the only answer. It felt like noon, considering he'd been semi-functioning for over half a normal workday already. The library would open at nine, so they could be off at last.

He stowed the backpack and a small cooler in the rear of the Jeep. No scavenging for lunch at that diner today. His stomach trembled. Surely they served good food as long as you ordered what they expected you to order. But their version of good and his may not be in the same galaxy. The sandwiches tucked away in the ice chest, with roasted chicken, red peppers, hummus, spinach, and a dab of aioli piled onto crusty oat bread, would taste delicious while not hardening any arteries he might need later.

Plus, it had given him an ounce of usefulness while Audie organized the binder and arranged their day of ghost hunting.

He closed the door and headed for the driver's seat, giving the fallen panel a glare. *Bet it was the skunk. Too bad about the corn.*

"To town, James," Audie, already situated, gave him her best British accent as he climbed in.

"You talk like that and they're really not going to believe this is a job."

She laughed. "True. But let's face it. Our line of work isn't at the top of the Labor Department's list of viable occupations."

He pulled out of the site's gravel driveway and onto the winding asphalt running to the highway. The tenters were already de-camped, tying down the last tote to the roof of their car. One frosty evening and a getaway no longer feels like any fun. *Been there.* The warmer nights of spring would see their own blue-and-green dome erected at each site they visited. But in the meantime, boy, were the comforts of the trailer nice: a real kitchen, no need to use the communal bathhouse, and heat.

At least, until the heater bit the dust. He pressed harder on the accelerator as they hit the road to Renarde. After the library, it would be straight to the hardware store. They'd need to hunt and gather to ensure they, too, didn't become popsicles overnight.

Audie pointed. "Check out all the tracks!" The turnoff to the Durand cemetery was coming up quick. The entrance was pure slop, even after the freezing temperatures. A fleet of vehicles must've moved through since yesterday afternoon.

"Popular place."

Audie didn't respond. She didn't have to.

"You want to go, don't you?"

"Do you mind?"

He slowed and steered the Jeep into an existing set of ruts. "What are you thinking?"

"For starters, I'd love to learn how they identified the body so fast."

"They can't get a lot of murders."

"No, but they still need some sort of forensic proof before they can be sure." The left front tire dropped into a pothole, and Jude's hair skimmed the ceiling. He clutched the wheel tighter, fighting to keep their spleens from becoming dislodged. "I mean," Audie continued after tugging her seatbelt taut again, "the poor girl is nothing but a skeleton, and one that's been in the elements for up to thirty years. That's not much to go on."

At last, they found a used-car lot in the middle of a cornfield. The sheriff's SUV was there, along with a four-wheel-drive Gator, a navy Chevy pickup, and an older model Ford Focus edged with rust. The Ford had seen more than its share of bad days.

Considering the half-mile expedition down this so-called road, this was one of them.

Jude pulled the Jeep over to the edge to let anyone who could escape the ruined terrain pass by. He climbed out, zipping his jacket, and turned when the other door didn't open. Audie was staring trepidatiously through the passenger window. His wife was seldom trepidatious. He walked around to her side and saw the problem—the angle at which he'd had to park would leave her dangling several feet above the ground. He grinned, negotiating the ditch and grabbing the handle.

"Need a lift?"

She bit at her lower lip. "A catch might be more useful."

He reached up, and she put her hands atop his shoulders. "Jump!" She did, and he got her to terra firma without disaster. It helped she weighed less than your average robin.

They climbed the embankment to the rutted path and dodged puddles on the way to the cemetery. Jude rose onto his toes but couldn't see anything past the stalks. *Higher than an elephant's eye, for sure.* No one would find this place if they didn't know it existed.

Merely one of a hundred curious things he'd seen since starting the family-tree business. They never knew what mystery would come next.

Yet a shiver rippled through him as they passed the sheriff's vehicle. The next mystery had never been a spare skeleton left topside.

In a low-toned conversation near the Durands' final resting spot was Carmichael, with his back to them, and two men Jude didn't recognize. *Surprising. I thought the entire town had been at the diner last night.* One man was dressed in overalls and a heavy-duty tan work coat, a faded John Deere hat topping off the ensemble. Average in build, his weathered cheeks were a ruddy color in the cutting breeze. The other man, shorter, rounder, wore a black windbreaker over his jeans. The cut of both said they weren't made for their current setting. Jude figured him to be a few years older than himself. He stood with his hands on his hips, his haggard face angled up at the farmer.

"Kirby, you can't believe that's true," the tired man was saying.

"Of course I can! It's my own dang field, ain't it?" The farmer's mouth clapped shut as he noticed the Wests. The sheriff, catching his narrowed gaze, swiveled, boots squishing in the muck.

"You two? Didn't you get enough of this yesterday?" Though he reached out his hand, the rest of him hinted heavily for them to skedaddle. No matter. They wouldn't be leaving until Audie asked her questions.

And if the group really wanted privacy, they wouldn't beat around the bush with the answers.

"We saw the new tire tracks at the road and wondered if you'd be here, Sheriff." Ah, she was radiating one of her patented angelic airs. Jude buried his hands in his coat pockets to keep from applauding the performance. "We were just wondering if we could be of any help."

"Help?" Carmichael scratched at his chin. A nick there said he'd cut himself shaving that morning. "Not sure how."

The man in the windbreaker coughed. "Owen, are these the folks—"

"Oh! Sorry, Tom." He took a step backward. "These are the Wests, Jude and Audie. They're the ones who, uh, found Cassie." An unsettled expression passed over the big man's face. "This is Tom Powers."

"Cassie's brother," Tom said as he, too, offered a hand.

"Our condolences, Mr. Powers."

"Thank you. And thank you for finding her. It's been such a

long time. I don't think anybody had hope anymore." He gestured to the farmer beside him. "This is Kirby Dinhart."

He waved off the obligatory handshake, showing dirty palms. "Sorry. Been a crazy morning. This is my field."

"Not how you thought harvest was going to go, I bet."

He shook his head. "That's a fact. This was the last ground I still needed to bring in, but it's the wettest of my land. I was letting the crop dry some more before combining."

"Thank goodness you hadn't gotten to it yet." Tom's focus traveled to where the graveyard fence met the corn.

"Yep," Kirby's mouth twisted. "Of all the fields for her to show up in."

Tom grasped the farmer's shoulder, and eight more eyes turned down the field. The weight of the silent memorial pressed Jude further into the mud, and he wished they had no part in it.

Out of nowhere, Kirby smacked his neck. "Ow, dammit!" He blushed. "Sorry, ma'am. The biting flies here are terrible." A small swarm buzzed near his green hat. Jude glanced around, but those were the only ones he could find.

"They must like you, Kirby," Carmichael said.

"If this is what they do to people they like, I've got to start being less friendly."

"We should be on our way," Audie spoke up. "We shouldn't intrude more than we already have."

Who are you and what've you done with my wife?

"You're not intruding, believe me," Tom said. "Owen says you were in the area to search for these plots?"

"Yes. A client of ours is a descendant of Madame Durand here. We're trying to put together the pieces of her puzzle. Records for this cemetery are hard to come by."

"Somebody should've asked me." Kirby swatted another fly. "I've been farming this land for twenty-plus years and knew it was here. I guess if you don't, it's like looking for a black cat in a coal cellar, and right in the middle of ground my family's worked for generations."

"Do you have Durands in your line?"

"No, which is strange, but if you go by the dates on those stones, my people settled here after the last of them passed on. The area was turning more German by then, and my ancestors emigrated from Bavaria in the later 1800s. The French were getting outnumbered. I can't think of any Durands around here these days." Another fly, another swat. Audie's head tilted, watching the frantic swarm. "Tom?"

"No, me neither."

"Or me," Carmichael added. "It must be one of those families that finally died out. You see the kids' graves."

"I hate finding those," Kirby grimaced. "They always have lambs on them. Makes me kind of sick." He caught himself and spun back to Powers. "Hey, Tom, I didn't mean—"

"It's okay, Kirby. Cassie's disappearance is just part of our history. It's hard for any of this to come as a shock now."

A manic voice sliced the moment in two. "Easy for you to say, you bastard. You're the reason she's dead!"

CHAPTER 6

Out of the woods burst a faded camo jacket wrapped around a skinny man whose gasket was in the process of blowing. *Ironic that I saw the camo first.* Deep grooves across his forehead and the first silver hairs at his temple contrasted with boyish—but flaming—blue eyes. He vaulted over the short fence, fists clenched, a scorched trail in his wake. Jude grabbed for Audie and pulled her behind him, every muscle's memory launching straight to DEFCON 1.

Genealogy didn't often require fisticuffs. *What's the right way to punch without breaking a metacarpal?* It had been a while.

Tom Powers stood his ground, but his own hands stretched out, open-palmed, toward the human locomotive. "Brice, you need to calm down."

"I need to calm down?" He batted away Tom's fingers. "You've been calm enough for both of us ever since Cassie disappeared."

Tom stumbled over his loafers as the shorter, younger man set up camp in his personal space. "Good grief, Brice. It's been thirty years!"

"Yeah, thirty years. Thirty years of everybody we ever knew whispering when they thought we couldn't hear. Pointing out *that* family, telling any stranger who happened along all about the nightmare we were living." The two moved together like a bad tango. "All that time I had to watch our parents die more every day from the questions, the wondering. And where were you? Clear across the state, hiding from what you did."

Tom's back smacked against Philippe Durand's monument, and cornered, his face flushed scarlet with a fire to match his brother's. "I didn't kill her, you moron!" His arms crossed his chest, probably the only thing keeping him from taking a swing. "How dare you say that."

"You ran away. You may as well have been the one to leave her out in this." His arm swept toward the cornfield, and Kirby Dinhart had to duck to avoid being clocked. "You left when we were still searching, when there was still a chance to find her."

"There was no chance, and you know it. Kane killed her and took off, all on that one night."

Jude bristled. The locals *had* already condemned a seventeen-year-old kid, still missing himself.

Maybe he did the deed.

But maybe he didn't.

Brice swiped unbidden tears off his cheeks, but he quit talking. Or he'd exhausted his ability to form words. His face angled up at his sibling in pathetic accusation, a mix of misery and weary sorrow rolled into one.

The awkward silence was too much for the burly sheriff. Softly, he said, "Brice, these are the folks who found Cassie."

From the reaction the younger Powers gave, the Wests had sprouted, fully ripened, from the farm field. "Oh," was the most he could muster.

Audie crept from the background and conjured up the voice that could soothe a rabid wolverine. "Sheriff, may I ask how you identified the body so fast? We just discovered her late yesterday."

Maneuvering himself into a less vulnerable position now that the level of local rage had lowered, Tom answered. "A stroke of bad luck that ended up being helpful. Brice and Cassie were the athletes of the Powers crew. She'd been a track and cross-country runner since middle school, graceful and silent as a deer. But in eighth grade, she got tangled with a pack during a race and went down hard, breaking her left forearm and the seventh rib on that same side. The, uh, skeleton showed the healed bones right where they should be."

"Combine that with the fact she's our only missing persons case," Carmichael added, "and it appears you two have solved Renarde's worst mystery."

"Only missing person? What about Hunter Kane?"

Jude knew he shouldn't have said it even before Audie cringed. The forge relit in Brice Powers as confirmation.

"Don't you talk like that kid's anything more than the rotten scum who killed my sister," he spat. "He doesn't need your pity. He needs to be in an electric chair. I'd kill him myself if I ever found him."

The sheriff inserted his full body between the walking torch and Jude. "I understand, Brice, but you see I'm standing right here, yes?" The reflection from his badge shone into the reddened blue eyes.

"I don't care." Another tear, hurled to the ground. "I don't care about any of it anymore." With a parting scowl, he turned and stalked toward the cars. Jude watched him climb into the beat-up Ford, spin his balding tires, and finally fling enough mud rearward to move in the direction of the main road.

Tom exhaled decades of drama. "I apologize for that. He was just sixteen when Cassie went missing. I was in college already and not as tied to home as he was then. He gave up a lot to try to find her." Too much, it seemed.

Kirby swatted another fly, and a blood droplet slid from his neck into the flannel showing at the top of his coat.

"You were away when she disappeared?"

"That particular weekend, I was home," Tom said. "I studied at Northwest Missouri State, but it was fall break. And everybody here was talking about the first Cinders and Cider. Heck, Brice was the whole reason I drove down from Maryville. He was playing JV baseball at the time. The festival's proceeds funneled into the athletic programs, so the teams helped set it up. Nowadays, several organizations get a share. I'm an accountant, and since I'm living here again, I help handle the distributions."

He paused. "Got off track, didn't I? Brice's group was putting the bonfire together. In the week before, he called me every night, telling me how big it was going to be. I thought I'd better come see what baby brother was doing." He pursed his lips. "Fat lot of good that did me."

"He blames you for not searching?"

"He blames me for a lot of things, but I did search. Of course I searched. I took off two weeks of school to hunt through woods and climb through crumbling barns. But Mom and Dad both told me to leave. If I didn't keep my grades up, I'd lose my scholarship. Would've been tough to finish without the money. Yes, Cassie's disappearance was horrible. Devastating. But we knew what had happened. She should've never been hanging around with that trash. He was bad news."

Kirby shook his head. "You did what you could, Tom. You told Kane to stay away from her. Right up to the end, you tried." He shoved his hands into his coat once more with a frown. "He was one of those kids. Didn't matter how clear you made it. He was never going to listen."

"I warned *her*, too, though. Cass blew me off. What did I know?" Tom kicked at a broken chunk of gravestone lying near his feet. "It's no use worrying about it now. Bad things happen every day. You never expect it to be your family."

Amen. Other than a twinge at Audie's jawline, the person with most cause to react didn't.

Progress? Difficult to say.

Jude slipped an arm around her waist.

"Did you move home after school?"

Tom snorted. "Definitely not. I'd met a girl. We got married and moved to Kansas City—close enough to come for major holidays, far enough to avoid scenes like that." He gestured to the spot his brother's car had vacated. "We lived there until seven years ago, when Dad's health nosedived. Soon after we relocated, he died, with Mom not far behind. Neither of my parents lived past sixty-five. They'd tried to move on for me and Brice." He grimaced. "Both lasted longer than I would've if she was my daughter.

"I ended up taking over Dad's firm. He was the local CPA and had been a fixture for decades. I couldn't leave his clients hanging. Those people had supported us through it all, but now they'd get stuck working with someone twenty miles away."

"That'd be tough."

"It's not just the distance. Financial folks see the nitty-gritty of a person's life. No one wants to start over with an outsider."

Another weighty pause, and Jude felt a nudge at his side. "We'd better get going. Duty calls." Audie reached a hand to Tom, and as he took it, she placed her other on top. "We really are sorry for your loss. Thank you for sharing a bit of your sister's story."

His shoulders, tense from the sibling spat, relaxed. "I love talking about Cass. Maybe we'll see you around in the next few days, and I can tell you more. It'll make this week go better."

"Sounds lovely. Mr. Dinhart, nice to meet you, as well."

"Yep." He squinted across the rustling cornfield. "This acreage might be a lost cause 'til next season."

Audie picked her way along the uneven path, Jude trailing her to the Jeep. She climbed in the driver's side and crawled over the center console, a smarter plan than fashioning stilts from the stalks. As he shut his door and reached for his seatbelt, she was already buckled in and staring at some invisible thing in the distance.

"I don't like any of what's being said around here."

He started the car and did a three-point turn to escape without demolishing rows of future silage. "It's pretty grim, for sure. Why—what else are you thinking?"

She waited as he wrestled the Jeep through the worst of the existing ruts. Mud splattered across the windshield, smeared by wipers not up to the task. "I want to know two things. One—why were the biting flies so fixated on Mr. Dinhart?"

His laugh—as uncontrolled as Brice's tears—was a welcome release. "Okay, didn't see that coming. And two?"

She peered through the arcing streaks. "Did Tom Powers kill his little sister?"

Chapter 7

The highway split, and Jude followed the sign toward Historic Downtown Renarde. Dense forest gave way to the first mown lawns, followed by St. Michaelis Evangelical Lutheran Kirche, roughly the size of a lemonade stand. When they drove by the shed housing the volunteer fire department, he knew they'd hit the city limits.

Every maple tree was dressed to the nines after most of their early-turning neighbors had become nudists. Three days of battering rains and wind accounted for the undressing. But he couldn't take in the brilliant fall colors without seeing red, then blood, then the drama of the Powers clan, past to present.

And I thought my family had problems.

Sadly, it wasn't an exclusive club.

He swung onto Main Street, soon met by chrysanthemums lining the residential walks and American flags waving from many porch rails. The rare building with curling paint and mildewed shingles squatted like an angry troll between the Stepford homes, giving neither two hoots nor a holler about city ordinances.

Well, somebody had to keep the code enforcement officers occupied and out of trouble.

The speed limit dropped to twenty-five just before the business district. This gave the octogenarian at the last house too much time to watch them pass. He leaned on his rake while mentally recording every detail for lunchtime conversation with the wife. Then a leaf had the nerve to land within his radius, and the chase began anew. No errant flora had sat on that yard since November of '98.

Jude felt their next neighborhood watch captain before he saw him. A younger man stood in front of a mechanic's shop, filling a blue-gray jumpsuit with impressive muscles and topping it off with the requisite buzz cut. He, too, twisted his neck to follow the unfamiliar vehicle, only he added a heavy-browed glower for theatrical effect.

If their physical description, VIN, and last cholesterol screening weren't plastered on a billboard by noontime, someone was falling down on the job.

The Jeep swerved to the right as Audie grabbed onto his arm and pulled. They bounced into a parking lot and he regained control of the wheel. "You could've just said something, you know."

"You were elsewhere."

"I was driving the car."

"And you were passing the hardware store."

He rolled into a space. "Wait—weren't we going to the library?"

"I'm worried about that fan. If we have to go to Plan B, I'd rather find out now than when it's too late this afternoon."

The storefront had a fluorescent orange "Come on in!" sign suctioned to the glass door. Surrounding it was a mosaic of advertisements. This week's specials: autumn lawn fertilizer and leaf blowers. Two upcoming concerts: one by the high school band for Veteran's Day and an a cappella choir slated to perform at St. John's Catholic Church on Sunday afternoon. A large poster bearing the image of a burning straw man filled most of the window beside the entrance.

Thirty-first Annual Cinders and Cider Festival
Saturday, October 31
Costume Parade at 4 p.m.,
followed by trick-or-treating.
Food, Crafts, and Entertainment opening at 6 p.m.
The Best Ever bonfire scheduled for 6:15!
Bring your own chairs.

Bells jingled over his head as they entered the store. The interior was as cluttered as the door had been, and that familiar bouquet of paint, lumber, weed killer, and galvanized nails sent Jude sneezing. This conjured a dark-haired, bearded man from a rear storeroom.

"'Morning!" He walked up the aisle, rubbing his hands together. The first customers of the day and strangers to boot—jackpot. "Can I help you folks find something?"

"We sure hope so." From the hobo bag slung across her body, Audie extracted a parts list and an exploded view of the trailer's environmental unit. *Exploded. How fitting.* "The fan on our camper's heater broke overnight, and it shredded the wiring on its way out."

Her slim fingers smoothed down the drawing and pointed to the diagram and the fan model number. The man scratched at his beard.

"The wires I've got, no problem. That fan?" He clicked his tongue as he thought. "We can order it, but it'll take at least two days to come in. Are you passing through?" He studied Jude more than was strictly necessary. That expression…

Oh brother. Strangers? Who was I kidding? Why don't they ever simply say we've made it into the grapevine?

"No," Audie responded, understanding the game too well

herself. "We're here doing some research and are staying over at Fillion State Park."

"Ah. You need to get this fixed ASAP. It's dropping another five degrees with the cold front moving in." He rolled his eyes. "Next week, it'll be in the eighties. Welcome to Missouri—if you don't like the weather, wait an hour. I'll go pull the wires for you. Do you need help with the installation?" Again, he turned to Jude and again Audie answered.

"No, thanks, I've got it." She didn't even try to resist the small smile.

The man paused for a moment, then shrugged. "Sounds good."

They followed him into electrical supplies and watched as he cut the lengths required for the hot, neutral, and ground wires. Wrapped together, the colored sheathing made an exotic—yet chewy—candy cane.

"I'm Lionel, by the way. Lionel Graymeyer."

"Thanks for your help, Lionel." Maybe it was a reflection from the tin snips hanging beside her, but Audie's irises twinkled. "We're the Wests. Jude and Audie, but I'm guessing you already knew that."

Under his beard, Lionel reddened, and after the briefest hesitation, he gave them a sheepish grin. "Sorry. Yeah. I knew who you were when you walked in. Word spreads fast in a community this size. I was selling a house once, had a realtor from the next town over hounding me for the business. I'd told her a dozen times I wasn't ready to list because the place still needed a lot of work. One day, I'm standing on my front lawn, shooting the breeze with a fellow about turkey hunting, and I get a panicked phone call from this woman. My neighbor had seen me talking. Must've had her on speed dial, telling her I was selling without benefit of her services."

Audie laughed, Jude groaned, and Lionel shook his head. "It

usually isn't a problem. But a few folks sure could use something to fill their empty hours."

"We did catch a long look or three driving down Main."

He waved it off. "I'd lay money one of them was from Travis next door."

"Travis?"

"Travis Bell. Owns the tow truck and repair shop. Never heard a kind word he couldn't growl at. He barks more than he bites, though." He led them back to the cashier counter. "My clerk's running late this morning. I'll ring you up. Anything else you need?"

"Only that fan." Audie frowned as she folded her paper and stowed it away. The two exchanged bag for a couple small bills.

"I'm sorry I can't help. Travis won't have it in stock either. You may need to go to the RV dealer south on I-55, but it's about a ninety-minute drive from here, one way."

"We've got a lot to do today," Jude said. "A detour isn't in the schedule."

Lionel's thinking cap must've been tied to his Mason jar pen holder, because he picked it up and repositioned it three times before saying, "You know who might have something for you? Harold Carver. I should've thought of him sooner. He's a junker a ways outside of the city limits. Takes whatever scrap he can find." The jar returned to its original spot. "Recycles some for cash, keeps most of it for a rainy day, his or anyone else's. It's how he makes a living, though once you see his place, you might question how that's living."

"Yeah?"

"Don't get me wrong. He's a good ol' boy, no problems there. But he can be rough around the edges, and his house and yard are his storefront. It's just that his store deals in junk. You better tell him I sent you over. He doesn't see a lot of people from out of town coming by and can get a little suspicious."

"Thanks, Mr. Graymeyer. Will do." Audie tucked the wires into her purse and headed for the door.

"Lionel, please. And, hey!" They both stopped and turned. Shelves of candy—chocolate bars, taffy squares, those sugary button things where eating the paper is part of the experience—stood between them and him. "You were the ones who found Cassie?"

That skull had a name and a story and a family. Breakfast shifted uneasily. "Yeah, I did, unfortunately."

"Unfortunate for you, but a big relief to us. She was in the class above me in school. That's one question that took too long to answer." He reached over the counter, grabbed a hefty potluck of sweets, and stuffed them into a bulging sack, handing it over to Jude. "It sure isn't reward money, but it might leave a better taste in your mouth for Renarde than finding that poor girl."

At least the nightmares he was going to have for a while had brought some comfort. Jude took the bag. "Thank you, Lionel."

"It's a shame the relief didn't last more than a minute."

And just like that, comfort beat a path for the interstate. "What do you mean?"

"I figured you would've heard," he stumbled, blushing again. "They said you found her wrapped in an old blanket, right? With the Renarde high school insignia on it?"

"Some sort of symbol was sewn in, yes."

"Sherri Powers makes those. Tom's wife. She's been a crafter for a while, but they only moved home here about six or seven years ago. If Cassie was in one of Sherri's blankets, she hadn't been in it for three decades. Somebody put her in that field within the last seven years."

CHAPTER 8

"Library or junker?" Jude waited as a Case International combine trundled past. He didn't have much choice—the behemoth occupied the full width of Main Street. At least the recent rain kept the dust trail down. He pulled out of the hardware store's lot and checked to ensure his wife had actually joined him in the car. "Audie?"

"What?" She rotated toward him in slow motion, the tiny crease between those gray eyes deeper than usual.

"Do you want to go to Harold the Junker's or over to the library?"

"Right. Library first."

"You're not worried about the fan?"

"I am, but we need to at least pretend to work a little this morning. If the junkyard is like Lionel described, Mr. Carver is bound to have something we can kluge together."

"I'm just hoping he doesn't shoot us on arrival. I've got a few mental images of this guy, and in each, he's holding a shotgun."

"And has a pack of snaggletoothed dogs waiting to attack?"

"Hey, I'm not kidding. Graymeyer said he was the suspicious type."

"I wasn't kidding either."

The library stood a block off the main drag. Its previous life must've been as a church—white clapboard siding, tall, narrow windows topped with stained-glass semicircles. The two front doors even glowed a bright, inviting red.

Inside, the reverent silence suggested sanctuary too, but not because of any black-clad ministers or stern-faced librarians with cat-eye glasses and severe hair buns. It was merely devoid of patrons. Folks had other pressing business on a Tuesday morning.

So did the staff, it seemed.

"Hello?" Audie's voice echoed off the vaulted ceiling. From behind a row of shelves, a head appeared like a jack-in-the-box.

"Ooh, sorry!" the head answered, emerging into a complete person and without the accordion neck. "Didn't mean to startle you." A woman as thin as Audie and with wisps of curls fluttering from around a well-intentioned hairband came to the front with an armload of books. She rounded the counter and dropped the pile on top with a bang. "Must've stuck my brain on a shelf along with the returns."

Jude smiled back and noticed the librarian grow more distracted than she'd already been. "We're the Wests. We'd emailed someone here about looking at genealogy records?"

She tucked three curls into the band before remembering she needed to answer with words. "Oh yes!" With pink cheeks, she turned away from him. "You're Audie. You write lovely emails. No one else bothers with proper correspondence anymore."

"Thank you, but that makes us both sound like we're ninety."

The woman leaned against a tall stool and laughed. "There are days."

"You must be Sherri. So you know we're here researching the

Laroque and Durand families from the mid-1800s. We're hoping to dig up info on homestead locations and any vital statistics: births, deaths, marriages."

"Dig up! I get it—family-tree humor. Since business isn't booming in here, let's get you to a table and see what we can find. Care for a cup?" She lifted the carafe of an ancient Mr. Coffee peeking from beneath the counter and filled a yellow-and-green polka-dotted mug. On its side glittered the words "Librarians have the best stories." They both declined, having already been caffeinated more than usual since the heater debacle.

Mug in hand, she ushered them to the rear of the building, where an alcove held the musty smell of old documents. Sturdy wooden tables—long etched with "Mary-heart-Jimmy," "School stinks," and the occasional prehistoric emoji—were paired with the most rickety chairs ever conceived. Jude weighed his lean frame against their structural integrity and declined that too. He circled around and designated himself the runner for the morning's digging.

Family-tree humor indeed.

Braver than he, the ladies took their seats as Audie extracted the binder and notebook from the Rucksack O'Everything. Running her fingers over the tabs, she flipped to the list of info they were after and pushed it into view.

"The Laroques are direct ancestors of our client, but they've been elusive, to say the least. Henri and wife Elise, plus a child named Gareth." Granted, Gareth's movements as a youth could best be described as elusive too. "Are there directories or registries from the time that could tell us where they lived? Seems like it's only the one couple, no other relations nearby."

"That's unusual. Families were big back then. Even with immigrants, we often find they traveled to the new country with siblings."

"Everything about this case is unusual. The Durands haven't been any easier. We finally stumbled on part of Elise's first husband's land yesterday, when we found the graveyard."

Off flew the mug, crashing onto the floor in a heap of bright ceramic bits and steaming coffee.

"Oh my goodness!" Sherri leapt to her feet, and Audie grabbed for the research. "I'm so sorry."

Jude glanced around—behind spiral stairs, a restroom adjoined the alcove. He ducked in and scavenged a stack of brown paper towels.

"Are you okay?" Audie asked the librarian kneeling to gather shards of the cup. "You didn't cut yourself?"

The hardwood planks had seen worse, which was lucky since the towels dissolved as he attempted to mop up the liquid.

"I'm fine, I'm fine." But her hands trembled as they worked.

Jude stood, taking her with him. "I've got this," he said. She let him guide her to a chair, tears clinging to her lashes. "Hey, no crying over spilled coffee, remember?"

She sniffled, adjusting the stretchy hairband from where it had slid onto her forehead. "I think that's milk."

"Sherri?" Audie asked. "What's wrong?"

Another sniffle, and she raised a towel to her nose. "You're the ones, aren't you?"

"Which ones would that be?" Jude's knees crackled as he crouched to resume swabbing the deck. Rude.

"How stupid of me not to put it together until now. You found Tom's sister yesterday. Out by the graveyard you were working in."

Audie bowed her head. "That would be us."

"I'm being dumb. It's—gosh, it was ages ago." She brushed at her cheek.

"It's hard to lose someone so close."

"Oh, it's not that." She cringed. "That sounded awful. I mean, I never had the chance to know Cassie. Tom and I met in college, up at Northwest. We hadn't been dating for more than a month or so, both sophomores when she went missing. I'd never been to Renarde, let alone been introduced to any of the family."

The way she inflected the last word... Even from down on the floor, Jude wondered if she wished she'd never met them at all. He rose in search of a trash can, hands full of papier-mâché and the mortal remains of the mug. When he returned, he found Audie had rotated her seat to face Sherri. The Laroques would wait awhile.

"Were the Powers kids close?"

"Like normal teenagers. Being sandwiched between two boys couldn't have been easy. Cass was popular, ran on the track teams, that sort of thing. Tom didn't talk much about the younger ones. He wanted to complete his degree and get—" She blushed.

"Get?"

"I was going to say 'get away,' but that sounds awful too." She swung her gaze between the Wests. "Where are you from? I mean, originally. Where did you grow up?"

"I was born and raised in St. Louis," Audie answered. "And Jude comes from southwest Ohio, the Dayton area."

"I grew up in Kansas City. We moved there after Tom and I married. Good area for jobs."

"KC has a fantastic library system."

Sherri allowed herself a small, wry smile. "I wasn't always a librarian. I have a master's in mathematics and was working at an insurance company. One of the 'big three.'" Burgundy fingernails formed the air quotes. "When we had to move down here, well..."

"I guess there aren't a lot of those jobs nearby," Jude finished for her.

"Don't get me wrong. I love this work. I love the research and the stacks and the hunt for that perfect source. Always have. But it's not how I'd expected my career to go."

"Life throws curve balls."

"That's for sure. Anyway, we're here, and it's for the best. Tom took over his father's accounting practice, and I found a new world among the books. I also started a little crafting. Thought it might help me fit in better."

That undertone—the sewing hadn't helped.

"We were told the blanket Cassie was found in was one of yours."

Sherri's weak coloring paled more. "One of the high school ones?"

"According to Lionel Graymeyer. Sorry, guess your husband left out that detail."

"Yes." Nervous fingers scratched at an old glob of glue on the table. As she focused, the gears started turning. "But that's not possible. We haven't been in Renarde for long. Cassie's been missing for decades. She couldn't have… *died* that recently, could she?" Her eyes widened, hand rising to her throat.

Jude watched it pass straight through her bones—the girl might've still been alive until seven years ago. Trapped somewhere, tortured, who knows what. There had been stories like that in the news. It was possible. She paled again, and he slipped beside her, expecting a catch to be required any moment.

"No, no," Audie reached for her arm. "The sheriff said the crime scene folks were sure she died close to when she disappeared."

"But how was she wrapped in one of my blankets?" Her confused expression traveled around the room for an answer and landed once more at the table. She picked up a pencil and began tracing the amateur graffiti unsteadily. Who was going to scold her—the librarian?

Pulling from her own well of trauma she'd rather forget, Audie answered quietly. "It seems to say her body's been moved sometime in the last few years."

The pencil continued its circuitous route as that sank in. Then it snapped in half.

"Sherri?"

"No."

"No, what?" Audie flashed Jude a worried look.

"It might not have been that long ago."

"But the blanket—"

"That's what I mean. I've done at least four versions. Describe the embroidery."

In his mind floated the wet, ash-colored fleece, caked in mud splatter and corn dust. "It was pretty dirty. It had reddish stitching in the shape of a one-room schoolhouse, with the letters 'CC' underneath it. I assumed you'd made it as a fundraiser for the cross-country team."

The curls shivered as Sherri shook her head. "No. The C's are Roman numerals. It's for the two-hundredth anniversary of the school district's founding by the French." Those puffy eyes darted between the Wests. "The anniversary is this school year. I started making those blankets three months ago."

A concussive crash rained prehistoric grime on them from the rafters.

"Oh my gosh," she whispered. "He's back."

CHAPTER 9

More stormy weather passed through as the front door slammed shut. From the central library came an agitated bark. "Sherri!"

She jumped from her seat and darted into the stacks. Audie mouthed "yikes."

Indeed.

"I'm here, Tom. I was in the alcove."

"Aren't you supposed to be out here guarding the place?"

"I was just—"

"I don't care. We've got bigger problems. Brice knows—"

"Tom, there's—"

"Dang it, Sherri, I'm trying to tell you—"

"There are visitors here!" Her words pinballed off every nook and cranny.

A long pause followed, and Audie nodded her head toward the commotion. *Does it count as eavesdropping if we can't help but hear?* He tiptoed out of their corner, and from amongst the bookcases he could see the two figures at the desk. Sherri was taller than Audie, and Tom about his height, but the wife had shrunk beside her husband. They stood in silence, with the newcomer breathing heavily and the librarian staring at the worried paper-towel remnants in her hand. Tom cleared his throat and spoke in a calm—if forced—tone.

"Well, you should've said something. Nobody comes in this early, and I didn't see a car outside."

Jude emerged into the aisle, smiling like it was Sunday afternoon at the fair and he'd won the pie-eating contest. "Hey, Tom! We'll have to stop meeting this way. Audie and I came in from the east side and didn't realize there was a lot behind the building. Jeep's parked on the street."

"Ah." The man struggled to collect himself.

"Is everything okay?"

"What? Oh yes. I mean, other than my dead sister being in the morgue down in Cape Girardeau." He returned to his wife. "Reverend Hickenbocker offered to hold a memorial service this evening."

Sherri's mouth fell open. "Already?"

"It's not a formal funeral. Just a minute to get the town together where we can try to catch our breath. We'll do the family thing next week, when we can bury her right."

To Jude, he said, "You and your wife should come tonight. Without you, we might never have gotten Cassie back."

"We'd be honored to attend." He gestured to the reference room. "I'll go let Audie know."

"Seven p.m. On the lawn outside of the First Community Church on Fleur Street."

"Got it. We'll see you there." He strolled away as casually as he could and took a hard right between the shelves, trying not to run. At the table, Audie anxiously waited. "You heard all that?"

"Difficult not to."

Furtive murmurs—no longer intelligible—drifted through the

space, followed by the door opening and closing a smidge harder than necessary. Footsteps approached, and a more haggard Sherri reappeared.

"We've gotten off to a lousy start on your research, haven't we?" The weak smile hid nothing.

"Not a problem. We're sorry to be intruding during such an awful time for you and Tom."

She shrugged. "It's going to be a strange few days, but it'll pass. With the poor girl being gone this long, it hardly seems real now. I guess a memorial will help start the healing."

"I'm sure," Audie said. "It's pretty short notice. How many people do you think might come to the service?"

Such an innocent-sounding query. Yet warning beacons lit throughout Jude's nervous system.

He knew, of course, it was going to be a problem. He'd simply hoped it would take longer for his beloved to work that out.

"Short notice isn't a thing around here. They'll come. When the Walters boy died in that car accident a couple years ago, the whole town and three counties descended on the candlelight vigil. I'm not certain we'll get quite that many, with it being such an old death."

"Folks will want to support you two," Jude added. "And Brice."

Sherri bit her lip at the brother's name, but simply said, "They probably will." She sighed, and fatigue in her marrow deepened the lines on her face. "We'll have pies from here to June."

Audie smiled, but it was a tight smile. That muscle in her jaw was twinging again.

Tonight would not end well.

The three of them pored over logs, dug into local genealogical society publications, and hauled boxes down from an attic storage area for hours. Or rather, Jude hauled boxes. After a few near catastrophes, he learned the secret to navigating the narrow, code-violating staircase without snapping his neck: move like a sloth and pretend your feet are the size of a toddler's. But all that caution didn't keep what felt like a white-hot dagger from stabbing through his left shoulder. The throbbing wasn't getting any better as the stack of cartons grew.

Neat piles of documents covered the table where Audie worked, stirred-up dust hovering overhead and giving her a halo from the window's weak streams. She'd declared eminent domain on her surroundings, and the files had expanded to a second work surface by the time lunch came around.

"The break whistle's blowing, dear." Jude set down a scrap of cardboard that couldn't handle many more trips from above. He rolled the shoulder and bent backward with his hands on his hips, released vertebrae snapping, crackling, and popping down his spinal column.

Audie's nose was inches away from a 170-year-old record, black pen bouncing like a teeter-totter in her right hand. "Sure. In a minute. I found death certificates for the two Durand boys. Emile died of whooping cough, Eliot of pneumonia."

He plucked the pen from between her fingers.

"You said 'in a minute' twenty minutes ago. My stomach's growling, and the quieter it is in here, the louder it's going to get." And it was plenty quiet. Sherri had needed to duck out to the front desk only twice so far. Presumably, things would pick up after school dismissed.

"Kids still read, don't they?" he asked no one in particular.

Sherri entered the room, carrying another stack of folders and nodding. "Sure! But some have seen mostly e-books. They come here and think paper is trendy. My favorite part of this job will always be watching new readers set off on an adventure and return begging for more." She winked, obviously recovered from Tom's fly-by. "You get them early, and they're hooked for life."

Audie had resumed examining the death certificates, substituting a pencil for the pen Jude had plundered. "Look at Becca and Connor. They've always been bookworms, and it's served them well."

"Your kids?"

Jude chortled, brushing the errant fringe away from his left eye and stealing the pencil away too. "Definitely not. Audie's niece and nephew. Both in their twenties now. Connor is an IT specialist, and Becca is finishing her first year at Boeing in Seattle. Mechanical engineer."

"Wow. We could use them on a poster for Literacy Week."

He turned to the table. *No wonder people become career criminals.* He filched the Durand records to add to his booty. "Lunch, Aud. Please. I'm dying here."

"Okay, okay." She scooted her chair and reached for her bag. "Sherri, is it all right if we leave our tornado? We'll be back after a quick bite."

"Or a slow bite," Jude amended. "Food is to be savored."

"As you've said. So, Sherri?"

"Gee, with all those eager patrons lined up outside, waiting? No, it's no problem. Take your time."

"Can we get you anything?"

"Thanks, but I pack my own."

"A woman after my own heart." Jude put a hand to his gut. "Besides, it's self-defense after dinner last night."

The librarian cringed. "You ate at Metcalfe's?"

Audie slipped the bag's strap over the shoulder of her coat. "It was fine, really."

"Fine, yes. Good? Questionable."

True. "Are there any public spaces that might be nice for an in-car picnic?"

"Best spot would be Bluff Park, since the city square is getting prepped for the festival. Signs will lead you right to it once you get onto Main. It's not far."

"Great, Sherri. Thanks."

Jude pushed open the cardinal red door, and Audie passed through.

"The sun!" she said, stopping at the top of the steps and squinting against the brightest sky they'd seen for a week.

He reached for his sunglasses and remembered leaving them in the trailer days ago. Using his hand as a shield, he examined the horizon. "Bask while you can. Clouds are rolling in from the west."

"Of course." He followed her down the stairs to street level. "You know how much more we'd get done if you could learn to ignore your stomach?"

"A boy's got to eat if he's going to schlepp twenty boxes from a life-sized Tetris board for his darling wife." Leaves skittered along the sidewalk as they approached the Jeep. "Oh for the love of Pete."

A folded piece of paper rattled under the windshield wiper on the driver's side. He pulled it free with more than a little aggravation. "Doesn't solving the town's biggest mystery earn us any street cred with the sheriff?"

Audie inspected the area near the car. "There aren't any markings or hydrants. What did we do wrong?"

He unfolded the paper and stopped.

"Jude?"

"It's not a ticket. It's a note."

She walked around to join him. "From whom?"

"Excellent question." He handed her the sheet—a single line, typed in large, bold font, underlined with a dark marker.

"'Don't let it die,'" Audie read. "What on earth does that mean?"

Nothing good, that's for sure. Jude's pulse pounded in his ears as he scanned the street in one direction, then the other. A dog barked at them from behind a chain-link fence a few houses over, but it was the sole sign of life. "Someone has a vested interest in something we're doing."

She shifted closer to him as that eagle-eyed focus took in a full three-block radius. The paper rattled in her hand. "But which plot has thickened? The Laroques of 1847 or the two missing teenagers of thirty years ago?"

CHAPTER 10

Wrought iron signs with curlicues and arrows led the way to Bluff Park. Jude pulled up to the metal railing in the empty lot.

At least we know how it got its name. A yard or two beyond their front bumper, the ground disappeared. He set the emergency brake and opened his door. "Want to view the scenery?"

Audie's head was buried in a map. "I'm good."

He walked to the fence and leaned over. Other than a few thin ledges, the limestone face was a straight vertical drop. From here, the entire world lay below: the town behind him, a glittering creek at the bluff's foot. The creek must've been the moneymaker for the early French trappers. How awkward would that have been when they realized they were in beaver territory? They'd already named the area "Fox."

The trees on both sides of the lot had lost most of their leaves, and the branches whistled with the breeze. Enough sightseeing. From the cooler in the trunk, he fished out two sandwiches and a pair of shiny Gala apples, then climbed into the cab.

"Too bad it's nippy. Would've been nice to sit out and get some air."

Audie unwrapped the origami-like butcher paper swaddling her lunch. "The library was getting pretty close, wasn't it?"

"The Powers' marital problems didn't help the vibe." He bit into the sandwich—the aioli enhanced the roasted red peppers and grilled chicken in one elegant mouthful. Not bad for a hand-held meal. He exhaled contentedly.

"And Tom had seemed like the more stable of the brothers this morning." Audie plucked a baby spinach leaf from her bundle and nibbled.

"Compared to Brice, anybody would've been more stable." He took another bite and reached for his water bottle. "What do you think?"

"About lunch?"

"No—well, yes, but that's not what I meant. What do you think about the world of crazy we've stumbled into? Brice accusing Tom of negligence, if not straight-up murder. Tom being a different man when no one's around except his wife. Sherri's reaction to Cassie being found. And now an anonymous note on our car. Take your pick."

She bit into his culinary creation, and Jude held his breath. At the second bite, he gave himself a mental fist bump. "It's a lot, for sure. They've all but convicted Hunter Kane. I wish we had confirmation he made it out of that night alive."

"That's bugging me too. In this age, it shouldn't be hard to find a living person."

"See, that's the thing. It isn't." She resumed reaping ingredients one by one. This time, it was a red pepper.

"Those are supposed to be eaten with the other parts of the sandwich. That's why it's called a sandwich."

She tilted her head. "From the Latin, *santo-vici*? Meaning a stack of edible tidbits combined such that one must unhinge one's jaw to eat it?"

He put a hand to his heart. “You’re a cruel woman, Audra West.”

“You understood the dangers when you married me. And I thank you for doing so, because this is delicious.” She popped in another bite. “As I was saying, it’s challenging but not impossible to find most people anymore, as long as they’re living. Being one hundred percent off-grid is almost a myth. Then why, when I was poking around overnight, couldn’t I find a single pointer to Hunter Kane?”

“That’s what you were doing instead of sleeping?”

“Until the heater exploded, yes. I ran a bunch of searches and came away with nothing. Not even a rabbit hole to fall down.”

“He may have changed his name.”

“I’ve heard some people do that. No one I know, of course.” She patted his knee. “But even with a name change, I should’ve been able to find a trace. The internet is better than an elephant at holding onto data.”

Jude crunched into the last third of his lunch and chewed for a minute. “Sherri implied she thought he could’ve been back in the area. Like Hunter could be coming after people still today. Very Michael Myers-esque.”

“’Tis the season.” She gestured toward the hillside across the creek, the remaining foliage a watercolor of scarlets, ambers, and corals.

“What if he didn’t do it? What if he didn’t kill Cassie but had to run for another reason? He’s had to hide who is for years, his hometown ready to go after him with torches and pitchforks. After three decades, could a mind snap? Now he’s returned and put a bullseye on those who’ve condemned him?”

She re-wrapped her half-eaten lunch. “Whether or not he killed her, I think Hunter Kane died the same night Cassie Powers did."

Peppers and greens shot in every direction as Jude's hand crushed the last of his masterpiece, the window beside his head jolted under sudden, violent pummeling.

CHAPTER 11

Owen Carmichael stood outside the Jeep, laughing with his entire body. Jude shoved the door open, forcing the sheriff to backpedal a few paces. He wasn't particularly sorry about that.

The man in tan wiped at his eye as he tried to compose himself. "Boy, you sure are jumpy this afternoon."

"Yeah." Jude grabbed a napkin to wipe a large smear of aioli off his hand. "This town has that effect on people."

The sandwich was a lost cause, a thumb-sized tear ripping through the bread, half the ingredients sticking to the front of his leather jacket. He mourned the mess, then crammed the remaining morsel into his mouth anyway. Who knew when his next meal would be if his wife—who subsisted on air—got on another roll?

Better safe than hungry.

Audie harvested errant produce from his sleeve as he plucked another napkin from the console. "Sheriff, did you need something?"

Carmichael calmed enough to say, "Sherri pointed me here. I wanted to let you know I talked to Lionel, and he told me you might go see Harold Carver for that busted fan. So I ran out to his place real quick. Told him to expect you and not be oiling up his shotgun in the meantime. I've got enough bodies to worry about."

Jude licked his last three fingers. The napkin disintegrated as he wiped at the residue. "Thanks for that, at any rate. We'll head over in a bit."

"Don't forget we left a path of destruction at the library," Audie said, handing him a mislaid pickle. "I'd rather not get on Sherri's bad side."

"I wouldn't worry much about it. Kids don't read anymore."

Jude and Audie exchanged looks as the sheriff walked toward his vehicle. He stopped halfway, calling back, "Did you hear they're holding a memorial service tonight?"

"Yes. We ran into Tom." Had a run-in with Tom? Same difference.

"I hope you come. The reverend, now, I ought to warn you about him too. He can get a little worked up when he's preaching. But he's a good man. Don't hold it against him."

A good man. How often had that described people ultimately responsible for the worst atrocities on earth?

The sheriff waved to them again as he climbed into his car and pulled away.

Jude slumped in his seat and found half a sandwich waving under his nose.

"You can have the rest of mine."

"Now you don't even like my lunches?"

"I love them. The demise of yours was a travesty."

"Thanks." But he returned it to her. "I'm fed enough for the time being. We better get going to the library. There's still a long day ahead."

* * *

"Newspapers."

"Hmm?" Audie paged through another set of charts, Jude pacing behind her in the alcove like the Queen's Guard. According to the records, Elise went through her third and fourth spouses in less than ten years. Thank heavens this county did a mid-decade census. In the 1850 federal listing, Husband Three was alive and well, but by 1855, Elise was married to Husband Four. She was a household of her own—a widow once more—in 1860.

"This town has a newspaper, right? Weren't there copies at the restaurant last night?"

"Good grief, was that only last night?" She laid down her pen, reaching around to massage her neck. That never worked as well as it should. "Yes, there was a stand for them by the cashier. The *Renarde Gazette*."

Jude's warm hands pushed hers away and started working at the kinks. *God bless the man.* "I wonder when it began publishing. In those days, papers would print anything. A lot of it was loaded with errors, but that society column could be gold. 'Mrs. Peacock welcomed her thirteenth child. Colonel Mustard and Professor Plum enjoyed a spirited game of chess on the mercantile's front porch.' Maybe we'd have better luck going that route instead of the official stuff."

"That's a good idea." *Don't stop rubbing, don't stop rubbing.*

Sherri scuttled into the room, carrying a steaming, blue enameled cup, handle missing. "Ouch, ouch, ouch." She set it down fast and blew at her fingertips. "I remember why I replaced that one. Now, what's a good idea?"

"How old is the *Renarde Gazette*?"

"It's the oldest in southern Missouri. Dates to around 1830, I believe."

"Perfect. Do you have access to historic copies?"

"Here? No. But the *Gazette* has archives that'll make you cry happy tears. Organized and vigilantly protected by Marshall Baden, the current editor. He'll tell you stories that have nothing to do with your research, but it'll be worth it."

"I'm always up for a decent story. Amazing the info we accidentally learn that way." Audie rolled her head to the side, not wishing to disturb Jude's work, and checked her watch—2:23 p.m. "We've got to see about getting that heater fixed first. I don't plan to wear all my layers at once tonight." Her sideways view of the tables covered with files and registers made her wince.

"Don't worry about all this." *Handy, librarians reading minds.* "I wouldn't dream of making you put away this work of art. If Jude would help me stack a few of the boxes in the corner, the rest can stay right where it is. I assume you'll be here tomorrow." She grinned. "I know you genealogy types."

Jude gave Audie's neck a final squeeze and moved toward the boxes. "You're a godsend, Sherri." Audie unzipped the backpack and stowed her notebook and binder. "That'll be a big help."

"I'm thrilled to have someone to talk to during the day." She laughed, but behind her, Jude raised an eyebrow and Audie concurred.

Sherri Powers needed someone to talk to, period.

Tom was not winning any Husband of the Year awards. And Renarde was definitely not Mayberry R.F.D.

CHAPTER 12

Harold Carver lived on the other side of the creek, past a narrow concrete bridge that had to have been on MODOT's Grade F infrastructure list for fifteen years. With the main part of town behind them, the terrain grew more rolling, the road more winding, and the number of neglected residences more, period. Some fought a daily battle to keep nature from reclaiming the sagging cottage, single-wide trailer, or outdated farm building. For others, the next steady breeze would end the war.

That's why Carver's house was such a shock. It sat before a fenced-in expanse piled high with every cast-off scrap from here to the Philippines. But the house? Though small, it was painted a brilliant white. Cobalt blue shutters framed the windows, complementing the aquamarine door. Alternating gold and burgundy mums lined the porch rail, three large pumpkins and a few gourds cascading down the stairs. Jude parked the car and followed Audie along the path. Leafless bushes, neatly trimmed, graced both sides of the stoop.

Thorns. Those were rosebushes.

Mr. Carver had quite the green thumb.

High-pitched yapping grew in intensity as they neared.

Through the glass to the left, a curly head of fawn-colored fuzz appeared—and disappeared—at intervals.

The screen door opened before they'd reached the bottom step.

"I suppose you're the Wests." Sausage fingers pulled a cigar from a mouth hidden behind a steel gray beard. A man fond of a hearty dinner, his denim overalls and forest-green plaid shirt said he'd teleported straight from Hazzard County. The General Lee would be revving up any minute, exploding over the mounds of junk with a full-throttled "Yeehaw!"

"Yes, sir." Carver hesitated before taking Jude's outstretched hand. "Jude West. This is Audra, my wife." Audie nodded at him from the walk. After another puff or two of the cigar, he responded in kind.

"I hear you got a camper giving you trouble?"

"Heater fan broke last night. Lionel Graymeyer hoped you might have something to get us by for a while."

More puffs as he chewed things over. "I don't know what you need. And I sure as heck ain't letting you loose out back by yourselves."

Because we'll die of tetanus? Audie brushed past to give Carver the environmental unit diagram and parts list. "I need a six-inch replacement fan with a D-shaft. It appears pretty standard. I still have all the hardware except the fan itself."

The man choked on his cigar smoke.

"Don't look at me." Jude raised his hands as two white eyebrows questioned what kind of witchcraft was this. "She's the mechanic of the household."

Audie tilted her head in the most cherubic of poses, and her husband had to swallow a grin. This would never get old—his petite, ethereal wife making grown men choke on their cigar smoke.

Carver considered these two lunatics on his step, skimmed over the paper and returned it to her. Opening the screen, he reached inside, drew out a hand-turned walking stick, and lumbered off the porch. The doggy in the window—what appeared to be a Pomeranian with a caffeine problem—redoubled its alarm.

"Betty, you be quiet!" he called over his shoulder. Jude nearly cut his lip trying not to snicker. Snaggletoothed junkyard dog, Betty wasn't.

She'd still bite your ankles if given half a chance, though.

Around the rose bushes they went and into the yard. No padlock or chain. How did one even start a collection like this? And how in the world would one stop?

They trailed the overalls through a narrow but clean track barely wide enough to allow the man's hips to pass. Junked cars spanning several eras, a whole section of appliances, a pyramid composed of lamps both modern and primitive. Over here, broken dishes. Over there, iron pipes from a torn-down building. If you needed it, Harold had it. But it might be fifty years old or under a pile of decaying box springs.

"Here we go," he panted, heaving to a stop. This was more exercise than he got in a week. Several tubs overflowed with a potluck of mostly mechanical parts. He extracted a pair of work gloves from his rear pocket and handed them to Jude. "She points, you pick."

The gloves were three sizes too large for him. He pulled them on anyway. "Yes, sir."

Audie walked from bin to bin, peering into each with laser focus. She tapped on the fifth one. "This looks promising."

Jude squinted but saw nothing resembling a fan.

"A couple layers down," she added, unhelpfully.

"If you say so." He knelt in the dirt, removing a pair of rusty brackets, three cordless screwdrivers, and a penny loafer. Sure enough, under a few geological strata, he unearthed three fans, all in better condition than theirs wallowing at the campsite. Standing, he held the three where she could see them. She took a last peek at the diagram and chose the middle one.

"Perfect. It's the right size, and the bolt pattern matches what we've got now."

"Good." Harold nodded as Jude replaced the other parts in the bin. "Five bucks and it's yours."

Audie handed him the money. "Thank you, Harold. I wonder—would you mind if I poked around a smidge? This is better than any archeology dig I can imagine. You have some amazing pieces."

Pieces? Only Audie could make a junk heap sound like the Metropolitan Museum of Art. Carver beamed a little behind the bushy gray beard, then stuck the cigar back in his mouth. "As long as you promise not to go tripping over anything. I don't need a big city lawyer coming after me because you went and got yourself killed."

She raised her right hand. "I hereby swear not to get myself killed."

As she made a beeline toward a heap of archaic doorknobs, Jude was left holding the fan and struggling to make small talk. "How long have you been doing this, Mr. Carver?"

"Collecting trash, you mean?" He sneered straight down his nose.

"Hey, you saved us from either a lengthy trip for parts or a freezing night in a trailer. Sure isn't trash to me."

Audie skirted a pile of rusting milk cans and disappeared into the east end of the lot.

"I've been at it about thirty-five years. I had some beater cars I kept for parts, but the ball really got rolling with my wife. She loved her antiques. Now, that's nothing more than a fancy word for junque, with a 'q-u-e.' She got to where it hurt her to let anything go to waste. We moved here to the sticks and converted the land into what you see now. After she passed, I found I couldn't break the habit." He surveyed the cache and grimaced. "I pity the poor sucker who has to clear it all when I'm dead."

They heard a small avalanche followed quickly by Audie's voice: "I'm good! No worries!"

A wry smile came from deep within the beard. "Bet you've got an interesting home life, son."

"True words, Mr. Carver. May I ask how long your wife's been gone?"

"Six years, five months." He took another puff. "Not that I'm counting. But I am. What else do I have to do around here? I take care of the house and the roses and Betty, so Maisel doesn't come haunt me. I wouldn't put it past her. Frankly, I had an interesting home life too."

From further away, a second small crash, but without the reassuring follow-up.

"Audie?" Jude called, shifting in the direction of the noise. "You okay?"

No answer came, and Jude's heart rate doubled. He quickened his pace, picking between the piles as fast as he felt able without being buried alive. Carver labored behind him. The yard was a maze. Paths merged and diverged, and he didn't know which to take. "Audie! Where are you?"

He rounded a corner and found her—upright and apparently in one sound piece—beside the pile of bricks and iron they'd passed earlier. She was staring at a heap of dusty, orange-red masonry.

"Are you all right? Why didn't you answer?" But her attention remained fixed on the heap. He turned to see what she was seeing, but a jumble of disassembled building didn't seem that captivating. Harold finally caught up to them.

"You all right, Mrs. West?" he wheezed, taking a handkerchief from his bib and wiping his face. Even in the late October chill, he flushed beet red.

"I'm fine. Yes. Sorry." Her voice radioed in from the next county over. "It's only—" Words failed her. Instead, thin fingers gestured to the bricks.

Something off-white lay in the shadows. Jude pulled out his phone and opened its flashlight, leaning closer and directing the beam into the masonry.

The phone slipped from his hand as he stumbled backward. He bounced off the belly of their new friend, rebounding toward the empty eye sockets silently appraising them from yet another human skull.

Chapter 13

The three of them sat on metal milk cans, ten yards from the county crime scene investigators noting, marking, and photographing each brick and metal rail before setting it aside. The pile of bones, lying a couple feet inside the building detritus, came into the open after ninety minutes.

Jude pulled the zipper of his jacket close to his chin and buried his hands deeper in his pockets. Audie's cheeks were a rosy pink, but she was now wearing an insulating layer, a fleece sweatshirt, and a vest under her puffy coat. Along with the knit hat and gloves, she was dressed for the Iditarod.

"No such thing as bad weather," he'd defended himself once when he was going for a run in sub-zero temperatures. "Only bad clothing." She'd taken that to heart.

A figure trudged its way from the makeshift tomb. The sheriff chose an unoccupied milk can, half-heartedly wiped at the dust-rust combo on top, and settled onto it.

"Why does every skeleton around here come with a side of you two?"

"Hey there, Sheriff." Harold shifted his girth forward. "You watch how you talk to them."

Carmichael put up both hands. "I know, I know. I just mean, dang, we haven't had a murder in decades. The Wests arrive, and we have a pair."

"I'm guessing you still haven't had a murder in decades," Audie said.

All gazes followed hers to the trio in lemon-yellow jumpsuits probing the jumble of remains. As neatly as Cassie Powers had been arranged, enshrouded and warm, this one wasn't.

"Yeah, it sure doesn't appear fresh. Could've been here for ages." He turned to Carver. "I guess you would've noticed something strange, huh?"

"Like a dead body?" Harold folded his arms across his overalls. "You've got to be kidding me, Owen. Besides, it couldn't have been here 'for ages.' Don't you recognize all that?"

"Why would I recognize a pile of, uh, stuff like that?"

"Because it's the old elementary school, the firetrap they took down a month ago. The crew asked if I wanted the demo'd bits, and I said sure. Those are quality bricks, and the wrought iron from the entrance still has life in it."

The sheriff's lips parted, then closed again.

"Good Lord, son." Harold drew on a new cigar, the end glowing deep orange. "That load's been here less than a week! And I guarantee there weren't any human bones lying there when the building was demolished, scooped into a truck, hauled eight miles over here, and dumped into my backyard."

Taking off his hat and scratching at his blond hair, the ridges on Carmichael's forehead deepened. "And I don't guess you've been moving material around any since it arrived."

Harold puffed out a billowy cloud and patted his denim bib. "Do you think I'm getting my daily constitutional shoveling tons of masonry? No, I haven't touched any of it."

"You still keeping the gate unlocked?"

"Somebody needs what I've got bad enough to steal it, it's theirs."

"You didn't feel that way in the past, Harold."

Jude glanced at Audie, but the conversation had her rapt attention.

"Well," the plaid-shirted mountain redistributed on the milk can, "I figure if they're up to no good, they'll get their comeuppance in the end."

A tech approached, carrying her camera. "Sheriff, I think we found what you were asking about." Jude peeked over the officer's shoulder at the screen, but couldn't see a thing at that angle.

"Shoot. I was afraid of that. Any ideas on cause of death?"

The woman—prematurely gray thanks to her career choice—flipped past a few more photos and stopped. "Got a pretty strong guess. That's the right parietal of the skull, with one angry set of cracks radiating off a central point. Looks like blunt force trauma. The lab will do more analysis, though."

"Okay. Thank you, Tory."

She rejoined her group, and soon the remains were boxed and the specialized equipment toted away to the vans parked on the road.

Carmichael stared at the ground, lost in thought, until Jude cleared his throat. When the lawman raised his eyes, six others watched him with anticipation.

"What was it they found, Sheriff?"

He hesitated, removing and replacing his hat twice before he said, "I guess it doesn't hurt to tell you. There's a series of healed breaks on the skeleton's right hand—four of its fingers—and a poorly healed break on the other arm. The hand trauma is from getting slammed in a car door at age twelve, and the arm is a defensive injury that didn't see a doctor until it was too late to help much."

"You got that from a couple of photographs?" Harold asked.

"I got that from knowing things I wish I didn't need to know." He gestured to the plastic tub carried away by Tory. "That skeleton is Hunter Kane."

CHAPTER 14

"That puts several things to rest anyway."

Perched on the tow bar, Audie scooted half an inch to the right, aiming for a clearer view of the environmental unit while not upsetting her delicate balance. Jude brought the flashlight closer as she wriggled the new fan into place. Round One of heater repair was complete. She'd installed and tested the new wiring and performed the customary happy dance when nothing exploded. They were down to the final steps.

Perfect, because with the latest surge of clouds that arrived about the time the body was found—how's that for coincidence?—darkness was falling fast. And it was only 5:30 p.m.

At last, the fan settled onto its collar with a satisfying click, and she reached for the screwdriver clamped between her teeth. "It certainly says Hunter isn't the one who moved Cassie in the past couple of months." She tightened the first fastener at the hub.

"Those bones were the same color as hers. I'd lay money he's been dead as long as she has. And since he was mixed in with bricks from a just-demolished school? Somebody's anxiety kicked into overdrive recently if they decided to relocate him from who knows where."

"What about how the two were arranged, one as tidy as a skeleton can be and the other dumped in a trash heap?"

"This same someone was more attached to Cassie than they ever were to Hunter."

The light beam drifted as he pondered. She redirected it to its proper position. "If a person were shifting bodies around, why wouldn't they put them both in the same spot?"

"To confuse people?"

"It worked."

"To keep the suspicion on Hunter for Cassie's death?"

She swapped him the tool for the flashlight. "Want to show off your muscles and finish those?" As she leaned backward, he edged in. "Everyone was dead set on him being guilty. But I don't expect either of those remains was meant to be found. It's pure luck we came across them."

"How fortuitous." She could hear his eyes roll. "I agree with the sheriff—why did we have to find both?"

Audie lifted the metal cover to the front of the unit. Jude took one side as she placed the first tiny screw into the hole in the upper right corner. The threads didn't want to mate. Rude. "From the sound of things, Hunter had little in the way of good luck himself."

The formed sheet shifted, and the screw dropped to the ground.

"Sorry," Jude muttered, plucking the hardware from the gravel. When he returned it and positioned his edge of the cover again, he rolled his left shoulder.

Oh. "You're thinking about how they identified him."

He stuck the next fastener into the remaining top hole and turned to the tools lying nearby. "You don't need the wire cutters anymore, right?" He gathered them along with the broken fan and made for the Jeep.

"Jude."

"It's a heck of a way to ID a kid. That's all."

It wasn't all. "I'm sorry." Unmoving, she stared at the hardware in her lap. She heard him zip up the gear bag, stowing it in its spot behind the cargo net. Everything as neat as it should be.

If only.

"Light's almost gone. Good thing you're about done."

She called on three saints to stop her from saying what she wanted to say. Maybe tonight, pressing on was best. "You'd better eat something real quick. We can't be late into town."

He walked back and leaned against the front of the camper with his legs stretched out and arms folded.

"We don't have to go, you know."

Deflecting your past traumas with mine. Touché. Placing the third screw in its hole, she tightened it and moved to the last. "I think we do. It should win us an ounce of trust, and we still need help with Elise and Henri."

His foot tapped on the rocks. "But there's no reason for both of us to make an appearance. You stay here."

Done—*with the work and this conversation, if possible.* The screwdriver rejoined its siblings in the kit. "It'll be fine." She lifted the bag to him but didn't let it go. "I'll be fine."

Three Mississippis before he half-heartedly nodded, and she released her grip. He tucked the kit into the vehicle, closing the hatch.

"I'm just saying it isn't necessary."

"Nothing's going to happen."

He must've been conversing with the heavens too, because he didn't remind her that wasn't the point.

"If you're sure." He brushed hair away from his eye. "I'll be right there with you. You give the command, and I part the crowd like Moses."

She reached for his hand. "My husband, the fighter of pharaohs."

From the freezer, Jude mined a storage container marked "chili" and turned the contents out into a pot. The frozen square won no prizes for presentation, but he knew it scored well on taste. Research days meant less than perfect eating, and the past two had surpassed imperfect by a long shot. So cryogenically prepped meals were his best friend.

As the beef and kidney beans warmed on the stove, the aroma of ancho pepper with a dash of cocoa wafted through the camper. Another save, courtesy of Jude West.

Behind him, Audie changed into a pair of nicer jeans and a sapphire sweater that floated around her like mist.

"Everyone's going to be bundled up tonight," he said, breaking up the block in the pot. "Nobody will notice what we're wearing."

"But it's a memorial service. I wish I had something better than denim for the part sticking out of my coat." She slipped past him to the mirror hanging on the bathroom door.

"Bad clothing, remember? You'd freeze in anything dressier. Plus, it'll be dark. And I already know you're beautiful, no matter what you're wearing." He stirred, trying to forget most of the day, and finally poured the steaming mixture into two bowls. Placing them on the table, he took his seat on the bench. "Your dinner awaits."

"I'm not really—"

"Yes, you are, really. I gave you, like, half a bite. Quit insulting my cooking."

She slid in beside him. "I would never do such a thing. You're the best cook on earth."

Through a mouthful of chili, he said, "Then eat it already!"

Up went the spoon. After a moment, she sighed. "Divine, sweetheart."

"Thank you." He wiped tomato sauce from the corner of his lips. "Too much spice?"

"No, it's perfect. And the cocoa is unbelievable. I would've never thought of that."

"Aw, shucks." He ducked in to kiss her cheek. "That's just because your mind is full of too many other things."

"There are a lot of things to think about." Her utensil swirled designs into the creamy dish.

"Didn't anyone teach you not to play with your food? Please finish that. We're not leaving this table until you do."

"Yes, Dad." Another nibble. "It's going to be hard not to say anything tonight about finding Hunter."

"I don't know what Carmichael's point was—as fast as news travels here, it must've gotten around by now."

"Harold is pretty isolated. Folks might go to him if they need something, but nobody's dropping by with banana bread. His neck of the woods may not be on the tell-a-neighbor network." She refilled their water glasses. "Anyway, the sheriff asked us to keep quiet until after the service, so we'd better do it."

They ate in silence for a few minutes. Jude tilted his bowl to scrape every last morsel and checked the clock. "We'd better get moving."

"You cooked. I'll clean up." Audie cleared the table and ran hot water in the little sink.

"That cut on your hand isn't going to like the water."

"I promise not to get gangrene." By the time the suds reached the top, she'd washed the two bowls, spoons, and glasses. The pot could soak. Jude buttoned the cuffs of the lone long-sleeved dress shirt he had with him and slid into the shoes with the least mud. He put on his jacket and lifted hers from the hook beside his.

The scent of her shampoo lingered on her hood. Raindrops and morning glories. Fresh and clean and pure. He held the coat for her, looked up to heaven, and quit biting his tongue. "I truly believe this is a bad idea, Aud."

She pulled up the zipper and swiveled around to face him. "It's a terrible idea. But I'm going to try, okay?"

Her soft gray eyes had hardened to marbles, the determined expression he'd seen too often in their ten-year marriage. It was useless to argue. Besides, if she wanted to try this, it was her choice.

And if things didn't go as hoped? *Just call me Moses.*

CHAPTER 15

At 6:55, Jude took Audie's gloved hand as they crossed Fleur Street to the large, open lawn beside the First Community Church of Renarde. At this point, though, it was far from open. It had taken ten minutes of driving in circles to nab a spot for the Jeep. Cars and pickups filled the church's lot and lined the streets for blocks in every direction. He watched a beat-up white sedan from the late nineties pull in next to the adjacent public cemetery, stopping beneath a no-parking sign. It still had its headlights on. Maybe they figured they wouldn't get a ticket that way.

Sherri's prediction had been right—the whole town and multiple counties huddled on the dewy grass between three enormous oak trees. At least the mass of humanity blocked the wind.

That's good and that's bad, Jude thought, a thrumming interior voltage demanding he stay on high alert. He couldn't yet gauge the level of bad.

"Hey, Jude!"

Without letting go of Audie, he twisted around to see a figure emerge from the shadows. Tiki torches at the perimeter of the lawn bathed everything in orange; the only name that came to mind was Jack, as in O'Lantern.

They'd met too many people over the past couple days, considering the ones they searched for were long dead.

The familiar man chuckled. "'Hey, Jude,' like the Beatles. I bet you get that a lot." He offered his hand, and the leathery skin conjured up a strange image.

Swatting flies…

"Kirby! Yes, you have no idea. At least it's a great song."

"Did your parents name you after it?"

"Lord no. The name comes from the saint. Patron of lost causes."

Kirby Dinhart didn't know what to do with that. He nodded down at Audie instead. "You a bit overrun in all these folks, Mrs. West? You want to move closer so you can see better?"

Her grip tightened. "No, thanks." Her head barely reached most of the chests around her. Jude's jaw clenched harder.

"Probably just as well. When ol' Hickenbocker gets going, it's best not to have a front-row seat. He's more, say, traditional than most preachers anymore. A big fan of fire and brimstone. You don't hear too much of that, not that we couldn't use a reminder from time to time."

Dinhart checked his watch and shifted his weight to his right leg. "I reckon I might not make it through the full service anyway. Been on my feet for three straight days, fixing fence while it's too wet to finish the harvest. Legs are killing me."

Jude's shoulder burned, and his own groaning spine reminded him it was there. Weather had worn the farmer's face before its day—they had to be close in age. Wood splitting and trail hiking kept Jude as fit as a man in his early forties should hope for, but he wouldn't want to be mending fence for three days either.

"I'm surprised you'd come and stand in this." On cue, the dying leaves in the oaks rustled with a gust of chilled air.

A bundle of candles reached the group, and each took one, passing the rest along. A woman wearing a coat with a lavender ribbon pinned to the lapel lit Audie's, and she in turn lit the others.

Kirby removed his hat as someone performed a sound check on an unseen microphone. Shadows fell into ridges on his cheeks and forehead that mimicked the corn rows on his land. "I had to come. Cassie and I were in school together. That summer, we'd been, uh, we were close."

Jude squinted in the darkness. Pairing the middle-aged farmer with the fresh-faced girl beaming from memorial posters hurt his brain. *But we were all teenagers once.*

It just felt like a hundred years ago.

A voice boomed from the branches above them, and the surrounding crowd jumped. Jude peered up—speakers roosted in the oak trees, like God Himself was holding the service. He pressed his wife's thin hand within his and said a quick prayer of his own that had nothing to do with Cassie Powers.

Audie squeezed Jude's hand in return. That face, with his deep hazel eyes and tan skin inlaid with worry lines caused by her… She smiled up at him. I'm fine, it lied. *Of course I'm fine.* A bunch of people gathered in sacred solemnity—what could be more loving and safe? Good-hearted folks wanting to support Tom and Sherri and Brice. A spiritual shepherd, sharing Christ's message and embracing his flock as they began to heal.

Nothing would happen in a group like this.

Besides, how long has it been since, well…

Seventeen years, three months—*what's today?*—and eleven days.

Give or take.

She shook her head. The past needed to learn its place.

The speakers crackled, and Audie pivoted to face forward, though she wasn't sure why. She was staring at the back of a hunting jacket. A stage of sorts must've been assembled up front, because if she rose onto her toes, she could make out jet black hair moving above the rest.

"Ladies and gentlemen, thank you for joining us tonight."

Audie's brain hiccupped, grappling with the contrast between the voice and the color she'd glimpsed. The words came with a more mature man's throatiness. Someone's cosmetic rituals didn't adhere to the commandment about bearing false witness.

"We're gathered this evening not to mourn our loss, but to rejoice that our dear Cassie has been in the Lord's arms all these many years." A murmur of agreement carried through the congregants, heads nodding, noses sniffling. "Tom and Sherri, Brice, this day has been a long time coming for you. I hope you know you've never left my prayers, and now, Renarde will bear you up like the angels ministered to our Lord."

The speakers cut in and out, the herd shifted forward, drawing closer to hear the preacher. It jostled Audie into Jude, but he held firm as a pillar, never letting go of her hand. His tension seeped through their gloves.

He shouldn't need to worry. But she guessed he always would.

"Many of you were friends or kin to Cassie Powers. I was privileged to provide spiritual guidance to her people early in my ministry. I led her confirmation class and witnessed her growth into an upstanding young woman. Everyone expected great things of our Cassie—a Christian life of service and virtue. We will never understand what drove her into such bad company that we must gather here today."

The pack pressed further forward, the mumblings shifting in tone. Off to the left, a single male voice raised a loud "amen." Audie forced a deep breath, counting to five as she released it. Her candle flickered, but didn't extinguish.

Words boomed from the trees, the remaining leaves shivering. "The devil is always among us. We must be constant, keep at the ready to fight his evil ways. This innocent girl let her guard down and was taken in by his dark angels." The speech's strength built with each sentence now, and an electric current leapt from body to body, licks of fire swaying as the energy multiplied.

"She chose the path of temptation, of earthly desires. They blinded her, and she knew not what she did. And what happened? A life snuffed out like these candles!" A blast through the speakers made Audie jump—he must've slammed the mic against something on-stage. The horde's murmurs grew to full voice.

"The devil's work!"

"He must be stopped!"

"Lord, save us!"

Jude's arm slipped across her, but she didn't look at him. Her teeth clenched, and her heart couldn't decide on a rhythm. Once more, the population lurched, the two pressed along with it. Black figures and dancing licks of orange caged them in. They were closed in, cut off.

A shudder rocked her sideways, vision flickering to television static.

Not now. Not again.

"A family torn apart by a moment's weakness. A mother and father sent to an early grave because bearing the loss of one they'd brought into the world was too much. Brothers heartbroken and filled with righteous vengeance. Friends, classmates, teachers, coaches—the list goes on like a thousand saints beaten, crushed under the weight of Satan's work. And why? Because of human frailty. Because she looked away from the gift of God's eternal splendor and hid herself from his light."

More "amens," with an angrier edge than the word should ever carry.

"Jude?" The air didn't make it past her vocal cords.

"Yet, we cannot put the blame on this unfortunate girl alone, abandoned in one of our life-giving fields to rot. She has already had her punishment and rests now in the bosom of Abraham. No, we must put our focus on the devil himself and on his empty promises, and especially on his operatives here on earth." The crowd anticipated the words. "Hunter Kane."

Shouts and fists went up in the mob, and they surged again. Jude stumbled as he was pushed from behind by someone's raised arm.

"Jude?" Her cracked voice couldn't rise above the swell. *Hunter Kane is dead. Hunter Kane was not the devil!* A car engine started out on the periphery, audible only because a loose belt squealed high through the night's cold air.

"This wicked, wicked boy stole our beloved Cassie from God's kingdom on earth, but in doing so, ushered her straight to the gates of heaven. His intentions were evil, as all *his* helpers are evil, but he understood not the rapture she would soon enter."

"Preach, Reverend!"

"But to him? To this wicked man who stole away her life and the heart of her community? Will he see joy?"

"No!"

"Will he revel in the loving embrace of Isaac and Jacob?"

"No!"

"He will burn! He will burn in perdition for what he did, and we will rejoice in his writhing as he cries for mercy!"

The congregation shouted and cheered. Faces around her melted into scarlet horrors.

Here were the devils. And among them, Audie and Jude stood, pilgrims in an unholy land. At any second, the demons would see the truth, and the flames would rise to consume them.

"Jude!" Her voice broke through. He grabbed her shoulder.

"We're going. Hang on." He tried to spin her toward the rear of the pack, but the mob was tight as a drum. "Move, people! Let us by!"

The figures convulsed and heaved. The noise of the throng deafened her until that high-pitched screech sliced through the din.

It was getting closer.

From the western edge of the group rose a collective scream, and the pack shattered into chaos as the white car bucked across the lawn toward them. Its headlights illuminated panicked faces as candles dropped and shrieks rang loud. Audie got shoved hard by a running man, and her knees hit the wet ground before Jude lifted her up and pushed forward, arm around her waist. The car skirted past the corner of the crowd, veering back onto the open lawn, bouncing over the curb, and tearing into the night.

Shadows and solid bodies crisscrossed in the tumult, a house of mirrors straight from the underworld. A new voice took over the microphone, giving orders with authority. It was Babel to her ears. Tears blinded her, and though she recognized her husband was pushing them through the melee, bellowing at people to get out of the way, she couldn't feel his hands anymore. Her feet couldn't feel the grass beneath her. All she knew was wild drumming in her chest and her head, and as she fell to the ground and into blackness, she didn't think the drums would ever stop.

Chapter 16

Jude braced himself on the side of the car and fought to open the passenger door without dropping an armful of wife. Her lids were fluttering by the time he pulled it wide and perched her sideways on the seat.

"Aud? Are you with me?"

She was white as a ghost. Whiter, probably, if the city had installed decent streetlamps. But her hand reached out and grabbed onto his shoulder as her eyes opened. He held his breath, and she did the same, the two hanging in the balance between pandemonium behind them and the quiet of the car. Finally, she focused, and the well of tears made a break for it.

"Aw, sweetie." He gathered her close to his chest. That morning-glory fragrance, faint and delicate. "You're all right. It's over." She trembled, but the tears were silent. She nodded. Stepping away an inch, he scanned her over. "You're not hurt, are you?"

With a swipe at her cheek, she whispered, "I'm so sorry."

"I don't want to hear it." He jerked a thumb toward the lawn. "That is pure insanity." *We never should've come.* He knew it would be bad—the crowd, the grief, the darkness. He didn't realize it would be a cult revival.

We never should've come.

Her color—what little she had—returned, and as sirens and red-blue strobes swarmed the streets, she started scrutinizing him as well. "Are you okay?"

"Yeah." He reached across her and into the glove compartment. Moses may have had manna in the desert, but baggies of salted almonds and M&Ms would have to suffice. "You need to get your sugar up."

She waved off the emergency rations. "Jude, I'm fine."

"It's a biological fact, Audie. You fainted. You need to eat something. Humor me, or I'm taking you to the hospital."

She opened the bag and popped a handful.

"Good." He took a few pieces himself and leaned back against the car, at last convinced she wouldn't nosedive from her seat. The spinning police lights added to the otherworldliness of the scene. From what he could tell, the homicidal lunatic hadn't run over anyone. He merely scared the bejeezus out of them instead. There had to be trampling injuries, lots of falls, but no bodies appeared to have gone under the tires.

Thank heavens for small miracles.

The skinny figure of the deputy, all drink-of-water beneath his official hat, stood beside Sheriff Carmichael's robust frame. Both with hands on hips, they assessed what lay before them. The boss dispatched his protégé across the grass as he took stock of folks gathered under the nearest oak. They sent him on to others, rattled but not wounded.

"I don't understand what that preacher thought he was doing." Jude's fists clenched, his muscles spring-loaded. "Spewing that filth in the name of God. That was one of the sickest things I've ever seen."

"Jude?" Her voice was hollow. "I want to go home."

"Right. Sorry." She brought her legs into the car with her, and he closed the door. Climbing into the driver's seat, he pulled onto the street and pointed them east toward the campground.

The Jeep passed through Fillion's entrance gate, high beams piercing the pitch-black asphalt winding through the woods.

"Would you build us a fire?"

"Of course." A fox skittered across the road in front of them, and Jude eased off the gas. Hitting a critter wouldn't improve the evening's mood. On their right, a pair of yellow discs, deer height, approved.

"A big fire."

"Is there any other kind?"

They arrived at the campground, and he backed into their space.

"I'm going to sit in here while you get things burning, okay?"

"Yes, ma'am." He climbed out, zipped up his jacket, and headed to the fire ring. The stack of logs he'd worked on all week was about to come in handy. He gathered a load of kindling from the stash beneath the picnic table. The sulfur smell of the match conjured up too many images of Gehenna, and his breath caught in his throat. *Get thee behind me, Satan.* In moments, the sticks took to the flame, and he added bigger logs in a tepee shape. A controlled inferno roared in less than ten.

The car door creaked open. Coming in from the gloom, she sank into her cherry red camp chair. "Share a blanket?"

He brought his chair beside hers and accepted the offered edge, even though he didn't need it. For a while, they sat in silence. He watched the sparks rising from the pit, burning bright and then dropping as dirty white snowflakes. His focus wandered around the sites—still no tent campers, perhaps none for the rest of the winter—but the two RVs were in their expected spots. The LED pumpkins hung dark. The group might've gone into town for a meal. Bet they were surprised when they found the place locked up tight.

"I'm okay, Jude," Audie said quietly. "I am."

"Great."

"Really. I'm sorry I freaked out. But with the crowd and the preacher—"

"Love, that wasn't a crowd. It was a mob. We should've left well before the…" Before the refugee from Mad Max tried to flatten a hundred rioters?

She shuddered. "Yeah, I could've done without that part."

"I don't know which was the worse atrocity. I should've screamed that Hunter Kane's been dead as long as Cassie has."

"I would've cheered you on right until they burned us at the stake for heresy. What that man said was vile."

"They'll learn tomorrow. Wonder if it'll change any minds."

"For some, it will. Tonight, hurting people got riled up by a snake who preys on that sort of thing."

"I wonder who was driving the car. They had to be the only soul in southeast Missouri who wasn't on the lawn." A log popped, and a shower of orange and yellow rained near their feet. "You think it was the killer? Or whoever moved the bodies? They might not be the same person."

She didn't answer, and Jude shifted enough to check on her without appearing like he was checking on her. A deep crease ran between her brows. "It could be," she said at last. "But it also could've been someone tired of hearing Hunter's name raked through the mud. One person in this community might not believe he's the wicked, wicked man-boy Reverend Hickenbocker has condemned him to be."

"I hope so. Driving into a flock of angry villagers was a poor choice, but I'd like to think there's someone who believes he's innocent."

The blaze leapt again.

"You warm enough?" He tucked the blanket closer to her chin.

"Yes, thanks. Smokey the Bear would not love you like I do."

He raised three fingers. "I swear to restrict my pyromania to sanctioned rings and to let forest fires end with me. Unless my wife is freezing. Then Smokey's on his own."

A small smile softened her worried expression. "Thank you. But that was the Boy Scout salute. And I know for a fact you were never a Boy Scout."

"Maybe it was also the Tibetan hand signal for 'I swear upon the graves of my ancient ancestors.'"

"Tibet?"

"Maybe. Maybe not. I've been around."

Her face screwed up as she studied him, and he tilted his head downward, radiating his best enigmatic air from the top of his eyes. "I almost believe that one."

The embers crackled, and Jude rose to add more logs. They would be out here for a while. He retook his seat and found her hand under the blanket.

"Who would've guessed Renarde was bursting with mysteries?" she said. "We're still behind on uncovering the story of Henri and Elise for Bob, and now there's something far more current and terrible going on."

"With creepy-crawling tendrils reaching back thirty years."

"That's a disturbing mental image."

"Inappropriate?"

"Disturbingly appropriate."

"I'm sure you're dying to do a round-up, Miss Poirot."

"I am." Good. Let her distract herself with facts, order, method. Anything but brimstone-spewing preachers. "Don't call me that."

"Yes, boss."

She squeezed his hand and took three deep breaths before proceeding. "Hunter Kane likely died at the same time as Cassie Powers. In the past week or so, someone relocated both bodies. Why? And why not leave them together?"

"With Cassie wrapped with care and Hunter tossed like trash."

"Seems everyone thought Hunter was trash."

"Have you caught anything yet that suggests he was such a bad kid?"

"Not a thing. It's all too vague."

"And it reeks of pure prejudice. Personal story-telling because he came from a less than stellar home." Those broken bones. Jude rolled his left shoulder.

"What else do we know? Kirby Dinhart had been dating Cassie a few months before she and Hunter went missing. Hunter was the guy who took his spot, and her body was found in Kirby's field. That doesn't sound great."

"Not at all."

She chuckled. "At least we solved the mystery of the biting flies."

"We did?"

"The scene reminded me of a message board I'd read online. A genealogist wrote about a strange experience at the grave of a person who'd been impossible to find. It was an ancestor of hers that came with a lot of baggage. She'd searched for years, trying to uncover this person's details, and ultimately discovered the tombstone hidden away like Elise's.

"Elated to be on the spot, the descendant quickly found her legs being bitten by swarms of black flies. She'd never had that problem at another site. It felt menacing to her—the ancestor was not happy and wanted her to leave. This morning, when the flies went after Kirby alone, all I could think of was that story. I wondered if Cassie was sending us a clue about Mr. Dinhart."

"An intriguing prospect."

"But Kirby mentioned tonight he'd been patching fences for the past couple of days. That's long hours on your feet, bending over, walking, working with your hands. His body built up lactic acid, which draws flies. So the local population bombarded him instead of the rest of us."

Jude paused to do the mental math. "Did your archivist degree come with a minor in biological minutia?"

"Yes," she said, straight-faced.

When her lips finally broke into a grin, tension dropped from Jude's muscles in a torrent.

"Now, Tom Powers and his brother had it in for Hunter too. But how could Cassie have been hurt? They wanted to protect her. Unless Hunter killed Cassie, and the boys killed Hunter."

"No. They wouldn't have let their sister's disappearance be a mystery for this long."

"But if they told folks about Cassie, they'd be implicating themselves in Hunter's murder. I'd bet certain teenagers could keep their mouths shut to save their own skins."

Her gaze fixed on the flames, the gerbils raced. "Tom anyway. He's the sibling who left for twenty-five years."

"True." Jude would've paid real money to not say what he was about to say. Beneath the blanket, he ran his thumb over her hand. "There is one more person holding some intense grudges against Hunter Kane."

"Reverend Hickenbocker."

She said it resolutely and flatly, and the strength of it darn near broke his heart.

"He's a piece of garbage, Audie. You know that. And I don't think for a second all those people out there were bad, but he's a master at pushing buttons. In any case, the dear reverend has deep-seated hatred for a kid no one's seen in three decades."

"How can a man of God say things like he said?"

"He can't." Jude's jaw clenched. "And he isn't." He leaned forward to poke the logs, and the blaze grew brighter again. Above them, their resident owl hooted his approval.

"Who do you really think was driving the car?"

"A disgruntled person who dislikes the town or the preacher? A bored kid wanting giggles?"

She shook her head. "It was way too direct. That was somebody who cared for Hunter. Somebody who knew he wasn't responsible for Cassie's death or who would've loved him regardless."

"At least, it can't be too much of a mystery. The car was pretty distinct and several hundred witnesses got a close-up view. The sheriff will have a body in the brig by morning." He stretched into the canvas seat and sighed, struggling to push away the angry faces and the vile words. "You did good tonight, Aud."

"I passed out."

"Not until we were being chased by a maniac in a Chevy. That was a pretty normal reaction, considering."

She didn't answer.

"I still say you did good. People with a lot less reason to lose it would've lost it in that circus."

Nothing.

"And we can stay right here all night." It wasn't a matter of craving the solace of Mother Nature. She couldn't go into the confines of the camper. Not into something small, even with two means of egress. Not yet. Maybe not ever.

At least they had a use for the logs he'd split. He glanced at her sideways, and she chewed at her lower lip.

"Let's talk about tomorrow. We should get a coffee mug to replace the one Sherri broke while helping us."

"We passed a florist near the police station. They'll carry things like that." A vase of Audie's favorite zinnias for the camper wouldn't hurt either.

"I'll bet the drugstore has something too. Plus, we need to resupply the medicine cabinet. Band-Aids, aspirin, that sort of thing." So she'd seen him take the last tablets for his shoulder. Couldn't help that now. And God knew it wasn't going away.

"All right. Then what's our next move?"

This deep breath came with a quiver. "The reverend."

"What?"

"We have to, Jude. We need access to church documents for the Laroque history. According to Sherri, he's the gatekeeper."

"No. You're not going. I'll go myself."

"Jude."

"No! That man's a lunatic."

"You don't always find things in the records that I do. You're so great, but you can't see it all. I need to be there."

"Audie, he's going to be less than helpful."

"I'd much rather he *not* be helpful. I need him to point us to the files and get out of my way."

Leaning forward now with his elbows on his knees, he shook his head. Before he could find the loophole that would win his case, she rapped the gavel.

"Jude, hon, we have no choice. It'll be fine. I'll be fine. It was the horde, not him."

"I don't like him."

"I'd be horrified if you did, but he's a necessary evil."

"Evil, at any rate."

"As soon as the shops open, we'll get on our way."

"All right." Though it wasn't. "But that bastard says one stupid thing—"

"—and your wife shall swoop in and protect you from his wicked ways, okay?"

A losing battle, he bowed in defeat. "Yeah, okay."

CHAPTER 17

The last light in the big RV had fallen dark two hours ago. Even the owl had flown off for a nap. When Jude left the warmth of the blanket for another visit to the woodpile, Audie peeked at her watch—two a.m.

"Don't feed the fire. I want to go in."

He picked up one of the split logs and tucked it under his arm, bending for a second. "No, you don't."

No, I don't. But he'd been stifling yawns for forty-five minutes, and that shoulder would be useless in the coming days if he sat in the cold any longer. "I do. We can go in."

He straightened, studying her through the rising smoke. "There's plenty of wood."

"We repaired the heater; might as well use it. And you need sleep." Stiff bones argued with her as she pushed herself from the low-slung chair and folded the blanket. He hesitated, but laid the logs back on the stack. *The smartest choice he had. What rotten spots I put him in.*

When he was behind her on the stairs, he finally asked the question. "Have you talked with Sister Philomena lately?"

She opened the door and stepped inside, tucking the blanket

into the dining nook without facing him. "We chatted last week. And, yes, I'll check in with her soon." She snuck a glance in his direction. He brushed the fallen bangs off his face, raising the curtain on a mask of taut muscles. "Don't worry. I'll be all right."

"I know."

He was getting better at lying. Or the old prayer about accepting what one cannot change had finally sunk in.

Within minutes of turning up the thermostat, the camper grew toasty. At least one thing had worked today. Clothes changed, lights out, two heads on two pillows. Jude's breathing fell into a steady rhythm.

Lucky boy.

She lay under the comforter, eyes open, smelling the smoke in her hair. She'd joked they should install an accurate star map on the ceiling of the trailer. Someday, she might finally master the names of the constellations.

Now, is Altair the star or the constellation?

Altair's the star. It's in Cygnus, the eagle.

Got it. Until I forget again.

Just as well. A map would encircle the skylight—complete with working hinges for any emergency escapes—and the real stars would mix with the fake stars. In a cosmos that messy, it wouldn't matter if the eagle was named Cygnus or not.

Sigh.

Her nose itched, but she refused to scratch it. She wasn't about to disturb him.

The day cluttered her mind. The dual mysteries—bygone and bygoner. *New word—better contact the OED.*

Where was I?

Right. The pair of dead teens. A brimstone preacher. And the mob.

The crazy, claustrophobic, breathing, seething mob.

She shivered, and Jude shifted, turning over but not wakening.

Oh, Ollie, why did you have to go like that?

Would every crowd, every cramped space, devolve her into a blathering idiot until the day they were reunited?

For the thousandth time, she tried to picture it, her two husbands meeting each other on the other side. She knew they'd get along. She couldn't have married them otherwise. But what would they say? Oliver, a perpetual twenty-six, soft and caring expression, curly hair, a helper and teacher, guiding others as they relearned how to walk, how to live. And Jude—dear God, she hoped he'd be an old, old man before this celestial introduction. Would the black locks have grayed? Would that one piece still be falling into his eyes? Would his intense, always-on-edge-for-what-was-coming demeanor rattle Oliver? Startle him? She could see her first love watching her, questioning—this was who replaced me?

Not for many years, darling, and never replaced. But you left.

Yes, he'd nod. I left.

And then Jude would be reaching out a hand, an abandoned series of tattoos peeking from beneath the collar of his shirt as it shifted.

I took care of her when you couldn't any more.

I know. Thank you.

A tear formed, and she had to let it roll down her cheek. She blinked away its brethren. Nope. Not tonight. Tonight had been awful enough.

How did I get so blessed? Blessed to have loved twice, for each to have been—to be—great in its own right.

May greed not be my undoing. Because she did not want this one to end.

Truly, truly blessed.

Chapter 18

It took three hard yanks to open the glass door to Fisher Drugs. If pain relievers hadn't already been on the list, Audie would've been adding them now. *At least it's my right shoulder that's dangling from its socket.* Between the two Wests, they could almost account for one functional upper body.

"Sorry about that, hon." The clerk at the counter was stashing her purse below the register, the store having opened only five minutes earlier. In her mid-sixties, she was the bright center in a mosaic of lottery tickets, penny candy, "Hope for Susie" cancer awareness bracelets, and promotional items swamping the front end. "I'd tell you to give it a swift kick, but that wouldn't do anything but add a broken toe to your troubles."

Shades of autumn red that may or may not have been in the orbit of its original coloring highlighted the woman's voluminous perm. The curly flames burned above a lively face offset by dangling spider-web earrings. A chunky pumpkin pendant rested on her floral blouse, complementing the garland of ghosts draped around the potato chip rack.

In no way would those three rounds of morning java match this woman's energy. "I'll pass on the broken toe, thanks." Audie smiled with as much charm as she could muster. "I was wondering if you carry any small gift items?" Jude tipped a non-existent hat at the clerk and headed to the first-aid sign hanging from a drop-ceiling.

"Honey, you came to the right place. We've got one of everything you need and two of what you don't." She rounded the corner of the counter toward a side window. A table overflowed with last-minute options for a hostess or forgotten birthday party. Angel statues, bud vases with quotes about friendship, lavender-filled sachets…

Come to think of it, if the party was for the average rural man, pickings were slimmer. Not that they wouldn't enjoy the heart-shaped mirror etched with "Live, Laugh, Love." But the Sausage To-Go pack advertised at Metcalfe's would probably be better appreciated.

"Think you can find something you like? I realize we're not Hallmark, but since there isn't one of those for thirty miles, the boss makes sure to offer a few odds and ends." Her earrings swayed. "Now and then, I get to help pick products to carry. It's more fun than circling your Christmas list in the Sears catalog."

On the left half of the table sat an arrangement of coffee cups, some with funny sayings, others with abstract designs. Droopy lettering on one confessed "I'm allergic to mornings," accompanied by a cartoon ice bag and thermometer. Probably not the best choice for a work environment. Moving on.

"Have you worked here long?" A mug the width of a soup bowl read, "I have measured out my life in coffee spoons. T. S. Eliot." An author quote for a librarian? Promising. But as jittery as Sherri was after a regular-sized cup, this one could cause global catastrophe.

"Ages. The mop was ginger for real back in the day." The spiders bobbed with her full-body laugh.

Another mug showed an open text with bright blue covers. Typewritten words filled the two pages: "A well-read woman is a dangerous creature."

"Sold!"

"Great choice. And true, ain't it? My book club meets twice a month. We should change it to a wine-and-cheese club with a side of plotting, but whatever. Is that all you need, hon?"

"This and whatever my other half digs up." They returned to the register. Outside, a man whose spine hadn't been straight since the Korean War looked ready to swing his quad cane at the stubborn door. Audie pushed it open before Congress had to consider another international conflict.

The clerk greeted Mr. Bailey, who saluted with his cane. All-purpose, that thing. As he hobbled to the pharmacist by way of the barrel full of Horehound Candy, she turned back to Audie. "Okay, I've got to ask. Are you two the couple that found the Powers girl?"

Well, at least this one didn't beat around the bush. "Guilty."

She clicked her tongue and shook her head. "To tell the truth, I never thought we'd know what became of that poor thing."

"Did you live in Renarde when it happened?"

"I've lived here since I was fourteen. My daddy moved us into town when his crops went south three years running. To be honest, Daddy wasn't the greatest farmer. I got married young, divorced as soon as I knew better, married a second time to a man with character and a savings account, and had a few kids. When they got big enough to fend for themselves, I started hunting for a job that let me escape domestic life for a while. Luckily, this one had just opened."

"That's good timing."

"It was for me, but not for Faye." The woman's bright face darkened.

"Who?"

"Faye Bell. Her husband runs the tow truck and repair shop down on Main."

"Oh, Travis, right? I think we saw him yesterday."

The redhead glanced toward the rear of the store where the druggist was engaged in conversation with Jude. She lowered her voice and leaned in. "Faye got caught stealing pills. Travis's business was doing bad—the entire town knew it. He never had any of the simplest parts to fix your car, and the tow truck he'd bought secondhand was always breaking down.

"Faye was selling the drugs down the interstate for extra cash to keep them afloat. I almost couldn't blame her. They had three little ones at home and not a penny to their name. It was all they could do to clothe the kids during those years, even with hand-me-downs from some of us other moms."

Nothing short of a hurricane could stop this river of consciousness now that it was flowing. As Missouri was not recognized for its tropical climate, the steady flow was in no danger. *No complaints from me.* This was more information than they'd get in a week at the library.

Too bad it wasn't about the case they were actually supposed to be working.

"Anyway, Mr. Powers, the accountant? The old one, not Tom. He was doing the taxes for the repair shop and saw these strange sums of money coming in. The books showed them being for legitimate work, but in a community this small? Everybody knows everything about everyone else. He tried to keep his concerns discrete. But after dropping subtle hints around Dennis—that's the pharmacist there with your cutie-pie of a husband—they put two and two together."

"She lost her job?"

"Dennis didn't have a choice. He handled it kindly from what I heard, but the state would've taken away his license if he'd kept her. Travis felt terrible. He went to Mr. Powers, saying he'd clear up the money with the drugstore over time, and there was talk Mr. P had negotiated some terms to make things right between all involved." Her face, animated by the ancient gossip, resumed its worrying. "But then Cassie disappeared. Folks panicked, and her father was never the same. I think a lot of financial details slipped through the cracks while he, Alice, and the boys struggled to wrap themselves around what you'd call a 'new normal.'" Air quotes and all.

"If Travis Bell still has his shop, I guess they climbed out of the hole eventually."

"It took a while. Things improved after he had that chat with Mr. Powers. But both of them—the Bells, I mean—they keep to themselves, even nowadays. Their kids moved away; Travis and Faye stayed put. They don't take part in any kind of social life. And I haven't seen Travis without that scowl on his face for thirty years. He wasn't always like that."

Abruptly, her focus shifted to the aisle before her, right hand rising to puff the curls even more. The familiar expression playing on her salmon-colored lips announced Jude's arrival. Onto the counter he dropped a bottle of aspirin, two boxes of Band-Aids—one flesh-tone and one covered with tiny motorcycles—and a tube of unknown content. Audie cocked her head.

"What?" he asked. "You're always saying I should have a motorcycle."

"Oh, darling, if anyone should, it's you," gushed the woman who wasn't his wife. Jude gave her a dose of patented smile, and the gush transformed into a bit of hot and bothered.

Don't mind me. I'm only the chick you're going home with. "I was questioning more the mystery tube."

"Mr. Fisher's recommendation. A new cream for various aches and pains." *Various, my left foot.* "He says it won't stink up the camper."

"Honey, that voodoo is the cat's meow. It works on joints where I'd thrown in the towel. But I can't imagine a young fellow like you having arthritis." Her eyes glimmered. "Of course, of all the Itis boys—"

"Arthur's the worst," Jude finished with a nod. "That joke never gets tired." He waved off her concern. "It's an injury from the Jurassic period that acts cranky now and then."

Such as when you're roped into moving an attic full of old documents and hauling your wife through a rioting mob.

She winked at him. "Sports, right? I should've known." She rang up the items and wrapped the coffee mug in extra paper bags. "Are you two in the area much longer? I heard you're doing some sort of research at the library?"

The grapevine had better reception here than their cell phones. "Genealogy. Helping a friend who can't get down here himself." *Another "is that a job?" and I'll need a straitjacket.* "We'll be here a few more days."

"If you need anything else, stop on by. I'm here most of the time and would love to chat." Not a huge surprise. "You should stick around for Spark in the Park too. It's the biggest thing this county has going for Halloween."

"Maybe we'll try," Jude said. "Thanks a lot, Missus…"

"Simpson, darling. Patty Simpson." She winked at him. "But you call me Red."

"You got it, Red."

Audie stepped on his foot and feigned surprise at his reaction. "See you later, Patty. Thanks again."

As they neared the door, a customer who clearly knew the secret to opening it on the first try blew inside. The harried man pulled up just short of bowling straight through them.

"Son of a biscuit!" She watched Jude mentally file that one away for later. "Sorry, geez. It's just—hey, Red! Is Dad back there?"

"Sure, hon, but what's the matter?"

He half-jogged down the first aisle, wind-breaker flapping behind him. "They arrested somebody on attempted murder for driving through the memorial last night."

Red raced from behind the register, salivating at his heels. "They did? Who was it?"

"Angel Faust. Hunter Kane's mother."

CHAPTER 19

"Roger, this is Jude and Audra West," Dennis Fisher made the introductions from behind the pharmacy counter. His white coat, crisp and professional, looked like it had been standing under the stained-glass "Druggist" sign for most of his life. A gold "50" pinned above the RPh on his name tag confirmed it. One earned that half-century award from the state after a lot of filled bottles. "They had the misfortune of finding both those kids. This is my son, Roger."

The younger man's cheeks reddened. "I didn't mean to almost run you over."

"No worries. I guess it's common knowledge now that Hunter's remains were found?"

"News travels darn quick around here, hon." Patty fiddled with the pumpkin hanging from her necklace.

"So that was his mom last night?"

"Were you there?" Dennis cringed. "You weren't seeing the best side of Renarde."

"We believe it, Mr. Fisher," Jude assured him. "All it takes is one person to set off the worst in a pack, things an individual would never consider."

"Hickenbocker might not have been part of Angel's

considerations when she plowed through the crowd. She wasn't always the most stable of women."

"He was laying it on thick regarding her son."

"But to drive right into all those people? What was she thinking?"

"Do any of you know Mrs. Faust well?"

"I'm not even sure she's a missus anymore," Patty admitted. "Her scumbag of a husband ran off within a week of Hunter disappearing."

Jude's eyebrows shot straight up. "He left? How did that not seem suspicious?"

The two older folks did that dance where they don't know quite where to look because—perhaps—they've been called out on a thing they never realized was sketchy until now.

The pharmacist cleared his throat. "Well, everybody assumed Hunter killed Cassie and then ran. They weren't really digging for other suspects." The word seemed foreign to his lips. Who needed a suspect? Hunter Kane had done it, and that was that.

"Why didn't people think they might've disappeared on purpose? They were dating, from what we hear?"

"The two were together a lot. But a girl like her with a boy like him? Those matches never work. Her parents were upset, but just kept hoping it would blow over when they graduated in the spring. She'd move away to college, and Hunter and this so-called relationship would be a bad memory."

"He wasn't college bound?"

"That kid? I'm sure he wasn't. Not what you'd call academic. And where would his mother get the money?"

"What about the stepdad?"

"Like Patty said, a deadbeat. Always drunk, always getting into fights. Couldn't hold a job." Fisher stopped talking, an epiphany sinking in. "You don't think he could've had anything to do with their deaths, do you?"

Audie surreptitiously felt for Jude's hand and rubbed at the base of his thumb. Her own frustration meter glowed a deep crimson. His would be brighter and more explosive. "We can't say, of course. We're not from around here. But have any of you heard how they identified Hunter's remains so fast?"

Three blank expressions.

"A poorly healed break on his arm and four fractured fingers on his left hand." Jude managed to keep his voice steady, but only because Audie was working his palm like bread dough. "Somebody enjoyed using young Hunter as his personal punching bag."

The sunlight, though filtered through the ever-present clouds, thawed Audie's soul after the chilling conversation. But as they stepped off the sidewalk in front of the drugstore, Jude still wore a frown.

"Red?" she teased. "Really?"

Either a snicker or a smirk would've been acceptable. She got neither.

"What?" Jude opened the car door for her but didn't meet her look. "She said it was her name." Audie climbed in, and he circled around to the driver's side. He buckled his seat belt and took the wheel. "Where to, boss?" But his posture suggested a rod-fused spine, and his knuckles burned white hot.

She reached over and placed a hand over his. "You okay?"

For a moment, he held onto the sting of all those senseless words, an interior dialogue screaming *"Someone's got to mourn this boy. Someone has to be angry for him."* Then the safety of their own car and his own wife at last broke through. His shoulders released. "Yeah," he exhaled, relaxing into the seat. "I'm okay."

"You're a fine man, Jude West." She let go as he started the engine. "To the library, dear. And make it snappy before Mrs. Patty Simpson finds herself a third husband: mine."

The big red door opened with far less argument than the drugstore's.

"If you're not supposed to talk in church and you're not supposed to talk in a library," Jude whispered as they entered, "what's the penalty for making a peep in here?"

"Welcome!" A cheerful but unfamiliar face sat behind the checkout desk. She pushed lime green reading glasses up into her auburn hair, setting aside a publication thicker than *War and Peace*.

"If the librarian isn't worried about it, neither am I." Wait—that was a book of Sunday crosswords. Another slow news day in the Renarde world of literature.

"But you have a library science degree, and therefore immunity. What about us mere mortals?"

"You're immune by association. Good morning!" Was it still morning? Wowzers. "We're the Wests. We left a tornado in your reference room."

The freckles on the woman's nose bunched up as she laughed. "I'm Missy Aikman, the other half of the staff here. Sherri told me about your visit yesterday." A somber hue colored her smile. "The family is grateful beyond words you gave them closure on Cass. I am too."

Jude slipped the pack off his left shoulder and set it at their feet. He needed Mr. Fisher's cure-all ASAP. "It was dumb luck on our part. You knew Cassie?"

"Back in the day, we were what they'd call BFFs. Slept over on weekends, took camping trips with each other's families. It was awful when she disappeared. It was like I lost my own arm."

And half your heart. "I'm so sorry. It's a long road, becoming whole after such a thing."

Jude's fingers on her lower spine... *I'm not projecting, I'm not projecting...*

Fine. See right through me. That's rude, you know.

The librarian didn't notice the silent marital dispute. "Amen. And it didn't help that we had no idea what happened to her. Or to Hunter."

"I understand we've been in town only a couple days," Jude said, "but you're the first person to mention Hunter's disappearance was a mystery too."

Missy's lip curled. "I've never seen such a bunch of closed-minded people as the ones who've crucified him all these years."

"Were you at the memorial last night?"

"You bet I was. It was a disgrace. Here we were, ready to say goodbye to a great girl after decades, and that imbecile with a pulpit spits on both their graves." Her cheeks flushed, and she reached for a clear blue water bottle covered with kittens wearing space helmets.

"I'm sorry, Missy. We didn't mean to upset you."

She took a drink and closed the cap. "No, no, it's all right. I shouldn't talk like that about a supposed man of God, but he's not a man of any God I was raised with. Hunter was a good kid."

Retrieving their jaws from the floor must've been obvious, because she leaned in. "He was. That nonsense the preacher spouted was nothing but lies. Hunter had gotten into a little trouble in his early teens—stealing a few bits from the junker, Harold Carver? A couple of cheap parts for the car he was building. He couldn't even drive yet, but he already understood he'd need to make his own way.

His mother wasn't any help, and his stepdad was less than useless. If Hickenbocker wants to name devils, he should start with Ray Faust, not poor Hunter."

The felines had to be getting dizzy as she fiddled with the bottle under the desk lamp. "Anyway, Harold had cameras in the junkyard then, and the sheriff at the time brought the boy over with the parts in hand, scared to death. Say what you will about Harold and that maze behind his house, but he's a better Christian than Hickenbocker could ever be. He gave Hunter a job helping with the yard."

"Hunter worked for Harold?"

He hadn't said a word. After Carmichael identified the body, he'd grown quiet, puffed on that cigar with more determination. But who wouldn't need a moment to collect themselves, finding a long-dead teenager dumped on their property?

"He had a way with mechanical things. He worked for Travis too, over at the auto shop. Hunter was saving for college, wanted to be an engineer."

And there go the jaws again. "We were told he wasn't the academic type."

"I'm sure you were." She sighed. "But he was smart. Super-smart. He hid it because of where he came from. A brainy kid on that side of town needed to be even tougher than usual to survive. Of course, the entire school called him a loser just because of his mom and stepdad. Some things never change."

"That's for darn sure," Jude muttered.

Missy returned her hydrating fidget spinner to its home amongst the paper clips. "But you two aren't here to talk about Renarde's sad history. Are you starting with the files where you left off yesterday?"

The coffee mug shed Patty's careful swaddling as it slid from the Fisher Drugstore bag. "We're here with a peace offering. Sherri broke hers while working with us. And now we're hoping to leave our mess for one more day. We need to go dig through church records. They might guide us more intelligently through your info here."

She picked up the mug, read it, and giggled. "Sherri will love this. And, of course—the boxes aren't bothering anyone. Believe it or not, we get busy on occasion, but closer to term-paper time when teachers still require books as sources. You'd think the students were being forced to rediscover the Rosetta Stone when asked to reference something other than the interwebs."

"Thanks much, Missy. I'm sure we'll see you later."

As they made for the door, she said, "Wait—you're searching the church records?"

"Yes. Why?"

"You know Hickenbocker has them, right? His admin office is the depository for all of Renarde's religious documents, no matter the denomination."

"Unfortunately, yes, we know."

Missy's lips screwed up once more. "Then good luck. You'll be in my prayers."

CHAPTER 20

The gravel surface of the parking lot crunched under Jude's shoes. Audie walked ahead of him, and he forced his unwilling feet to follow.

Nothing good— that's what was going to come from this visit, no matter how chipper the response had been from Joleene Devonshire, church secretary.

With russet-colored brick and the as-expected ivory steeple, the house of worship lay to the left of the admin building. Tangles of leafless vines climbed the downspout. At the top of a short, non-ADA-compliant stairway hung the arched doors, breaking canon by being forest green rather than red. A bronze bell peeked from the belfry.

Between the two buildings sat the parsonage, a cottage silent and sober. Coal-colored shutters and no flowers on the stoop, a shiny black sedan parked beside it. Affixed to the rear window was a white cross decal with "clergy" printed underneath.

Jude's breakfast threatened revolt.

Focus on the job, focus on the job.

A breezeway attached the parsonage to the west wall of the office building. Weathered and flaking, a hand-painted sign announced the structure also served as an event space for the congregation. The office's wrap-around porch breathed life into the large, bleached edifice, and a gentler touch had prevailed here than at the not-so-good reverend's abode. Pots of mums graced one side of the entrance. Scarlet bushes burned in a line below the railing. Blame the owner of a well-traveled minivan over near the Jeep for their diligent care.

Hickenbocker didn't seem like the pruning type. *Though he's certainly full of fertilizer.*

A parade of past brides marched by, all photographed on that porch. Nervous and excited and worried and happy. The city cemetery, beginning yards away, would've made a powerful view before saying those vows.

Until death do us part. He climbed the stairs behind Audie.

Movement to their right drew his attention. Leaves blew in cyclones on the open expanse of lawn below the graves—or the scene of the crime, as it were. The temporary stage still stood, though tendrils of black bunting had torn from the metal framework overnight and flapped in the gusty wind. Starting near the side street, two deep ruts sliced through the yellowing grass.

No, nothing good was going to come from the First Community Church of Renarde. Not today.

More swirling foliage chased him onto the porch and into the office.

"Don't worry about a few leaves," a voice said as Jude shooed some out, only to have more blow in. "It's just God's creation making an entrance."

The woman behind the desk wore a warm smile on a plump, weary face. A faded beige stain on the left shoulder of her otherwise crisp pink blouse said a baby had rested there post-mealtime. "I'll bet you're the Wests. I'm Joleene. It's great to meet you!"

Audie drew a folded paper from her hobo bag, probably from a pocket between the pyramids at Giza and a spare Winnebago. One day, she was going to go missing and he'd be forced to tell the authorities to check that bag. No, not for clues—for the five-foot-two wife it had swallowed. "Thanks for letting us come by on such short notice, Joleene." She handed the list across the desk. "We're doing genealogy research on the Laroque family, from the 1840s. We're wondering if you have any church-related files for Elise and Henri Laroque, or their child, Gareth. Elise married a Durand before Henri."

Joleene skimmed over the sheet. "That's going back a ways, but nothing's ever been thrown away around here." She spun in her chair and lifted a thick ring of keys from the wall behind her. "Each congregation used to keep their own archives, but then family-tree work got popular. All the historical records found their way into our basement, since we had the space and are right next to the Renarde cemetery. It makes it easier for folks to find what they need instead of traipsing to eight different churches across town."

The entry to the lower level was a chipped oak panel on iron hinges dating to Missouri's entry into the Union. The lock was no newer. Joleene sorted through the keys and selected one larger than the others. The king of trolls must live down there. A rush of stale air blew up from below.

Her nose crinkled. "You get used to it. I'll leave the door open for circulation."

Jude slid into the rear of their three-person formation as they took to the creaking stairs, praying each step wouldn't be the one that ended life as he knew it. Divine intervention got them to the concrete floor without disaster. Joleene flipped on lights as she went.

"My brain's fled the country since the last baby came along," she said, vaguely recalling days before spit-up stains. "There's a master switch at the top I should've used."

It wouldn't have made a difference. Stadium lighting couldn't help this space, loaded to the gills with file cabinets and bookcases, stacks of mildewing paper and leather-bound volumes with failed bindings. Audie had to be ready to call emergency services to save all this from a tragic end. After weaving through a labyrinth not dissimilar to Harold Carver's backyard, they arrived at a series of vertical files stenciled "Weddings."

"Here's a starting place for you. These cover the 1830s and '40s."

Jude dropped the rucksack onto a metal table from Thomas Jefferson's presidency. The table rocked as the load settled. From a chain above them swung a single naked bulb. He took off his jacket and hung it over the chair where Audie had done the same.

"I'll leave you to it," the secretary said, pulling open a drawer. A captive and irritated genie didn't burst free, which was surprising. "Everything's unlocked. Feel free to dig through whatever could be useful."

"Thank you, Joleene."

"I'll be right upstairs if you need anything." Not five seconds passed before her head reappeared around the corner. "Hey, you two are the ones who found Cassie and the Kane boy?"

Who knew it took so little to become celebrities? Grauman's Chinese Theatre should be asking for their handprints soon. "Yes, we found Hunter and the Powers girl."

The sarcasm blew straight past Ms. Devonshire. She pursed her lips and began fidgeting with the gold cross hanging around her neck. Finally, she steeled herself and dove forward. "Did the Kane boy really have—I mean, I heard his forehead may have had, um…"

"Had what?" A low, deep thrumming arced between his temples, and Audie's fingers arrived from nowhere to wrap around his upper arm. *Never did have a poker face.* His featherweight wife intended to ground him to earth, recognizing every explosive component amassing for days threatened to ignite.

"Well, there's talk that there may have been something sort of, um, etched or maybe burned onto his forehead. Like… numbers."

"Numbers?"

"You know." Her gaze flickered up at him, then down to the floor.

"Like, mark-of-the-devil kinds of numbers?" The pitch of his words pointed to the utter insanity of her question.

In defense, she straightened her posture and raised her chin. "I'm just repeating what I heard."

"No, Joleene," Audie said in a voice meant for toddlers. "There were no sixes or horns carved into Hunter Kane's skull. I saw it myself."

"Okay, then." She disappeared again, and this time, she scurried up the rickety stairs, racing closer to heaven and further from, well, ….

Audie stared after her. "Wow."

"That's one word for it."

"Let's find what we came for and get out of here."

"Yes, please." His attention had fled the area. *Maybe it's hiding here.* In the drawer Joleene had left open, he rifled through a few documents. They still didn't have a year for the Laroques' wedding, but first husband Philippe had passed in early 1844. Considering a widow's situation in that era? Elise's next nuptials likely were soon after.

Behind him, papers shuffled as they were slid from the pack.

Soon, they'd be arranged like perfect soldiers beside the binder and pen. Casually—*who am I kidding?*—he asked over his shoulder, "You're okay down here?"

A dingy, subterranean labyrinth with no air and one point of egress—heck, *he* was on edge. But she took a deep breath of dust and forgotten sacraments, and lied.

"I'm fine."

He opened the next cabinet. Still no moths bursting forth like an Egyptian plague. Wonders never cease. "Here we go, 1844." He liberated an armful of once-manila folders and deposited them on the table.

Audie took the one on top. The paper crinkled under her light touch. "Whoever archived the marriage licenses didn't realize April is customarily before June." She rubbed at the bridge of her nose. "While I'm sorting these, why don't you see if you can find Gareth's baptismal certificate?"

"Aye, aye, Captain." He walked past the wedding and funeral registers, then a cabinet marked "Baptisms" that turned out to be as empty as Reverend Hickenbocker's soul. The next bookshelf held more ratty folders piled high. He took one down and choked on the insect remains that fell in its wake. *So that's what happened to the locusts.* The light bulb over the work table struggled to reach this far, and after he wiped the dirt off his lashes, he squinted at the timeworn handwriting.

Christenings. Eureka.

At least this would require less sifting. Per his marriage certificate, Gareth Laroque had entered this world in June 1845. Baptism should've followed forthwith.

At Mission Control with his file, Audie's "in" pile had shrunk by half. As he dragged out his chair, she scanned another page.

"Finally!" she said, sitting up straighter. "Success."

He leaned across the table. "It's upside-down and in French."

"Right-side up, it's in French too. Henri Laroque, son of Pierre and Magdaleine Laroque, was joined in matrimony to Mrs. Philippe Durand, daughter of Leopold and Veronique Boursellier on August 12, 1844."

"Her dead husband even tagged along to her next marriage."

Audie's knuckles whitened around her pen.

And the trophy for Half-witted Spouse of the Year goes to—Jude West!

"Holy smokes. I didn't mean—"

"I know." But she didn't lift her eyes. She moved on while he silently self-flagellated. "August. That was only two months after Philippe's passing. Well, at least we have a couple more blanks to fill for Bob—a wedding date and names for four new great-great"—she tapped out the count on the table—"great-great-grandparents. If we can find confirmation of Gareth's birth date with his baptism, we'll have more spots checked off."

Another quarter of an hour passed. Audie, long understanding that words fell from his mouth without stopping by his brain first, wandered into the older documents further away. Jude skimmed page after page. "Hey! I found something."

"Yeah?" Her voice floated through the bookshelves.

"It's a baptismal certificate for a son of Elise and Henri, 1845, but the child was named after his father. He's also an Henri."

"Middle name?"

"Pierre."

"That's strange. Maybe Gareth was a nickname."

Jude shifted to the left, searching for a position that didn't throw shadows on the paper. From the top, he traced the old-fashioned cursive and French wording. He must be mistranslating. Not a shocker, as his foreign language skills came from three years of deciphering tombstones. *I might not be able to ask directions to the bathroom, but if you need "born," "died," or "God" in any European dialect, I'm your guy.* No, he was reading it right. "If it was a nickname, I guess it's better than just calling him the Laroque boy."

"Jude."

He leaned back in his chair, pushing the bangs away. "It's got to get to you too, Aud. The Kane boy. They make him sound like a stray dog no one wanted."

From the vicinity of her voice, a metal drawer squealed. "He *was* a stray dog nobody wanted."

"The mark of the devil etched on his skull? What was Joleene thinking?"

"I'd venture a guess."

"Wonder where she picked up that idea?"

"Got a guess on that too."

The bulb above Jude's head flickered and died. "Perfect." Standing, he stretched over the table, fingers brushing past the hot glass. The thing must've loosened from all the swinging.

Like dominoes, the rest of the lights fell dark.

"What the—"

He pivoted toward the west end of the space. A thin rectangular of yellow illuminated a section of the stairs. Thank God, Dieu, Gott, and Dievas for small favors. He took a step in that direction.

Then the door above them slammed shut, the concussion sucked into the foundation and sound-deadening tomes surrounding them.

Utter blackness.

"Jude?" Her voice had tightened like Ebeneezer Scrooge's purse strings.

She'd appreciate that reference if she wasn't on the verge of a panic attack.

"Don't move. It's okay. Do you have your phone on you?"

"It's in my bag, by you." As an afterthought, she added, "I'm all right."

And the Pope's not Catholic.

He tripped over a chair leg, straining to picture the last known location of any of their stuff. *She's the one with the eagle eyes, not me. Wait—can eagles see at night? Maybe I need bat eyes?* He swept in front of him, coming up with nothing but air. His own phone lay safely in the Jeep.

"Jude?" The pitch had risen again.

"Hang on. I'm gonna'—" do what? He couldn't remember where the switches were on the walls. If he could make it to the stairs without breaking his neck, the master switch was at the top. "Stay put."

Arms outstretched, he aimed for open space. *Was it cabinets then bookshelves then staircase?* His foot caught on something hard and unmoving, and before he could react, a cold stone wall smashed into his left shoulder. Maybe the shoulder smashed into it. No matter—one gave and one didn't. Stars blinded him more than the darkness, and a string of expletives escaped.

"Are you okay?" No scolding for the curses. Her voice was either far away or fading. Or both.

"I'm almost there." At least the damp rocks told him he'd arrived at the edge of the basement. Forcing down nausea, he shuffled as carefully as his pounding heart allowed. There—the bottom step. He clambered up the death trap, tripping twice, and flipped the switch at the same moment a new racket came from below. With the arm that wasn't flaming, he wrenched at the door. It held fast.

"Joleene!" The wood planks were as hard on his fist as the stones had been. "Anybody! Let us out!"

For the love of Dieu. Down once more, through the maze, past the worktable. Audie sat on the floor beside an open metal drawer, holding her lower leg. Jeans torn, blood seeped from a gash on her shin. Her eyelids were clamped shut, lips drawn tight.

Jude dropped to one knee. "The lights are on. Let me see." He pried her fingers away. The cut looked painful, but not stitch-worthy. He drew her close. "You're all right."

"Are you two okay down there?" Joleene's voice drifted from the first floor, followed by footfalls on the stairs. "I don't understand how the door locked. I stepped away to the ladies' room for a minute and came back to hear your banging." Rounding the corner, she stumbled as she caught sight of them on the ground. "Oh my gosh! What happened?"

Jude cocked his face up at her, Audie's still planted in his throbbing shoulder. "Somebody killed the power and locked the exit on us. It was like a tomb in here." Adrenaline burned through his veins now that the crisis passed. "Who else is in the building?"

"It's only me and the—" Joleene stopped.

"The reverend?"

The frightened shadow falling across her expression was his answer. "Is she hurt?"

"She cut her leg in the dark. We're coming upstairs."

"Yes, of course."

He practically had to stand on his head to get a view of Audie's downturned face. At least her eyes were open. "You're all right," he whispered again.

She nodded.

He rocked back on his heels, pulled himself upright, and reached his hand to her. Together, they limped to the table. Bags packed, they plodded to the stairs.

"I'll put the files away," Joleene said weakly, trailing them toward the daylight.

CHAPTER 21

Audie brushed off Joleene's fussing about a first-aid kit and walked straight outside. Lurched, perhaps. Behind her, Jude told the secretary they may or may not be back. *My shin should receive a medal for its sacrifice.* It was the only thing keeping Jude from a second-degree arson charge. If he hadn't been distracted by blood, he's be stealing matches from the church altar to burn the place down.

In the lot, she perched on the edge of the Jeep's rear bumper. Surveying the landscape over Jude's head as he bandaged her leg, one thing was noticeably missing: a certain black sedan.

"I grow weary of this town." Her gut churned, and her brain ached worse than her leg.

"You and me both." He completed his work, scrutinized it with a nod, and reached around her to the cooler. Extracting a Ziplok of baby carrots, he took three and handed the rest to her.

"Is there anything you don't try to fix with food?"

"No. I thought you knew that. Now, what just happened?"

An invisible lead weight hung from her wrists, her ankles, her neck. "Someone sent us a message." Was there such a thing as a reverse marionette? A doll that can only lay on the floor? She was becoming one.

"A message about what? If it was the preacher, does that mean what I think it means?"

"That he's been dabbling in corpses by moonlight? I don't know." She eased down from her perch, bent her knee a few times, and returned the veggies to him, unmolested. "I need to move."

Shake off the lead. Remind her lungs of their job description. Block the stifling darkness and the terror that would always come with it. Cemetery or lawn? Site of dead people or, if Angel Faust had steered three degrees to the right, site of almost-dead people?

Cemetery, it is.

Jude closed the hatch after swallowing two more carrots, and jogged to catch up. He could've crawled and caught up.

Sigh.

The day had clouded over again, and more leaves blanketed the graves. As dwellings for the deceased go, this one was pretty. Spacious, serene but not spooky, most vases filled with silk autumn flowers. She ran her gloved fingers over a monument worn smooth. Its better-preserved neighbor bore a date around the time of Renarde's founding. The rare, house-shaped crypt dotted the landscape, but the ground in between was carpeted with gray stones. Sprinkled in for contrast were rose-colored ones, carved from ancient, southeast Missouri pink granite.

There, a grouping of Metcalfes. To the west, three Bryants. A squirrel in full hoarder mode raced by, sprinting straight to the names Alice and Gordon Powers.

Cassie's parents.

Their marker could've been chiseled yesterday. In the undisturbed grass beside it, their teenage daughter would soon be buried.

What a nightmare.

In silence, they made a circuit of the grounds, following the fence line. The far corner held one of the mausoleums, sheltering the mortal remains of the Clayburn clan. The graves surrounding it had seen a century and a half; its masonry must've been laid generations ago. At the foot of the bronze door, the most recent engraving read 1975.

"Clayburn. Have we met anyone by that name?" Around the far edge of the building, a copse of trees encroached, leading into thick woods.

"In Renarde? I don't think so."

"It sounds familiar." Sculpted reliefs on the door depicted Judgment Day, Jesus taking the lambs with him to heaven and the demon-headed goats falling into eternal torment. "That's odd."

Jude stepped closer. "The goats? Definitely."

"No, that." Near the padlock, a patch of shiny, chestnut-colored metal peeked from the seafoam green patina.

"How the heck did you see that?"

Glove off, the surface felt rough, sharp. Then she remembered Elise's ill-tempered tombstone. No more blood loss on this job, or Bob would need to subsidize their health insurance. "This is the oldest section of the graveyard. It's got to be used less. How do you think this damage happened?"

"Lawn mower threw a rock?"

"But it must've been recent. This hasn't oxidized yet." Tilting back, she studied the letters near the roof. "I wish I could place the name. I'm lucky I remember my own right now." She pivoted on her uninjured leg and aimed them toward the car. "Did we learn anything useful today?"

"We nailed down Henri and Elise's wedding date, confirming their relationship existed. And we uncovered a Laroque son with the wrong Christian name."

"Maybe Gareth was a family nickname to keep him straight from Henri the Elder. He took it with him when he moved to St. Louis."

"If that's all we found, though, it sure isn't much."

And wasn't worth the trouble, he left unsaid.

"Wait—I never had the chance to tell you. Before my swan dive, I finished sifting through the death records from that period. They were in better order than the marriages, yet I still never came across Henri Senior's burial info."

"How can there be no documentation? Burial on consecrated ground was pretty crucial in the day. Did you see any big gaps in data? Like info was lost in a fire?"

"Not at all." She stepped off the grass and onto the gravel lot. "But Bob's third-great-grandfather remains a big mystery. And we don't have a clue where to find him."

Jude turned the wheel toward downtown single-handed, while his left shoulder continued to protest with the explosive fire of a thousand cannons. A star or two lingered from the hit taken in the dungeon.

Insult. Injury. A great day all around.

On Main Street, Metcalfe & Son's Family Restaurant hosted the expected lunch crowd. The sheriff's SUV occupied the corner space.

"How intrepid are you feeling?" Audie asked.

"The church plundered all my intrepidness. Intrepidity?"

"I meant gastronomically."

His gut wept. "Audie. Sweetheart. I made us an award-winning lunch—Greek salad and stuffed gyros. Our own brief escape to the Mediterranean, just the two of us, basking in feta and Kalamata olives, not discussing murder."

"Your meals are worth a wait. We can have it for dinner. But we won't learn what's going on around here if we eat by ourselves."

"And we want to know that?"

"To avoid being locked in future church basements, yes. And I think you're curious too, but you're letting your hunger do the talking again."

His stomach lodged a formal complaint, but he pulled into the lot. "What are you hoping to learn?"

"First, are there any more bodies we're expected to discover? Also, someone left us a note yesterday. Who's keeping tabs on our work?"

He parked the Jeep between a Ford F-150 and a Chevy Silverado. Frenemies at lunch—at least they'd provide entertainment. "That note we got. The man-in-the-shadows routine worries me, Aud. It might be our pal from this morning, which points in one specific direction."

"Then you should be eager to hear the latest." She climbed from the car stiffly and slipped the hobo bag over her head.

Until the day he died, he wouldn't figure her out. Equal parts porcelain doll and revolutionary. A terracotta warrior—fierce and fragile. She shouldn't be functioning after the basement, after last night's ordeal, after horrors past. But she was.

How? No clue. But the next person to hit her triggers is going down if it's my final act on this earth.

He held the door as she walked into the diner. Out came the usual sweeping stares. At least they moved on faster today; the Wests were getting to be old news. Rick Metcalfe waved at them from the kitchen as they took the empty table beside Owen Carmichael.

"Sheriff."

The khaki-clad man glanced up and groaned. "Don't tell me you found another skeleton."

"No. And we're sure not seeking them out."

"You couldn't prove that by me."

The day-shift waitress came by. Ginny must've been in school. Without a peek at the menu—because what good was that going to do?—Audie ordered a cheeseburger and side salad. Jude did the same. No, no fries, thanks. He'd like to live long enough to solve the Laroque mystery, and the burger already made that unlikely.

Audie refocused on Carmichael, who continued eating his lunch, pretending she wasn't staring at him. "Has Hunter's cause of death been verified yet?"

He chewed through a mouthful of beef, wiping mustard from his cheek with a blue checkered napkin. "As a matter of fact, yes. Blunt trauma to the skull."

"That'll do it."

"The ME said it was a single whack, thank God. I wouldn't want to be laying there, waiting for the follow-up." He continued shoveling the sandwich into his mouth, hoping for early release from this unexpected incarceration. Audie was undeterred.

"So, how are you proceeding? Since it seems Hunter didn't murder Cassie?"

"Who said he didn't murder her?"

"Sheriff, those bones have been sitting somewhere as long as Cassie's were. They died at the same time. Sure, Hunter could've killed her and then been killed himself, but it could've been the other way around too."

He laughed so hard, a bit of tomato flew onto his plate. Another swipe at his face.

"I'm not saying it's likely. I'm saying it's possible. A lot of scenarios are possible. In any case, someone moved both bodies in the past week. Sherri's new blanket and that brick pile in Harold's yard guarantee it. Somebody from your town."

"Hey, now, how do you know—"

"Sheriff!" Exasperation.

Thought she reserved that look for me.

The big man swallowed the last bite, reached for his iced tea, and sank back into the vinyl-covered booth with a belch. "Okay, fine. That could be true."

"Then who are you checking into?"

"I do not have to discuss suspects with you." Now the shiny silver star comes out? *After all we've been through together?*

"Because you don't have any?"

"Because you're civilians! And strangers."

"Pretty sure we no longer qualify as the latter." Carmichael swung his frustration around to him. Why let Audie have all the fun? "We've cleared your missing-persons list, met half the locals, and received a personal invitation to the memorial service. Plus, we've almost been killed twice."

"Twice?" The sheriff put down the tall, red tumbler. To his credit, he listened attentively to their narrow escapes from both the rampaging car and Hickenbocker territory. By the end, his entire face burned the color of his drink glass. "I couldn't venture a guess about the church, but last night was a fiasco."

"People are saying it was Angel Faust, Hunter's mother, driving the car."

"All that filth spewing from the reverend? Not a surprise it'd knock a parent sideways. She's sitting over in my jail cell now. I have to bring her up on charges, though she made sure not to hit anyone. With terrorism laws these days, she's going to be in for it, I'm afraid."

"Sounds like the woman's had a difficult life."

"Folks who knew her claim she was a pretty girl in her day. Then she got pregnant with Hunter before graduation. That used to be a bigger strike against you. The baby daddy ran off, and Angel went through a series of creeps, hunting for a way to survive. The jerk who stuck around the longest was the worst of them—a little rat named Ray Faust."

"AKA, the evil stepfather."

"That's him." The sheriff squinted through the window at the police station on the next block. "That is one piece of vermin nobody was sorry to see disappear." He turned back to them. "Ray was a scrawny, self-important idiot who wanted nothing more than to be a big man. And he'd pick on the smallest around to show how big he was. Those identifying breaks on Hunter's body? I'm sure you already guessed they were compliments of Ray. Slammed the kid's hand in the door of his truck once on purpose. All for getting dirt on the floor mat of his precious piece-of-crap Ford."

"With his history and disappearance, wouldn't he be a reasonable suspect in Hunter's death?"

Carmichael shrugged. "Maybe. He's on the list, for sure. The most incriminating evidence is he got into a fight with Hunter the afternoon of Halloween."

Jude had to pick his eyeballs up off the table before they rolled away.

"But the thing is, he was always getting into fights with Hunter. Or Angel. Or his boss. Or his neighbor. The man was an absolute—well, a donkey's hind-end, anyway. Does it mean he killed him? No idea. And if so, how did Cassie get caught in the middle?"

"If she was with him, she might've tried to stop it."

"Possible. But Ray Faust hasn't shown his face around here in thirty years. Even if he did kill them, who moved their bodies? And as much as I hate to admit it, there are other prospects. Have you heard about the Bells?" He pointed across the street where the mechanic worked beside the hardware store. "The guy with the repair shop?"

Audie nodded. "We're hearing a lot about everyone around here."

"Dirty laundry and small towns go hand in hand, unfortunately. Hunter did some work at the shop until Travis couldn't pay him anymore. Cassie's father, our accountant, was the one who discovered their money problems and realized the recent influx of cash didn't mesh. That was Faye's doing."

"We heard about that too."

"I always wondered if Travis might've wanted the Powers kids to get their dad to lay off his questions. He wasn't that much older than them back then, twenty-seven, twenty-eight? They might've felt more relatable than a white-collar bean counter. He could've confronted Cassie when she was with Hunter, and it all went farther than he intended."

"How are the Bells now?"

"They're making do. Had to declare bankruptcy at the time, but worked terms with the creditors and didn't lose it all. They're stable from what I hear, but they keep to themselves. It's what you do when the entire population has its noses in your business."

"I'm surprised they never left Renarde."

"I think they would've if they could've, but your hands are tied with three babies and no money. Like I said, if Hunter didn't do it, there are other places to dig. But after this long, it's going to be hard to make a case." He scanned the surrounding tables and lowered his voice. "All I'm sure of is someone in this town knows something. I just hope it isn't another few decades before we figure out what it is."

CHAPTER 22

Greasy cheddar lurked unquietly near Audie's liver. She readjusted her position in the front seat, hoping it would get the hint. One check of her chauffeur's unusually shadowed cheeks said all was not well there either, though for a different reason. "You need a nap."

Jude raised an eyebrow at her as he swung onto Main. "So I'm three now?"

"No. But some rude woman kept you up way past bedtime. And I have research I can do from the comforts of home. We'll give our lungs a break from the mildew."

"Who would've thought a camper would be the cleaner option?"

Two blocks from Metcalfe's, the business district opened into a large greenspace. A white wooden sign with moss-colored scrollwork read "Renarde Town Square." Clusters of workers assembled metal frames along one of the bordering streets. Booths for the weekend's festival? Past a decorative hedge, she got a better view. An immense pile of cut wood covered the center of the brick-paved plaza. The great bonfire had begun to take shape.

At least the party would be warm.

Main Street became Highway S as they passed the last antique store and the water tower. Five miles down, they rounded the bend into the campground. A large red squirrel zipped across their path.

"The welcoming committee."

"Better than Pepe Le Pew."

Two more RVs had pulled in since the morning, the primitive sites still a ghost town. *Appropriate.* Kids ran amok again at the trailer with the pumpkin decor. They shrieked and squealed, making the park their own magic kingdom.

"The wolf pack must be too young for school," Jude said, backing into their space.

"Somewhere, the parents are having their quietest week in years."

They weren't inside three minutes before her other half passed behind her with a bundle under his arm. "Where are you going?"

"To nap, on the advice of my nanny." He grinned from the top step, holding open the screen door.

"The bed is this way."

"And the hammock is that way." The navy-and-gray nylon billowed like a sail in the October wind.

"When you hung that on Monday, I figured it was for atmosphere. You'll catch double pneumonia."

"I want to be an overachiever like you, so I'm aiming for triple." When she was not amused, he nodded to the bundle. "Two blankets, wool hat, pillow—I will literally be a happy camper. Plus, I'll be out of your hair."

"My hair doesn't mind you being in it."

He winked. "Yell if you need anything."

"And that's why I love him," she said to the closed door. It didn't respond.

At the kitchen table-slash-desk, the laptop took more than ten seconds to awaken, so she flipped to the back of the case notebook, well away from the details of Elise and Henri. Time was too short to waste, and certain things about their talk with the sheriff ate at her worse than Rick Metcalfe's cooking.

Specifically, Ray Faust.

The man gets into an altercation with the stepson he's abused for years, the kid winds up dead, and Ray disappears. Yes, as Carmichael said, being a deplorable human didn't automatically make him a cold-blooded killer. But why the vanishing act? Black bullet points denoted a whole slew of questions before the computer decided to be useful.

She glanced at her watch. Bob's third-great-grandfather could wait another five minutes. She opened a search bar and began to type.

The hour passed faster than the boot-up time had—oops. And the number of unknowns had grown instead of shrunk. But her tapping pen kept a steady cadence as she stared at the screen, an idea percolating. *Could that really be what happened?* It would answer a few things, anyway. She set aside the pen and composed an email to the major newspapers nearest to Renarde: St. Louis, Memphis, West Plains, Cape Girardeau. On a whim, she ventured as far as Springfield, Missouri.

Fingers crossed.

She rose from the desk, refilled her water bottle, and peeked through the tiny window over the sink. Jude lay wrapped like an egg roll in the hammock, hat jammed over his ears and half-way down his face. The wind rocked him as he embraced toddler life. She smiled.

From her bag on the counter, she dug out her phone. First, a text to Connor, full of balloons and birthday cakes. Twenty-six. How in the world had that happened? She still remembered holding him hours after his arrival, herself a mere teenager, elated to be called Auntie. Vita had been lucky to have a built-in and eager babysitter.

Audie scrolled to find their sibling-only thread. She fired off a note, wishing a Happy Mom-of-Connor's Birthday. Vi replied immediately.

"Thanks, sweetie! Can't believe he's so old since I haven't aged."

"It's a miracle! ;-)"

"How are you two? Job going well?"

Boy, how to answer that via text? She'd need to call later with the details, but not now. The entire Callaway nuclear plant couldn't give her enough energy. "Same as ever. Bits of info, dead-ends, dust."

"Fun. You staying warm enough?"

The decade between them meant Vi would forever ask questions like that. "Yes, mother. Wearing my galoshes in the rain too."

A wild-eyed emoji with its tongue sticking out appeared, and Audie's laugh bounced around the camper.

"How's Beck?" she typed.

"Homesick, I think, but fine. Boeing is working her hard, and Seattle hasn't seen sun in a week."

"We haven't had much either."

"True. She'll be here for Thanksgiving. You'll be home then, right?"

Audie smiled again. Home, in Vita's mind, was her two-story brick abode in historic St. Charles. Since the Wests had sold the condo and bought the camper, they spent each holiday within those wonderful walls. And the lulls between jobs when they weren't traveling on their own, etcetera, etcetera. Both Vi and hubby, Simon, had said in no uncertain terms, "mi casa, su casa." Connor and Becca had seconded with unbridled enthusiasm.

Everybody under one roof. Heaven. "Yes. I'm bringing roasted sweet potatoes."

"Perfect. I'll get Jude to work his magic on the rest."

And he would, with glee.

"I'll let you go. Just wanted to send b-day greetings."

"Much appreciated, sweetie. I know C's age now can't be easy."

Audie's vision blurred for a moment. *Nope, nope, nope.* She did not need Jude walking in to find his wife weepy over her first husband. "C's living for both of them."

"He's doing his best. And he loves his aunt to the moon and back."

"His aunt's a lucky girl. Hugs to you and Simon."

An animated pink heart danced at the end of the thread. Her sister would always be full of the life for which she'd been named. Leave it to their mother to throw out the baby book with the bath water and be a sucker for good old-fashioned meaning. Otherwise, she may have christened her second child—the one arriving after nine months of nausea and an almost lethal delivery—Sally. But no, she went with Audra, or storm in Lithuanian.

Life and Storm. They made a great pair.

A flash from the laptop drew her from the phone. The banner of Cape Girardeau's *Southeast Missourian* topped the email. Must be a slow news day. No, they didn't have any information on a Ray Faust from the year she'd requested nor any immediately adjacent. *Crud.* She sent her thanks for looking. Strike one.

Another time check. Hmm. Well, she'd blown this much, what was a little more?

Bob, I haven't forgotten about you. Really. But I need to do this first.

She slid off the bench, her lower leg reminding her of the

morning's trials. *Like I could forget.* It protested louder as she crouched to open the drawer built into the bed frame. From beneath leggings and turtlenecks, she pulled a black composition book, half the size of her regular working spirals. A glance out the window—all still quiet on the western front—and she set the timer on her phone for twenty minutes. Flipping to the last page of highlighted data written with questionable penmanship—her mother would be horrified—she turned to the computer and typed in search strings that had nothing to do with Renarde history, old or new.

The duck quacking from the phone sent her through the skylight. She cleared the browser's history and stowed the book.

I'll tell him. I will.

Guilty much? When, exactly?

When I know more.

How much will be enough?

When it's… enough. Soon. I promise.

But not now. Now is not the time.

CHAPTER 23

The Greek salad and gyros transcended the hype, and Jude looked like a new man after a filling meal and some rest.

"Preschoolers have this thing down." He folded his napkin and pushed his plate away. "Sleep, eat, repeat."

"What about play?"

"Getting locked in pitch-black hell-cellars isn't fun for you?" He lifted his glass but stopped before his lips. "'Hellars?'"

"No, and it disturbs me that you think it is." Audie took the plates to the sink. Her phone, resting on the shelf behind the table, buzzed.

"You've got mail." He handed it to her.

"Probably another dead end." Passcode, email app, swipe, tap, read. "Or not…" She dropped onto the bench again.

Really?

"Everything okay?"

Her brain raced to process what the screen was telling her. "Yeah. Everything's good. I think I might've just discovered what happened to Ray Faust."

* * *

They walked into the police station, met at the door by Owen Carmichael. "You better have a doozy of a revelation, Ms. West. I left my wife and a perfect pot roast at my folks' house to come back over here."

Audie handed him a thumb drive. "I need to print something."

"We're not the office supply store." But he took the device anyway.

"It's one picture and an email."

They followed him to his desk, where he plugged it in. They'd need a forklift for how far his mouth dropped as the image splashed across his monitor. He clicked quicker now, skimming the text in the other file. "Holy—"

"Sheriff."

"Where'd you get this?"

"A bored intern at the *Springfield News-Leader*."

The printer behind him whirred to life, and the sheriff snatched the color print off its tray. "Come with me."

He led them along a short hallway where the building's maroon bricks transitioned to institutional green blocks. A single figure haunted the jail cells, a gaunt woman with iron gray hair, patchy weather-worn skin, and bags beneath both eyes. She wore holey jeans and a faded red sweatshirt with stains painting the ragged hem. The shirt, three sizes too big, had a central pocket, and her hands were jammed into it. She sat slumped on the bench at the rear of the second cell and watched them when they entered. She did not rise.

"Angel, I've got something I want to show you."

"Who are them two?" Several teeth were missing from the front row.

"I'll make introductions shortly. But you look at this first, okay?" He passed the photograph through the bars and held it there.

After a minute, she hauled herself up like she was doing him a great favor. "It's not enough you've got me locked in here. I gotta' smile at your family photos now too?" He rattled it at her. She glared and shuffled nearer, but didn't reach for the paper.

"I think we may be talking about your family photos, Angel, not mine."

A wary expression crossed her ruddy face. She took the sheet. Audie watched subtle fear creep into those dull eyes. "Where'd you get this?"

"They got it from the Springfield newspaper. It was taken two weeks after Ray disappeared."

"Way back then? What's it mean?"

"Tell me what it's a picture of."

She shoved the paper at him. "You know darn well what it's a picture of. It's Ray's tattoo, the one on his right hand. I should remember, I seen it coming at me enough." She stalked to the rear of the cell and sat, fists returning to the sweatshirt pocket.

Carmichael pivoted and nodded at Audie. She approached the bars. "Mrs. Faust, my name's Audie West. This is my husband, Jude."

"So?"

"The newspaper says the Springfield morgue had a John Doe come in, thirty years ago, around mid-November. He'd been kicked out of a bar for not paying. Stepped into the street and was run over by a truck."

The skinny woman snorted. "What a way to go."

"A missing person report was never filed on Ray, and he had no wallet or ID when he was hit. They cremated and buried him in Springfield as an unknown."

"About the same as the rest of his life. Unknown. Unfit. Un-…

whatever." Angel had exhausted her ability to describe the man without breaking into words that would make the reverend blush. "Why's this coming up now? That was a dang long time ago."

"Jude and I were the ones who found your son, Mrs. Faust."

Her eyes shot up to them, then darted to the concrete floor. "Oh."

"We're very sorry."

She didn't move for a moment, then shrugged it off. "That was a long time ago too."

"He was your son." Jude kept his voice low and level. "You wouldn't have done what you did last night if you didn't still care."

Now she was on her feet again. "What I did last night was nothing more than what those bastards had coming! That preacher said hateful things about my boy, you hear me? Hateful things. I could say a few hateful things about that man too, but I'm better than that. Better than him."

"Angel?" Carmichael's head tilted.

"Don't you worry none, Sheriff. It's neither here nor there. I'm stuck here, and he's out there. But you want the real criminals around this town, you go dig into them Stepford folks, the Pollyannas, the ones too perfect for the rest of us."

She paced the small cell. "They're grieving and crying for a girl who was like every other girl from the so-called good families. She wasn't nothing special. I'm sorry she died, I am, but my boy—he was special. He'd had a rotten upbringing—I'm no saint—but he was smarter than anybody. He was going places. But you see anyone mourning him? Were they praying for his eternal soul? Not on your life."

She sat down hard on the bench, leaning forward with her arms on her knees, her right hand holding her forehead. The three on the other side of the bars waited for a minute before she spoke, now more defeated. "So, why are you showing me a picture of that pile of garbage all these years later?"

"Just needed to make sure it was him, Angel."

"What does that tell you?"

"An important fact," Audie said. "If Ray died soon after Hunter and Cassie were killed, he's not the one who moved them this past week."

CHAPTER 24

Jude slung the trash bag over his shoulder and walked the path to the campground dumpster. Leaves crunched beneath his feet, the owl heckling him from above. "You don't see me taking out the garbage," it said.

No, but I had chicken for dinner. Take that.

He zipped his jacket to the top. Now that night had fallen, the microscopic amount of warmth distilled through the clouds had blown into the next time zone.

Anywhere he looked, he saw Angel Faust sitting behind those bars with her sunken cheeks and haunted expression. Carmichael said she had a rap sheet too. Drugs, negligence of Hunter when he was young. But most of the visits to the Faust home, if you could call it that, were for domestic violence perpetrated by her son-of-a-biscuit husband. His leaving was the best thing that ever happened to Angel. Unfortunately, her only son disappeared in the same blink of an eye.

Some folks can't win for losing.

Put yourself in his shoes. They felt slimy. Why would Ray run if he wasn't involved? A guy with a long history of beating his wife and kid, picking fights, unemployment, drugs—taking and dealing. A real winner of a fellow.

He pushed up the dumpster lid with his right hand, the left side not on speaking terms with him. After tossing the bag, he peeked over the rim to see if any raccoons had been beaned in the taking out of this garbage. The interior was surprisingly empty of the ring-tailed scoundrels.

Scoundrels. *And we're back to Ray Faust.*

A rotten waste of space like that runs. He had to know he'd appear guilty as anything.

The lid dropped with a crash.

Well, of course.

He did know.

Ray Faust may have been a devil, but he was no idiot.

He understood the town's opinion of him. He realized his history with the law. He figured there were witnesses to his fight with Hunter that afternoon, assuming he'd been sober enough to remember such things. Taking off was the best way to avoid getting burned at the stake after his stepson and the girl went missing. Unable to mend his sinful ways, he gets drunk and flattened by a pickup. Thus ends the repulsive life of one Ray Faust.

Dang.

The banging of a squeaky door tore Jude from his thoughts. That was their door. He'd been meaning to grease it for two weeks. He started toward their site. The lamp above their kitchen table threw an amber shaft out the camper's window, and in its path stood a black silhouette.

He picked up his pace. "Audie?"

Definitely not Audie.

The figure jumped, twisted toward him, then bolted around the edge of the trailer into the darkness.

"Hey! What do you think you're doing?"

But the visitor was long gone.

Jude took one leap at the stairs to their entry. A knife was driven into it, holding a sheet of paper against the wind. Jerking open the screen, he burst inside. Brandenburg Concerto, No. 3, blasted from the mini-speaker by the sink. "Audie!"

Like a gopher, she popped up at the front of the trailer, his under-bed drawer sitting open as she put away laundry. "What's wrong?"

The edge of the table caught his hip. He didn't care. Several words she'd never permit got lost in her hair as he smothered her in a bear hug.

"Jude?"

Several seconds later, he let her out for air. "Didn't you hear him?"

She reached for the remote on the bed and shut off the radio. "Him who?" The sudden silence was deafening.

How do I get back to the door while keeping her in arm's reach? Suddenly, the tiny home on wheels wasn't tiny enough. He grabbed the billowing paper.

She paled. "Is that a knife?"

A single-blade pocketknife, to be exact. Nothing fancy. No need for the corkscrew attachment when leaving notes under the cover of night.

With the blade on the table, they examined the sheet, cheeks touching. Last spring's championship baseball team from Renarde Senior High grinned at them from an inkjet-printed photo. Twenty boys held a trophy in the shape of Missouri, their bats arranged in a fan pattern on the ground.

"What on earth does this mean?"

"Shouldn't you be asking who decided to pull a Norman Bates on our door?" He shoved aside the picture and spun into the kitchen. Gripping the counter as he leaned into it, he watched his knuckles go white. With his head down, his loose hair blocked her from his view. Good. The roaring between his ears screamed at him enough without a reminder of what he might've lost.

Then she was there, slipping her arms around him from behind. "I'm okay, love," she whispered. "I'm sorry you got scared."

Her warm face rested against his spine, soothing muscles rigid and strained. How? How was he supposed to protect her if all it took was three minutes for everything to change? Three minutes for the universe to go up in flames? He'd risen from those ashes before.

He wouldn't do it again.

Chapter 25

The coyotes sang in chorus deep in the wooded hills. A dog closer by joined in. Audie stared at the ceiling, wondering how they agreed which key to howl in.

The things you think about at three a.m.

It was better than the alternative.

Jude rolled from his right side to his left, wrestling with the blanket in an uneasy sleep. His back faced her. It was the most he'd been apart since their unexpected visit.

She counted to one hundred. He didn't budge, breathing light and steady. Maybe a second hundred, to be safe. She'd start at the top and work down this go-around. They'd talked for hours about the note and the knife and the creepiness of it all. Waiting another minute or two wouldn't kill her.

She reached zero and inched out of the bed. Pulling on a purple fleece sweatshirt, she took her spot on the bench behind the table. The laptop came to life, electric blue bathing her face. She double-clicked on the file that hid well away from their casework.

Adelphe.

Sister, in Greek.

It opened beside a browser. *I'd said soon, right? I'd finish soon, tell him soon?* Too much hid in those torn up muscles of his. Too much simmering below the surface that would never let him relax, never let down that guard. If she could do this one thing for him, ease his mind about the biggest loss he'd long ago buried, would it lessen his grasping at the things he couldn't control? Lessen the fear?

It was either this or Sister Philomena.

And *adelphe* didn't mean that kind of sister.

Audie scanned the document, her list of ideas and dead-ends, narrow leads, utter defeats. Entire sections of possible narratives were slashed through in red, newer ideas highlighted in yellow. Green ink encircled the rare—very rare—verified facts.

It all made for a Christmas tree trimmed by a six-year-old on a sugar high.

She scrolled until she found the most recent lines of yellow. The notebook under the bed held a bit more, but waking the restless lion was not a risk she was willing to take. So few clues, so much reliance on guesswork and a human psychology that was nebulous at best. *Pure conjecture.* She reread the text, forced a deep breath, and typed as silently as she could.

"What are you doing?"

She jumped and her heart stopped. He hovered over her shoulder, staring at the screen. She hadn't even heard him get up.

"Audie."

His tone. She couldn't breathe. "I'm just looking." She glanced at the clock on the monitor—5:23. How could it be so late? "I was going to tell you. I've only been running a couple searches for her." The words couldn't get out of her mouth fast enough. They were all stuck behind a logjam of her own making.

"Been? How long?"

No, no, no. "A couple weeks. A month, at most."

"A month?" He ran both hands up through his hair and turned around in a circle. "Audie, she doesn't want to be found, and I don't want to find her. I thought I'd made that clear." He paced to the rear of the camper, as far away as he could get.

Miles wouldn't be enough.

"Jude, how long has it been? She's your sister."

"And she made her feelings clear too. She wants nothing to do with the family."

"But neither do you!"

"She doesn't care."

"Which is why I'm looking." She slid from the bench and approached, but he crossed his arms in front of his chest. Hours ago. Hours ago, he couldn't stand to be apart. Backing out of the no-fly zone, she said, "You don't have anyone else. Neither of you do."

"I thought I had you." The black fringe masked his left eye. The right one glowered up from his downturned face, stabbing straight through her stomach, her heart, any other organs in the way.

"You do! But you know that's not what I mean. We hunt for families for a living, for those connections you can't get any other way. You see how important they are. You two need each other."

"She doesn't need me and hasn't for years." The vein in his neck pulsed. "You shouldn't have gone there. You knew what I wanted. You should've let me lead for once."

For once. "I'm sorry."

"I'm sure you are." He straightened without so much as a glance at her. He grabbed his coat from the hook, the wool hat from its pocket. Yanking it over his ears, he opened the door, then the screen. Puncture mark in one, torn mesh in the other. "My boots are outside. Lock up behind me."

The door slammed but didn't catch on the latch, bouncing inward again. Audie's head dropped backward. *How could I be this stupid?* If she'd been able to complete the search, she could've laid the ground work piece by piece, told him the right way. He would've been open to it, not defensive, furious. She walked to the door and raised a hand to the angry slit from the knife. They had other things to be working on, to be worrying about.

She should've let it go.

But instead, she set off a train wreck. He'd be gone for hours trying to burn this one off, walking wherever the woods took him. Thank God the park had trails. Maybe he wouldn't wander too far off of them this time.

Or maybe he'd wander so far he wouldn't return.

She sunk onto the bench, the laptop a blur. She erased the search history and shut down the browser, then saved and closed the file. The white arrow carried it from its home directory to a folder named "Someday," where her side projects retreated to die.

This one should've died before it was ever born.

CHAPTER 26

The crash of a splitting maul on a metal wedge sent Audie through the skylight. 8:30 a.m. How many whacks would it take today? She peeked between the curtains. Weak rays spotlighted his swing. At least he was home in one piece. By the fourth log, he was rolling his left shoulder. With luck, he'd be in a calmer state of mind before he severed the damaged rotator cuff completely.

She plated four blueberry pancakes and poured maple syrup on top. A bunch of grapes lay beside them. She took his coffee mug, the one that changed from black to Cardinal red when warmed, revealing the phrase "You call it camping—I call it prepping for the apocalypse," and filled it to the brim. Balancing the teetering tower, she pushed her way out the screen door and down to the yard.

At first, he didn't look up. She set the offering on the picnic table near where he worked, then took a spot on the opposite end of the bench. Her hands buried deep in the pockets of her coat, she shrank with each heavy strike to the wedge. Amber leaves fell from the tree shading the trailer.

Nature is shuddering too.

A few more hits, and he let the axe rest on the ground, his right hand finally going to the left shoulder. He moved the split logs over to the pile and returned to the table. He studied the plate.

"I'm sorry I wasn't back to make you breakfast." His face flushed from exertion, the bottom of his jeans caked with mud.

"I'm glad you're back, period. And I'm sorry about a lot of things."

He sat and took a slow drink from the mug, steam rising off the coffee in the crisp morning air. His focus settled in the distance between them and the next RV. Not on her.

"Are the woods good?" Good woods had hills and bluffs, boulders to climb, caves to explore, deer and raccoons and woodpeckers. Missouri woods passed the test ninety percent of the time.

He reached for the fork and knife and cut off a corner of the pancake stack. "Good as any." He chewed the pancakes, then set down the utensils. "I'm sorry I got angry."

"You had every right to be. You told me you didn't want to find her. I thought I knew better."

"There's so much dredged up when we go down this road, Aud. In theory, you're not wrong. I wish things were different. It should've been different with me and her. But she swallowed the lies before I could stop the force-feeding. Now, it's too late."

It's never too late. "I understand."

He cut off another wedge with the fork. "Kate and I used to be all we had."

"That's what I meant."

"Yeah." He plucked a grape from the bunch. "But she needs to be the one to find me if we're going to be siblings again. Not because I don't want to see her. It has to be her choice."

Audie nodded. He stared at the plate once more. "These are the best pancakes I've ever had."

"Liar."

"About food? You really don't know me, do you?"

"Guess I'm learning. It's helpful to live with a pro."

Another bite and a swallow of coffee. The mug was fading to black. He swung his legs over the picnic bench.

"I'll go warm it," Audie jumped, but he waved her off.

"I'm not an invalid." He emerged from the trailer a minute later with a bright red cup and a second one for her. "Did you eat?" She took the mug, happy to be holding it in her chilled fingers, happier that he offered it.

"Enough."

"Sure." He moved his plate closer to her end of the table and sat alongside. "So what's the plan, boss?"

The knot in her stomach released a fraction. *On to business as usual.* One stupid mistake and poof—it all disappears. Wasn't she smarter than this? Hadn't she learned?

"I think we're due for a visit to the *Renarde Gazette*."

"Could be enlightening. We ought to find the day's scuttlebutt there, whether or not any of it's factually accurate."

"It was a different era in journalism. And those letters citing grass-cutting ordinances will never go away."

He finished the pancakes and broke off a stem of grapes, handing it to her. He started popping the rest of them in his mouth, one by one. "Since I've blown our early start, we'll be at the paper most of the day." Standing, he took the empty plate with him. "I'll put something together for lunch. Another meal at Metcalfe's is going to send me to the cardiac unit." He juggled coffee and dish as he opened the door and entered the camper.

"Thank you, Lord," she whispered.

You better get with the program, woman. The response was as clear as if the owl had hooted it. She nodded. She'd been given too much. There was too much to lose.

CHAPTER 27

A fleeting ray of sunshine beamed through the side window of the newspaper office, spotlighting the room's solitary occupant. A man wearing reading glasses bobbed his head up and down as he squinted at his computer monitor.

"I'm guessing you two are the Wests." With a frustrated grunt, he tossed the readers onto the desk.

"How did you know?" The old wood floors creaked under them as they crossed the open space. The inky scent of printing presses long gone lingered in the air. Lining the south wall, three empty drafting boards awaited relevance. Audie pictured layouts of bygone days gracing their surfaces before the process turned digital. Two tables in the rear held stacks of reference books, notepads, and a vintage Superman lunch box. Clark Kent of the Daily Planet beamed at her through black, identity-disguising frames.

"I wouldn't be much of a newspaperman if I didn't know who was wandering my town, would I?" He rubbed his eyes, stood, and shook both their hands. "Marshall Baden."

"You're the editor of the *Gazette*, Mr. Baden?"

"Marshall. And yes, editor. Reporter. Photographer, if you want blurry pictures. Thank the tech gods for Photoshop."

"Busy life."

"Not as much as you'd think," he sighed. "I'm busier on the Cinders and Cider committee this week than I am with the paper." He gestured to the monitor, and Audie glimpsed a flyer design, pointing visitors to parking areas and shuttle buses to the festival. "We publish weekly, and in certain issues, there's still not enough news to cover the pages. Ever questioned why many papers have sections called 'Remember when?' Where they print morsels from fifty or a hundred years ago to give us modern folks a chuckle? It's nothing but filler."

"We're big fans of that stuff. We're doing genealogy research for a client whose ancestors came from this region, and we hoped you'd let us do some digging."

"Mis papeles son sus papeles. What time period are you needing?"

"The 1840s."

He rose and walked toward the rear of the building, waving them along. The door he opened led to a flight of stairs leading downward.

As expected, she froze like a popsicle. *Lovely.*

Jude's voice was low in her ear. "Aud?"

Marshall stopped too. "You okay?"

Get it together. "I'm sorry. We had a minor hiccup yesterday. Got locked in a basement with the lights off."

Also, I have a bit of a thing. Confined spaces. Long story. Would take up half your weekend edition, if you had one.

"That'll do it. If it makes you feel more at ease, this doesn't lock, there's an emergency exit in the rear, and our lights are on motion sensors. They won't shut off unless the entire building loses power." He started down and she followed, Jude's hand never leaving her back. At the bottom, they arrived at an area far better maintained than the church's dank catacombs. "Since I've been in charge, we had a little remodeling done, making sure the foundation is as moisture-tight as possible to keep the collection viable. It's no museum, but it's leaps and bounds from what it was."

Overhead, LED panels activated as they walked, the room flooding with a soft, bright glow. The walls were lined with lateral files more like those of a city's central library than the cellar of a small-town newspaper.

Stark contrast to the dated, empty space upstairs.

Audie's shoulders relaxed, and she had to stop herself from drooling. Marshall noticed. "A woman after my own heart."

"I have a degree in research and archiving. This is nirvana."

He turned to Jude. "You've got a keeper."

She glanced over her shoulder. What would he say to that, considering? Those hazel eyes looked straight into hers. "I know it."

It was like she'd been underwater for an hour and finally surfaced.

She had a keeper too.

"Eighteen forties?" Marshall proceeded to the nearest wall. "The *Gazette* had been in business about ten years. Fortunately, I'm the tail end of a long line of hoarders." They came to a cabinet marked with their decade, then broken into two-year increments. "The paper has always been a weekly, so fifty-two editions per annum. Pull whatever you want. There's a copier in the corner and tables you can work from. I'll refile after you're finished." He returned to the stairs. "If you need anything, give a holler."

"Thank you, Marshall." The editor disappeared. Audie opened her mouth, but no words came out.

"Yes," her husband answered what she couldn't ask, "you're still a keeper. Besides, it would take forever to find another woman willing to put up with me."

"You are a rare find, Mr. West." She rose on her toes to kiss him. "Let's dig."

They extracted the full file of 1840 and split the stack in two. Jude took the first six months and Audie the last. After scanning through articles about weather and crops and trappers, checking names in obituaries and birth announcements, they got through the entire year without making a single note. Same with the next. Three hours in, she wanted to offer their life savings to whomever could get her coffee. Jude slid a paper across the table and pointed to a short item from May 1845.

"Mrs. Lawrence Grebe crossed the Great River to visit Mrs. Henri Laroque on Tuesday last. Mrs. Grebe reports the Laroques have felt the hand of our mighty Lord upon their house and await the arrival of Henri's first child, expected in the latter half of June. As the Laroque homestead is cut off from the Missouri side of the river during the long winter, and the spring's flooding caused further delay, this paper offers belated warm wishes for the blessed news."

"Brilliant. Check the editions from the end of June."

Jude extracted the bottom few issues from his pile, and they each skimmed through one. Nothing. "If they were across the river, it might've taken awhile before anyone knew the baby was born. See if it's in your stack for July."

Three weeks in, she found it. "Mr. and Mrs. Henri Laroque announce the most joyous news of their son's birth. Henri Pierre Laroque Jr., born June 28 in the year of our Lord 1845. Mother and child are well, and for that we give thanks. Since the child's doting father is our esteemed woodworker, the *Gazette* is certain their home amongst the trees of Chene Blanc Island is now the sight of a rocking chair made by his gifted hands."

Audie fished out the laptop. "Does Chene Blanc sound familiar to you?"

"Nope."

"Me, neither. Think there's any Wi-Fi down here?"

"Better try. We need maps."

As the computer booted, Jude jogged upstairs to ask Marshall about a password. "It's bonjour1830, all lower case," he reported back. Images of the Mississippi river bounding southeast Missouri were soon at their fingertips.

"Have you seen the Fisk Meander maps?" A layout of multiple colored lines painted her screen.

"Were those the US Army Corps of Engineers overlays?"

"Yes, created by Harold Fisk in the 1940s. They're beautiful, aren't they?" The muted hues lay twisted like the threads of every embroidery project she'd ever attempted. "These squiggles show how the river has changed over generations."

"My gut says something that big stays put. But I know it makes its own path."

"And the Mississippi, for sure. Floods, earthquakes. Its course changes constantly."

Jude took a sudden interest in the wooden beams crossing above them. "We're near to New Madrid, aren't we?"

"Not much closer than we were in St. Louis."

But he seemed to make mental notes on how to flee the building should the tremors of 1811 and '12 choose to repeat.

She leaned forward, squinting at the tiny print on the meander maps, and launched the USGS website. Their earliest archives dated to 1907, and the indices didn't list a Chene Blanc. "This is getting us nowhere. All we know is it was near Renarde and isolated during winter and floods."

"I can't imagine, especially with small children."

"No kidding." She skimmed her notes. "The only other thing we learned is that Henri was a woodworker. Maybe that somehow answers everything."

"Sure. And I have oceanfront property in Arizona for sale."

They resumed the hunt, but nothing else came out of 1845. Same for 1846. They ate lunch upstairs with Marshall, who told them stories about his tenure on the paper, his years at the state's J-School, his days as a bookworm teen fighting to survive Renarde Senior High. After a longer break than intended, they extricated themselves and descended once more.

"Back to the salt mines," Jude said, pulling year 1847.

It took him three-quarters of an hour to strike gold.

CHAPTER 28

"'May 19, 1847. The calamitous weather unleashed upon our region on Friday last has taken a toll beyond what any household should ever need to bear. As felt by all who read this account, that evening saw the countryside battered by winds, rain, and lightning born straight of God's fury. This, of course, came behind the constant flooding that has plagued the community since the late snowmelt of this spring. Storm reports from the east side of the Great River noted a tornado mere miles from us abiding on the west. The destruction manifested itself on more than half our family homes, with the loss of precious glass, entire sections of roof, and a fallen barn, to say nothing of injured livestock.

"Yet, by far, the storm dealt its cruelest blow to the Laroque homestead of Chene Blanc Island. From what details can be gathered, a firebolt of terrible magnitude struck the woods behind the house, the same woods from which Mr. Laroque drew his livelihood and crafted many of our tables and chests. The flames took fast to the trees and engulfed the island. Residents on our bank of the river witnessed the awful glow and knew the devil danced within the inferno.

"By the time those living nearby reached the docks, they found

Mrs. Laroque half-drowned upon the river's shore. The family skiff lay shredded and broken from her wild escape. She was carried to the Abraham home and Dr. Stroub called for with all urgency. A party gathered to search the shores for signs of Mr. Laroque and their young boy, Henri, but to no avail. No searches of the river could launch until the storm passed and the new day broke. Ultimately, no trace of either Christian was discovered.

"On Sunday afternoon, town residents made the sad crossing to salvage what they could for Mrs. Laroque. Few earthly possessions remained, but those collected were delivered to Dr. Stroub for her keeping.

"Mrs. Laroque, once again a bereaved widow, is reported to be in a poor mental and physical state, but convalescing. She suffered minor injury to her hands in the blaze. The doctor assures this paper that they were the sole burns she sustained and that they will heal, one miracle amid a thousand misfortunes. The wretched woman has been able to say little except the house caught fire and while escaping, the babe was swept from her arms as the skiff hit the river torrents. Her cherished husband, attempting to save the child's life, lost his own as well. We at the *Gazette* pray for their souls and for the widow Laroque.'"

Audie let the paper sag onto the table, and they both sank back into their chairs without a word. Jude studied his wife, the once widow Garland, but her attention fixed to the newsprint. Elise's story crushed every chamber of his heart. Audie's story. Then she met his eyes, her expression full of something bigger than sadness and tragic memories.

"The child didn't die."

He should be accustomed to the whiplash by now. "What?"

"If the child died, we wouldn't have Bob, and we definitely have

Bob. He's made a down-payment on our work, it didn't bounce, and he's not a specter. The boy—a boy—of Henri and Elise's was raised by Henri's sister in St. Louis."

"Wow. Of course."

"So why would she say the child died? How did the kid wind up in St. Louis?"

"Good questions." He reached for the paper. "And what really happened to Henri Laroque Senior?"

CHAPTER 29

Audie pushed open the big red door to hear a disembodied voice from the spirit world call to them.

"Be right with you!"

At least it was an accommodating ghost.

From an unseen nook, the chatter of small children breathed life into the space. *Or maybe they're tiny fairies come to play from the pages of the Fantasy section.* This is a library, after all.

They passed Philosophy, Social Science, and Languages before finding Missy Aikman reshelving Missouri geology.

"Hey! Glad to see it's you two. Somebody could come in here to murder me, and I'd still be yelling 'one second!'" She slid *Taken for Granite—The Ancient St. Francois Mountains* into its slot and turned to them with a treasure hunter's excitement. "Ready to unearth more goodies?"

"Sure hope so. We've got a new direction to take after visiting the *Gazette* today."

"Marshall is a wealth of knowledge, isn't he? You must've made his year. He's never found a story he didn't want to tell."

"He said you carry microfilm for old Cape Girardeau newspapers?"

"Yep! Not much of it's been scanned and put online yet. We keep it on-site until it is, since the freshmen need those papers for local history projects. Let's head to the reference room."

Through the stacks they went. One of the fairies darted from the children's section as Audie passed, almost sending Jude flying without benefit of pixie dust. The boy and his sister carried armloads of chapter books, while Mom bounced Baby Brother nearby.

"Sherri loved the mug," Missy said. "She was trying to figure out how to send a thank-you note to your camper at the park."

"We were the reason she broke hers in the first place. I guess she's not in today?"

"She was here this morning. But Tom needed her for something, so I took the afternoon." She frowned before she could stop herself.

"Anything wrong?"

"Oh, nothing but town talk." She waved it off. "Tom's one of those Type A personalities. And since Cassie turned up, he's been worse than usual. But he's got a stressful job, taking care of the finances of anyone who has any. Can you imagine the secrets you'd need to keep in his position? Knowing the nitty-gritty of everybody's business?"

"I'd be uptight too." Behind Missy's back, Audie nodded to the question flashing in neon across Jude's face. Aren't an absurd number of murders related to money in one way or another? Root of all evil, etcetera?

Cassie's father knew the Bells' dirty laundry—the creditors, the bankruptcy, the black market dealing of prescription drugs. Did someone want to ensure he wouldn't hang it on the line? Did someone try using his daughter to do so?

So many puzzle pieces, none of them fitting yet. Sigh.

In a corner of the familiar alcove, Missy stripped a plastic dust cover, brittle with age, from a yellowing box-shaped reader. She opened the top drawer of the cabinet beside it. "These are all the state newspapers we have, along with a few of the bigger out-of-state ones nearby. They're organized by city name, then date. What years do you want?"

"Eighteen forty-seven. May and June."

"Very specific. You must be hot on a trail." Out came a pair of three-by-three-inch film boxes labeled *Cape Girardeau Southeast Missourian.* The machine whirred to life and she loaded the reels. As they watched the bulb warm to full brightness like it was the Sunday matinee, she crossed her arms and tapped at her lip. "I can see how Tom would be out of sorts right now. And Brice, acting like his usual self, doesn't help."

"It sounds like the two have a complicated history." Troubling? Disquieting?

Homicidal? *No. Maybe. Well…?*

"Complicated like any brothers," Missy went on, ignoring Audie's internal debate, "but more so with their sister's disappearance. Brice will always blame Tom for not staying home when she went missing. Tom got his degree, married Sherri, and lived away for years. Brice—I think he's still stuck as a sophomore in high school. He wasn't a super-mature kid, and the loss sent him over the edge. He never left Renarde, didn't go to college though he could've, never married." Missy shook her head. "It's bad enough Cassie and Hunter lost their lives. Brice sort of lost his too."

She motioned for Audie to take the seat. "But that's not why you're here. You can work one of these dinosaurs?"

"In my sleep, yes. We've been in front of a lot of them. Thanks for setting us up." She slipped off her bag and shrugged out of her coat.

"Let me know if you need me." Missy vanished into the library proper. Her voice echoed off the vaulted church ceiling as she cooed at the baby.

Jude dragged one of the rickety wooden chairs closer. "So, Tom."

"Yes. Tom."

His fingers tallied the facts. "He was here for the big festival. He'd made it clear to Hunter and Cassie that he didn't like them together. His brother feels he wasn't distraught enough when the sister disappeared. And he abandoned his hometown for two and a half decades."

"And he's awesome at keeping secrets. I don't see how we cross his name off the list."

"It's quite a list. Tom Powers. The Bells. Kirby Dinhart."

"I think there's another we need to add, but I'm keeping it to myself for the moment."

"That's playing dirty, Aud."

"Me? Never. Tomorrow, we should go over to the high school, sort through what they might have for the Laroque case."

"Right, this job thing we've been hired to do. They'd store records that dated?"

"Sherri told me they hold on to everything, and education here used to be in a one-room schoolhouse. There could be class rosters from that period. It could add info to our missing dates."

"And this visit has nothing to do with Cassie and Hunter?"

"How could it?" She turned the knob, advancing the film to the front page for May 19, 1847. But the look he was giving her burned her cheek. "Okay, fine. Since we'll be there anyway, I'd love to flip through yearbooks from their school days. See if we find anything interesting. I've got a hunch."

"Of course you do." Jude shrugged and leaned in to start the hunt. "Who am I to argue with the hunches of Audra West?"

An hour later, she flicked off the switch. It took a full thirty seconds of blinking before her eyes moistened enough to see clearly. "All that microscopic print and nothing. Not a single reference to a body downriver for a month after the big storm."

Jude stood up, cracked several vertebrae, and paced the room. "That does answer one question."

"Which is?"

"If Henri—either one—had been discovered near Cape, someone there would've heard about the Laroque fire and put two and two together. It's the next significant town on the river."

"But Henri the Younger, aka Gareth, was alive and well in St. Louis, despite what his mother said. Also, Cape may be close-ish, but seventy miles was a much longer distance back then."

He raised an eyebrow.

"You know that's not what I meant," she sighed. "But the horse you were riding couldn't get you there in an hour like the Jeep could."

"True. So what does that tell us?"

"Nada. Too many variables. All it says is no one found Henri's body."

"Not near Cape Girardeau anyway."

"By the time a body would surface, it should've been close to that area." Jude didn't respond, but the gerbil wheel was spinning. "What are you thinking?"

"I'm not sure." He folded his arms across his chest as he walked. "Maybe he never made it as far as Cape."

"That's the strongest possibility. I'd hoped with the rush of water from the storms, the river would've kept things moving."

He stopped pacing. "That could be it."

"What?"

"They found him *past* Cape. The Mississippi was running hard. The body didn't get noticed until it was farther along."

"And folks at that distance wouldn't know about the fire." Once more to the cabinets. *Please have it, please have it.* Ah, third drawer. "*The Commercial Appeal*, out of Memphis, the first metropolitan river town south of St. Louis."

She touched faded box tops while reading dates. "We're in luck—the publication dates to 1839. In '47, it was called *The Memphis Appeal.*" She gathered boxes covering late May and early June. Retaking her seat, she loaded the first film.

Jude studied the label. "This paper published more often. More pages to sift through."

She turned on the projector bulb and adjusted the focus. The front page from May 17, 1847—three days after the fatal storm—came into view. "Better get to it."

Skim, scroll, skim, scroll. Politics, business news, crime reports, farm predictions. Zero unidentified relatives—spouses or offspring—of Elise Durand-Laroque. Thirty minutes passed before Jude's hand shot out and grabbed hers to stop the knob. "Eureka!"

She zoomed in on the small square of text in the lower corner, and he began to read.

"'June 1, 1847. Over the weekend, passengers on the Steamboat *Jefferson* sounded its alarm as the remains of a tragic soul floated upon the river. The body was caught on a snag of debris near the center of the channel. In that location, the current was dead, and so the remains could've been washed downstream at any point in the last few weeks. Authorities dispatched to the site drew the remains in, but no identifying information could be discovered. The unfortunate soul had obviously drowned and his body—as it was a man—was covered with lacerations from its terrible voyage. The injuries included a horrific split across his abdomen.'"

"Ew."

"Right? 'This spring's floods and the furious storms of mid-May have filled our waters with more than the usual detritus. Thus the sad state of the deceased can only be mourned. Because of his condition, he was given a quick Christian burial in the unknowns section of the city cemetery.'"

His words hanging in the alcove, Jude ran both hands through his hair. "Holy cow. Did we just find our man?"

"I'd lay money on it."

"Wow. To be torn from his family and drowned."

Audie reread the words on the screen. *I can't be right. Can I?* She shifted to the end of her seat and skimmed through the report again. Slowly, she shook her head.

"Tell me—you have another hunch."

Her lips pursed. "Yes. A messy one, based on a weird collection of information." A maelstrom of facts swirled inside her skull, and no matter how she sorted them, they funneled into this single, awful theory. She swiveled to face him. "We have a child with the wrong name and reported dead by his mother, but who was alive and well in St. Louis. We have a drowned man with massive cuts. And we have a woman who has gone through two husbands already and will soon outlive two more."

"All true. But I'm not seeing what you're seeing, Aud."

"This week might be making me paranoid. But I've got a strong suspicion that poor Elise Laroque was not the innocent widow in this story." She looked her own second husband right in those gorgeous hazel eyes. "I think she may have killed Henri."

CHAPTER 30

Friday dawned with rain rattling the roof of the camper. Jude bustled in the kitchen as Audie dressed.

"Eggs Benedict with homemade hollandaise." He slid the plate in front of her, a bowl of chopped fruit on the side, and joined her at the kitchen table.

"My goodness, dear. Fancy."

"A morning this dreary called for something bright. See? The egg is smiling at you."

"How am I supposed to eat it now? We've bonded."

"Eat already!"

She laughed and dredged egg white through creamy yellow sauce. "Oh, Jude. You do not disappoint."

"Chez West aims to please," he bowed. "So we're driving over to the school, right? Do they know we're coming?"

She stabbed at a blueberry that kept rolling sideways. "I emailed the office yesterday. They said it was fine."

"Fine? That doesn't sound like the warm welcome we've gotten elsewhere in Renarde."

"The secretary's dealing with a building full of adolescent hormones."

"Solid excuse." He cut into his second egg. The drumming on the roof grew louder. "Do you think we're going to find much about the Laroques? Mother Nature seems to be encouraging a day at home."

"Honestly? It's a wild goose chase. But since when are you worried about a little rain?" She appraised him with those eagle eyes. "Your shoulder acting up with the weather?"

He shook his head too quickly. "Nah." Hollandaise dribbled at the corner of his mouth, and he wiped at it with the napkin. "It's fine too. After all, I have Pharmacist Fisher's magic ointment. I just didn't want to get swept off in a flood and have someone accuse you of murder."

She cringed. "You think I'm going overboard with the Elise theory?"

"We're working with super-strange facts, so piecing together the puzzle is bound to result in a weird picture. Like a neon rooster with twelve wings, riding a surfboard down the Danube. But, no, I've been struggling to shoot holes in your story, and I can't yet."

"It's a stretch, I realize. Also, A-plus on the analogy." She took the last bite of egg and pushed the plate away.

"Be still my beating heart. You ate a full breakfast."

"Husband-killing is hungry work."

The fork of cantaloupe froze halfway to his mouth; the glimmer playing in those gray irises thawed it. "Oh well. It's been a nice life." He toasted his demise with the bright orange chunk and bit into it before she could carry out whatever diabolical plan Bob's ancestor had inspired.

Jude dashed through puddles to the covered entryway of Renarde Senior High, arriving seconds after Audie. She'd refused to be dropped off, insisting she wouldn't melt. He guessed the new, canary-yellow wellies on her feet, now christened, had something to do with her insistence.

Inside, the building smelled like every high school since the beginning of time. The lockers, the books, the tile floors and their cleaners, all mixed with fresh teenager. It shot him twenty-five years into the past, and he stood in the esteemed corridors of St. Francis Academy for Boys. The one difference was St. Francis must've owned stock in a lumber mill. That place was lousy with mahogany.

Apparently not lost in her misspent youth, Audie was already halfway down the hall, and he jogged to catch up. Narrow classroom windows offered snapshots of modern education. Animated teachers and sleeping students, burned-out teachers and antsy students. Ahead, a girl materialized from one side of the passage, studied them as they neared, then disappeared into the opposite side.

A space-time portal, masquerading as an institute of higher learning? Where was this when I was in school?

A few yards before the wormhole, they came to a door etched with the word "Office," and Audie turned right. Forced to abandon his plan to visit Ford's Theatre on April 14, 1865, he followed.

"Good morning," Audie said, with energy that matched her boots.

The freckled young man sitting at the desk, stapling a pile of handouts with intense concentration, jerked at the sudden intrusion. Half of the hard-won pile fluttered to the floor. "Miss Sperry," he called through an opening behind him, expression filled with stranger danger. "Somebody's here for you."

We don't bite, Jude thought, but he didn't say it. The kid was on office duty and that was bad enough. He needed to pay off cafeteria bills, or he was frantic for anything to fatten a college application. Either way, this wasn't his first choice of what to do with a study period.

A middle-aged woman with a messy bun and a wrist full of rubber bands appeared in the doorway, lingering with one foot and most of her body still behind her. "Can I help you?"

"Yes, thanks." Audie had turned on the high-beams for her smile. "We're the Wests. I emailed about digging through school history from the 1800s for genealogy research?"

"Right. The family-tree people." *A pox on your ancestors too, lady.* Charming personality. She dragged herself into the main office and plucked a ring of keys from a hook. "Come with me."

Was that exhaustion or boredom? *How can a building full of teenagers ever be boring?* Maybe Heather Sperry's idea of excitement was roller derby kite surfing. By comparison…

"Thank you so much for letting us steal you away." Audie continued the kill-'em-with-kindness approach. They tailed the slouching shoulders through the entrance to the hall and up a flight of stairs. With enviable one-handed phone skills, she didn't stop checking her social media the entire trip.

"All the records are in our storage room. It used to be the art studio, but budget cuts killed the class. Say, you said your name is West, right? Are you the two that found Cassie?"

"Unfortunately, yes. Were you acquainted?" The ages could've been about right.

Heather's voice hardened. "She was one of my best friends. What that monster did to her? I'll never forgive him."

"If you mean Hunter Kane," Jude spoke up from the rear of their procession, "we found him too. They've been dead about the same length of time." The stairs ran out, and they arrived at the third floor. It was a clone of the ones below. On one of the lockers, a hundred glittering signs shouted "Happy Birthday, Madison!"

"Murder-suicide," the woman shrugged. "He should've skipped the first part."

"He committed suicide by blunt-force head trauma?"

But Ms. Sperry was not to be persuaded by facts. "I'll never believe it wasn't him. That kid was a loser from the get-go."

"Why do you say that?"

"I have eyes, don't I? We were all seniors together. We'd been through a lot by then. Hunter never took part in anything. No teams, no dances, no service projects. Nothing. He didn't socialize. He'd stare at you as you walked by—"

"How could you tell he was staring if you weren't staring too?"

She hesitated. Just as Jude was about to award himself a point in the debate, she charged on undeterred. "He was weird. A loser, like I said. And he stole my best friend."

They reached a room with "Records" written on looseleaf and taped to the door. Through the paper, the word "Art" stoically reminded passers-by of the state of today's education. She unlocked the room but didn't cross the threshold into Wonderland. "You won't need me, will you? I'm sure you know what you're looking for."

Stacks of yearbooks leaned on each other in a corner, creating a structure only MC Escher could love. The layers had no discernible pattern. Crumpled papers hung limply from several metal file cabinets, themselves arranged like a labyrinth.

He watched his step, waiting for the Minotaur. This was going to trigger Audie worse than being locked in a coal black cellar.

"The drawers are marked." The admin was already escaping. "Stay as long as you need. School lets out at 2:30." *Be gone before then. Yep, got it.* She disappeared before Audie could thank her for her most generous assistance.

His meticulous wife absorbed the mess without moving, and he began planning an extrication STAT. But she took a deep breath and picked her way toward the cases beneath the room's sole window. "You start with the yearbooks. Organize them a bit, see if you can find anything old."

"Why do I get the feeling this place is going to be in better shape when we leave than when we found it?"

"That is quite the mystery."

And the sun doesn't rise in the east.

A round table with three chairs took up the center of the room, covered with paint spills from its previous life. He pulled a chair to the yearbook heap and began sorting. In the middle distance, drawers opened and closed.

"How can anyone live like this?"

"It's not a home, sweetheart."

"It's the files' home, the school's beating heart from the past."

"Someone's waxing poetic today." He lifted a book with dusty, spinach-green binding, blew off its cover, and put it with others from the 1970s. "Do you think they meant the dolphin or the heir to the throne?"

"What?" Audie was not listening.

"The yearbook name. It's *Le Dauphin*."

"Hmm." Nope, not listening. He reached for another and started a 1960s stack.

She mumbled as she read labels. The ones he could make out were less than descriptive. "Nothing," she ultimately pronounced.

"What about the boxes in the corner?" He glanced over and saw her pop up like a meerkat.

"What boxes?"

"Over there." They appeared to be the most forsaken of all and, ergo, might be the oldest. She maneuvered to them with a combination of ballet and parkour and opened a lid. Another cloud of dust rose in the gloom.

"Pay dirt. Somebody should give you a raise."

"Happy to be of service."

He took his books by decade and aligned them on an empty shelf, sorted again by year. Extra copies went straight to a box.

Oh no. I've caught archivism.

Audie sat on the floor cross-legged, her wellies pulled off and resting upright beside her. A high-rise condo development had sprung up in a semi-circle around her. She held up a yellowed paper. "Philippe Durand."

"Report card?"

"Attendance sheet for 1829, when he was in seventh grade. It gives the roster for the one-room schoolhouse that year."

"Any sign of Elise or Henri?"

"No, but that's not too surprising. Maybe both emigrated as adults. Plus, they often didn't educate girls outside of the home during this era." She paused, tapping at her lip. "I wonder."

"Wonder what?"

"We're getting nowhere with Elise's backstory, but at least we found her parents' names from the marriage registry. That may be enough for Bob, filling in a few more blanks on his tree. Maybe we don't need anything else from her childhood."

"The Mrs. Durand-Laroque-Smith-Jones years or whatever those last two husbands were called does seem to be the intriguing story so far."

"Didn't that article about the storm and fire say they recovered some of her belongings? I wonder if anything still survives. A family Bible, diary, old letters?"

"It's been a century and a half, Aud. Can you imagine the condition they'd be in? And we know there's no other family left in that line, preserving documents like the Smithsonian. Bob wouldn't need us so badly."

"True." She frowned. "But we're running out of straws to grasp at for her."

"The straw well has certainly run dry. I guess we can always look into it." The last volume slid into place, and he rated his handiwork. *Five stars, would recommend.* He bushwhacked a path toward her. "Yearbooks are set. Can I help with these?"

"Did you see anything in the books?"

"I haven't found any earlier than 1947. They won't give us info for Bob's tree."

She angled her face up to him, doing her best cherub imitation. "But it might shed light on Renarde, circa thirty years ago."

How did I not see that coming? "It's a good thing you're cute." Once more into the breach.

Ten minutes passed before a voice bellowed in his ear.

"What do you think you're doing?"

CHAPTER 31

Temporarily blinded by his own bangs, Jude whirled around, talking fast. Goliath filled the doorway. "Hey, now, we have permission to be—"

The words cut out like a dropped call as he took in the newcomer: a boy, sixteen if he was a day, wearing a football jersey over blue jeans and holding his ground with hands on his inexperienced hips.

"Oh brother." *Waste of a perfectly good adrenaline spike.* He pushed aside wayward hair and glanced over his shoulder. Audie climbed to her feet amid her recently-constructed fortress. "It's just a kid."

"And I'm asking what you're doing in here!"

Jude swung his head around slowly. The guy was a full half-foot taller and accustomed to winning by means of girth. This called for a leisurely once-over and his best withering glare. "I said we have permission." Voice even, low. Where were those motorcycle Band-Aids when he needed them? "What are you doing out of class?"

"I'm hall monitor." One pace backpedaled. The teen lacked age and a practiced scowl. "Nobody's supposed to be in here."

"No *student* is supposed to be in here. Do we look like students?"

"Um, no. Sir."

They can be taught.

Fingers appeared on the shoulder of the jersey, and the boy jumped.

"It's okay, Nathan. I'll take it from here."

He moved aside, and a woman dressed in a burgundy blazer and black slacks took his place. She offered a hand as Nathan scurried away as fast as his lumbering football legs could carry him. "Louise Keppeling. I'm the principal. Heather told me she brought you two up here, and I came to make sure an avalanche hadn't buried by now."

"Jude West. This is my wife, Audie." He turned to find her mere inches behind him. *Maybe that's who scared Nate.* The giant was smarter than first thought.

"Are you having any luck?" Louise closed the door to avoid any more hall monitor upsets. "Good grief, have you been organizing? It was not this neat when I last ventured in here."

Audie blushed. "Old habits. I used to work for the Missouri Historical Society as an archivist."

"Woman, we need to talk," the principal said. "I've got a full-time position for you if you want to relocate to Renarde." The two yearbooks lying open on the table drew her attention. "Oh my gosh. That was my first year teaching." She picked up the book and thumbed through to the staff portraits.

In grayscale, her light hair set off a bright smile and lively expression. The before-and-after versions weren't so different. Her face hadn't aged in all that time. Only a few wisdom lines now deepened the compassion in her clear brown eyes.

"You were teaching when Cassie Powers and Hunter Kane were students here?"

The woman paled as she turned and surveyed the pair. "You're the two who found the bodies, aren't you?"

"Yes."

"They disappeared my second year. I hadn't taught either of them because I had underclassmen science when I began. But it's not a big school, and I knew who they were."

"Cassie seemed to be pretty popular."

"She wasn't a cheerleader or dating the captain of the football team, not that kind of popular. But she was a good kid, ran track, worked over at the drugstore. Lots of friends."

"And Hunter? We're hearing the opposite."

Louise Keppeling squared her jaw and a bright-red flush darkened her features. "What this town has against such a beaten-down child, I will never understand."

"You liked him?"

"I knew enough about him to recognize the trash talk as nonsense. That young man had a hard, hard life. Because he lived on the poorer outskirts of Renarde, he would never be one of the boys, even if he'd wanted to be. He got into a little trouble with the sheriff, but it blew over quickly. He ended up working for both the junkyard fellow and the Bells. They never uttered a bad word about him. Unfortunately, they weren't popular with the townsfolk either."

"What was he going to do after graduation? We've gotten two different stories."

"I'm surprised you've heard two," Louise said. "But Hunter was smart."

"That's not the prevailing opinion."

"If this room was less of a death trap, I'd find his file and you could see for yourself. Straight-A student. An ace in math and science. He begged his teachers not to make any fuss about it, though, because the other boys were tough enough on him already. He had his stepdad to beat him up—he didn't need the jocks too." The flush wasn't fading any time soon.

"But no one liked it when he and Cassie started going together?"

She laughed. "They weren't going together! That's what everybody says, but they weren't. Cassie and Kirby Dinhart had broken up earlier in the summer, and then she was seen with Hunter a lot. People talk. But the truth was that he was helping her with her chemistry class."

"He was tutoring her?" If the week continued in this vein, Pharmacist Fisher was going to need to concoct an analgesic cream for dropped jaws.

"It was informal, but yes. And doing well at it."

"Then why did her family want to keep them apart?"

"They didn't know. Their minds went straight to the worst-case scenario. It was Cassie's doing. She rarely floundered in her studies, and it embarrassed her. She wanted to show them how much she'd improved by the end of the semester." The principal paused, a sad truth dawning.

For some, that semester had ended earlier than expected.

"Only two of us were aware that Hunter was tutoring her—me and Trudy Wechsel, the chemistry teacher. Cassie was aiming for the pharmacy college in St. Louis, so Trudy put her with the best chem student she had. I walked in on them studying after school one day."

"Then Trudy's mom died in mid-October. She had to rush down to Florida to help her dad. She was gone the rest of the year and ended up moving there to be with him."

"When Cassie and Hunter went missing, the gossip mill kicked into overdrive. I realized nobody else would know that tutoring tidbit, and it might be useful to the investigation. I tried to tell the police, but the search had thrown Renarde into chaos, and folks were already making up their own stories. No one listened. I finally told Donald Hickenbocker, who was police chaplain. I stressed that the two had strictly been study buddies. He said he'd make sure it got into the report."

"This is too much." Jude slid chairs away from the side of the table. "Would you two please take a seat? My knees are going to go out, and I'd like to sit without being a cad."

Both ladies complied, Audie patting his arm like the feeble old man he was becoming. Louise drew the yearbook close and flipped to the sports teams. "There's Cassie, by the way." A group of teenage girls emerged from the woods during a cross-country meet. The leader had "Renarde" plastered across her tank top.

Jude's chest seized—it was the first action photo they'd seen of the dead girl. Long, runner legs. Blond hair tied in a ponytail. A determined expression on her face as she led the pack.

At last, the skeleton in the cornfield evolved into a human being.

The principal turned another page. "That's her brother Brice." A thin boy, also light-complected, sat in the first row of the JV baseball team. "He desperately wanted to play varsity, but he hadn't hit his growth spurt yet. The bigger boys would've run right over him. Well, except for Rick."

"Rick?"

"Metcalfe. The one who owns the restaurant?"

"Oh sure." Heart-attack Rick, as he was now referred to in the West trailer.

"He played on the top squad almost his entire time here. Great hitter. Then at the end of his junior season, right after the state championship, he hurt his knee. Torn ACL, I think. Today, that means surgery and therapy. But thirty years ago, it could be a career ender."

"He didn't injure it playing?"

"No, but I never heard what happened. As a teacher who expected academics to come first, I wasn't the athletes' favorite. He grew into a great guy, of course. Involved in public committees and such, plus the restaurant. It's funny how they call the high school years formative. People can be so different later."

Thank God. Louise turned to a photo of the varsity team.

"Wait, Rick wouldn't be in this because he didn't play senior year." She reached for the other book on the table. "There he is." He was one of the taller boys, more on the cusp of manhood. At the center of the team's last row, he beamed into the spring sun. "After he got hurt, he started helping Brice. He'd been friendly with Tom, so he took Brice under his wing and was bulking him up, improving his swing. They spent a lot of time together that fall. Until the end of October, of course, when everything went to heck in a hand basket."

All those young faces, so strong, full of promise. Soon to win a state championship, then to be rocked by a classmate's disappearance. A scan of the caption gave surnames of half the people they'd met this week. A Carmichael anchored the end of one row—probably a cousin to the sheriff. They had the same nose. Lionel Graymeyer of the hardware store stood three boys away from Rick. The only thing that had changed on his lanky frame was the facial hair.

"Were there any theories regarding Cassie's disappearance that didn't involve Hunter Kane?"

"The rare soul who thought Hunter might not have done it were laying their money on his stepdad, Ray Faust. He'd been cussing Hunter that afternoon downtown, drunk and mean, and Cassie had been there when he did it."

"What did you think?"

"I had no idea. My goodness, I was, what, twenty-five? Not much older than the kids. And I'm not a native. I come from Bonne Arbre; it's even smaller than Renarde. I didn't have the history the rest of the community had, wasn't sure who was reliable and who was easily twisted by idle speculation. But what I knew, and I'd swear to today, is that Hunter Kane was a smart young man on his way to things far above his original station, if people still use that word. It's a terrible shame he lost the opportunity."

Louise closed the yearbook with a sigh. "I'm sorry. All of this resurfacing so many years later makes for strange emotions. I'd better leave you to your work."

"Thanks a million for sharing with us, Ms. Keppeling." Jude stood as she rose.

"My pleasure. Come find me if you need anything." She left the door open enough for air to circulate, but not enough to summon Lieutenant Nathan. The click of her pumps soon faded.

"That was… illuminating."

"You're not kidding." Audie approached the area he'd neatly arranged, her fingers running across the perfectly even bindings. His heart fluttered in anticipation of the glittering gold star to come. But all his adoring fan club said was, "I just remembered my other hunch."

He needed to have a word with the head of club membership. "Does it involve the wonders of that flawlessly curated shelf?"

She laughed and kissed his cheek. "Of course. It's so beautiful, I was blinded for a moment. Let me take it in." She gazed, stroking her chin as the eagle eyes analyzed his work of art. "Fantastic job, sweetie." A second smooch.

Eh. I'll take what I can get.

From the row, she pulled a few issues.

"You're messing up my masterpiece, lady." The covers listed years almost two decades before Hunter and Cassie's disappearance.

"I promise to properly reshelve." She handed him one and retook her seat, going straight to the index.

His fell open to a group of kids building a parade float. A girl was throwing candy at the camera, another wrapping crepe paper around a friend. "What am I searching for?"

"See if you can find any girls named Angel."

"Angel Faust?"

"We don't know what her maiden name was."

He joined her at the table and began with the seniors. After sifting through all four class years, he had a list of five Angels.

Audie inspected his heavenly host. "There she is." A fresh brunette, her hair straight and parted down the center like Marsha Brady, looked out at them from amongst her fellow sophomores. Her clear skin and bright eyes stood her apart from the rest. "Angel Randolph."

"If that was her at sixteen, she's had a harder life than we knew." In the next year, he found those bright eyes in six photos other than the junior class gallery. Playing volleyball on the school team. Filling buckets at a fundraising car wash, all sunshine and short-shorts. Painting sets for the spring play.

"Holy—"

"Jude!"

"Sorry, but you have to see this one." He spun the book toward her, his finger beside an image taken at the Renarde Junior/Senior

Prom. The theme? Underwater FantaSea, complete with cardboard waves and tropical construction-paper fish hanging from the gymnasium ceiling. A homemade backdrop overflowed with balloons and a giant oyster shell.

Near the shell danced a glowing, if mismatched couple, holding tight to each other and facing the camera with big smiles. Her glossy, auburn locks flowed over a pale green, spaghetti-strapped dress, a carnation corsage wrapped around her wrist. The boy had a mop top and a goofy grin, in a see-what-I-got-here kind of way. Under the picture, the caption read. "Angel and Donnie were in the FantaSea spirit!"

Audie's head jerked up, her mouth hanging open.

"Yep. Mr. Fire and Brimstone himself. Donald Hickenbocker."

CHAPTER 32

From his tidy shelf, Jude snatched the next chronicle. Two others slipped sideways. *Go ahead. Fall. We've got bigger fish to fry.*

This index listed only three photos for Angel Randolph. In the fall, the volleyball team showed her as cheerful as ever, as did her official headshot amongst the other seniors. But the last? Another prom pic, now in the background of a different glittering couple. She had a new escort, one who carried a similar size and shape to good ol' Nathan. They sat at a table on the dance floor's perimeter, both staring outward. He had his hand on her knee. On her face, the carefree Angel of autumn was long gone. Her dress wasn't the svelte affair of junior prom, but had a sweater over the straps, tied below her waist.

"She was already pregnant," Audie said. "That must be the original Kane boy."

"What a guy. I wonder what happened to Donnie?"

She drew the book closer. "Is that him? Off to the right?"

On the side of the frame, a shaggy-haired youth stood alone, arms crossed. While the others faced either the camera or their dance partner, the future preacher glowered in the direction of Angel and her date.

If looks could kill, it would've been a bloodbath. "Wow. Was this your hunch?"

She nodded. "He hates Hunter too much."

"Man, you're good."

"No. 'Hatreds are the cinders of affection.'"

"What?"

"Sir Walter Raleigh. Sometimes, human emotions are really, really telling."

"Here's the next obvious question, then. Exactly how much did he hate Hunter—or the concept of Hunter—from Day One? He's held onto a lot of anger for thirty years after the kid disappeared. That doesn't bode well. Did our dear reverend murder Hunter Kane and Cassie Powers?"

Audie said nothing, but the hamster wheel spun with enough energy to light Las Vegas. It was no use offering a penny for her thoughts, not until the blocks fell into place. In the meantime, she stared past the bookshelves, past the walls, past the present, her eyes matching the day's clouds and the storm for which Mrs. Marik named her.

As they closed the less riotous record room behind them, they were swept up in the lunch rush of a noxious multitude. Hair spray, body spray. The roar of voices and laughter and slammed metal lockers. Jude grabbed for Audie's hand, pushing through the pandemonium until they reached the exit.

"You all right?" Older students flocked with them to the parking lot. Seniors had off-campus lunch rights, for whatever benefit that gave them in a town with a single restaurant. No way was Metcalfe's speedy enough to serve a meal within a forty-minute window.

"I'm fine. Thanks." But she said it through gritted teeth.

The rain had dwindled to a mist, puddles filling potholes. He was dodging a large one near the Jeep when Audie gasped and tightened her grip.

"What is it?" They were through the adolescent horde. What now?

"Sorry." She let go and reached for something wrapped around the windshield wiper. "Caught me by surprise. I don't want you getting as jumpy as I am, love." She untangled a plastic bag from the wiper and opened it.

Oh grand. Another note. This one, though, was a newspaper article, cut from the current issue of the *Renarde Gazette*.

"The Vietnam vet story?" He vaguely remembered seeing it on their first night in town. "Why would someone leave that for us?"

She scanned the page. "Let's see, his remains are being brought home after five decades as MIA. There will be a procession next week—storefronts on Main are asked to hang their flags and Independence Day bunting. Renarde is acting as de facto kin for the poor guy. Parents died years ago, no siblings. He'll be buried in the family mausoleum."

Her head jerked up, and Jude fumbled backward. "What?"

"Mausoleum." The intensity of her expression could've melted lead. Returning to the article, she ran fingers along the lede like a greyhound. "Dillon Clayburn. The vet's name is Dillon Clayburn." She looked up at him like he should understand what on earth she was talking about.

"Aud, I'm missing something."

"The mausoleum in the cemetery, the one with the recently chipped bronze by the lock. The one that last saw a burial over forty years ago?"

"Yeah?"

"It hasn't been opened in forty years, Jude. But it's common knowledge that it'll be opened next week—the name on the tomb was Clayburn."

CHAPTER 33

"You two better be sure about this." Three sets of shoes crunched into the gravel, but the sheriff's boots ground the loudest as he led the parade across the lot to the church office building. The big man walked with purpose, but his attention lingered on the black sedan as they passed it. "Word spreads so fast, I'm going to get heat whether we find anything or not."

Donald Hickenbocker stepped through the door and stood above them on the front porch like a statue of Napoleon. Must be quite the view from up there. *Only way to look down on people when height isn't on your side.*

"Sheriff, this is intolerable."

"I know, Donald, but these are intolerable times. And you've got the keys."

"The church has the keys, Sheriff." The reverend leaned into the honorific, since Carmichael had omitted his. "Because we're next to the city cemetery. That is all. And nobody should be in those mausoleums except for kin. It's disrespectful."

"If the Wests here are right, somebody's been in one specific mausoleum already. Besides, the Clayburns have been gone for years. I don't think they're going to mind if we take a peek."

The pastor's lips drew into a tight line. He cast an air of harsh judgment on Audie, who gave him nothing back. Reddening, he redirected. Jude struggled not to laugh as he met the man's icy glare with one of his own. *I can do this all day, your ministerness.* He wished his tattoos were visible.

Carmichael interrupted the contest. "Come on, preacher. Lead the way."

He descended the stairs and brushed past them without a word.

The group slogged across the lawn, Hickenbocker managing to hit every puddle. With each splash, mud stained the hem of his crisp, charcoal slacks, and his face resembled ever more a circus balloon. That and Audie's bright yellow boots brought Jude a single slice of joy amongst the graves.

These people below their feet were more than their birth and death dates. They were the dash in between. Their hopes and dreams, families and friends, accomplishments and failures. He'd bet most of those once attached to these mortal remains would've been unable to resist smiling at Audie's wellies.

She had that effect on people.

She could also irritate the bejeezus out of a certain demographic. The good reverend was an excellent example.

"Mrs. West"—emphasis on the Missus, the tone saying what he thought of married women and their position amongst men—"I cannot fathom the impertinence you're demonstrating here. I've heard about what you and your husband"—more emphasis, but Jude wasn't sure if that was testament to a woman's place or a slight at him as a spouse unable to control his womenfolk—"do for a living. Invading people's private lives after they're long gone. Not letting anyone rest in peace. You come here digging through history like it's any of your business, and now you're tromping over a graveyard you have no connection with. Not out of care but pure voyeurism. It's a disgrace bordering upon blasphemy."

"Hey there, Donald," Carmichael warned.

"Owen, I'm the man of the cloth around here." He stopped, stabbing a finger at the lawman's chest. He had to lift his hand to nose level to do so. "Your jurisdiction and mine do not cross, and I would hope you'd remember that when you're letting complete outsiders run roughshod over you."

"Roughshod?" Audie's forehead crinkled. *Yeah, that's my wife. Boxing champion of the fleaweight class.* "You've got to be kidding."

Jude bit at the inside of his cheek to keep from snickering.

Hickenbocker turned on her. He must not have read the odds sheet. "Yes. You're a troublemaker. You want to dredge up things from past lives, defiling the names of Christians who have gone on to their reward and can't defend themselves from your baseless accusations. You two coming here and raking up dirt and rumors and innuendo is nothing but the devil's work. You're going to find a day where those ways won't succeed, and I can guarantee it will be too late to save your soul."

Jude wanted to deck him. Every muscle in his body yearned to punch the man's lights out, if that was still a thing. But Audie's face warmed from the Cliffs of Dover to a blazing vermilion, and he knew what was coming.

She didn't need a husband's protection.

"My soul?"

"Yes, your eternal soul, Mrs. West. You'd best be considering it instead of dragging the rightful children of God across cemeteries for your own sick amusement."

"My soul." The same two syllables, but transformed. Now cool, level, measured. Jude touched her coat. He wished he'd had the chance to sell tickets.

"Mr. Hickenbocker, my soul and I have a few words for you too. Never in my life have I met a man further from the word of God than you are." She advanced on him. "You stand before a town of believers, raising the banner of my God, and you condemn people like it's in your power to do so. No one but God can judge, and if anyone is doing the devil's work, it is coming through your mouth and your words and your deep, hateful ways."

She was within inches of the man. His puffed-out cheeks dripped with smug condescension, but Jude saw the fear they masked.

Fear of being uncovered, naked before the altar. Fear of someone speaking truth.

Fear of the Almighty coming in the form of a petite, forty-three-year-old woman.

She continued. "How dare you use my Christianity to judge me or anyone else, hurling insults like you're already beside the throne? I may be traveling south after this world finishes with me, but it won't be for a lack of trying. And I *guarantee* you, sir, you'll be waiting when I arrive."

The man's pupils burned beams of full-on hate. But he said nothing.

"Preacher?" The sheriff gestured toward the mausoleum. "If we could get this over with, please?"

Hickenbocker held his ground a moment longer, then pivoted to the crypt. Before he could reach the lock, Audie pointed to the chipped and unpatinated bronze. Carmichael took a picture with his phone and motioned the reverend to the padlock.

The heavy metal shrieked in protest as the sheriff hauled apart the doors. Inside, a single window diffused the afternoon light into a weak aurora, a stained-glass cherub guiding souls to heaven. Jude flipped his phone to flashlight mode and aimed into the space.

Within the small, musty room, marble slabs lined the walls from floor to ceiling, four on each side of the narrow aisle. Carved into seven of the slabs were names and dates, the grooved writing filled with gold paint. The Clayburns were few in number, but the line dated to the late 1800s. Dillon Clayburn's parents were at and above their heads on the left. The marble at the upper right was still smooth and blank, awaiting the long-dead soldier's homecoming.

Audie's fingers wrapped around his bicep as he began to step forward.

"Give me the light, would you please?" She shone the phone at the floor. The tile pattern was a chess board of cream and navy squares, but shoe marks disturbed the decades-old dust. Between the prints was a pair of larger, dust-free outlines, long and side-by-side.

Roughly in the shape of two human bodies.

CHAPTER 34

At Metcalfe's, Owen Carmichael sat across the table, a half-eaten cheeseburger and fries occupying the space in front of him.

"They've been in there all this time." He stared down at the meal. For once, the lawman had lost his appetite. Jude studied his coffee, took a token sip, and set it back down, as disappointed as he'd expected to be.

"The crime scene folks are going to examine the footprints, but their lead said she wouldn't expect much to come of it. They were pretty messy—couldn't be sure if it was one person or more. And with commercial footwear being what it is, probably half the town will have a match in their closet. Based on size, we can guess male, but even that's not a certainty."

"And that only eliminates fifty percent of earth's population," Audie added.

Jude leaned forward, his elbows on the tabletop. Extra ears listened in as usual. The energy to care had been sucked out at the graveyard. "Who has or had access to the mausoleum, either after the disappearances or last week?"

"Last week? Hickenbocker, for sure, because the keys are kept in the church office. And Joleene Devonshire. But the whole area knows First Community handles administration of the cemetery. Anybody could get the keys when nobody was watching. I doubt they lock up real tight most nights."

"What about thirty years ago, when Cassie and Hunter were placed there?"

"Don was the associate then, but sure, he could've gotten to the keys. The lead pastor was already ancient. I wouldn't put him at the top of our suspect list. Again, though, anyone who could get into the office could get into the crypts." Carmichael turned to Audie. "How did you know what we'd find in there? People have been walking by that mausoleum for decades with no idea."

"The chip in the bronze, close to the padlock, was the first clue. Since it hadn't changed to green yet, it was recent damage. We chalked it up to a loose rock thrown by a mower. But when we were reminded that the name of the veteran being repatriated next week was Clayburn, the story started coming together."

"I'm still not sure I follow."

Audie ticked off her fingers. "The Clayburn grave hasn't had a new resident since 1975, when Dillon's mother passed away. It was common knowledge that the Clayburns had one child, and as he was missing in action in Vietnam, the killer would've understood that the mausoleum would be ignored for ages, possibly forever.

"If I was going to stash a body—or two—it's perfect. No risk of being caught digging a grave or not digging deep enough or a body floating to the surface in the river. Add the newspaper copy about Dillon Clayburn's homecoming to the fact that someone might've been fumbling near the lock lately, and there you go."

Jude gestured to his right. "May I introduce my wife, Sherlock?"

Muffled voices penetrated the glass pane. Across the street, Travis Bell's arms waved in the air as Lionel Graymeyer leaned against the brick wall of his hardware store, swinging his head from side to side like a pendulum. Lionel said something to the mechanic, but the only discernible words belonged to Travis.

"What do you think that's about?"

The sheriff smirked. "Not a hill of beans. Their businesses share parking space, and Travis's short fuse is always going off about one thing or another. A simple property issue or hardware patrons pulling into the wrong spots or whatever. It's been like this for decades, won't change any time soon." He rediscovered his appetite—or felt guilty for not cleaning his plate—and gathered a haystack of fries, dredging them through the ketchup. "I'd love to find out who has enough info to be sending you these notes. You think it's the killer?"

"No, I can't see the murderer being remorseful at this late stage." Audie frowned. "I'm betting it's a local who can lead us in a direction but can't come forward on their own. Or doesn't have proof."

"You saw him, right?" Carmichael asked Jude. "Renarde's midnight marauder?"

"I saw a silhouette. It was dark. I was—well, I was more worried the dude had gotten into the camper in the three minutes I was gone." Audie's hand settled on his knee below the table.

"Male? Female? Anything?"

"In my mind, it was a man, but I can't swear to it."

"And the notes said what? Other than the one about Dillon Clayburn?"

Audie said, "The first told us not to let it die, like we should keep digging until we found the truth. At first, we weren't sure if it meant the Cassie-Hunter story or the job we're on. And the last note was a photo of the Renarde baseball team from this spring."

"Those kids weren't born until at least twelve years after the murders. What about their parents?" Jude asked.

Wiping ketchup from his chin with the back of his hand, the man in tan shrugged. "Could be, I guess. I'll check on it, but none of the boys' names leapt out at me as a connection. It's sure a roundabout way to lead us anywhere."

"Coaches? The team manager?"

"Who knows?" He glanced at his watch and retrieved his hat from the seat beside him. "I'd better see if the CSI squad needs anything else from me before they wrap up at the cemetery."

"Yeah, we should go too. We need to plan the next move in our other mystery."

"More dead ends there?"

"It can get maddening." Jude scrutinized his coffee mug, another maddening subject in his life. "We find enough information to be intrigued, then it's brick wall after brick wall."

"We're down to chasing long shots, the current being what would've happened to a woman's possessions from the 1850s if she had no children and all the kin finally moved on?"

Carmichael paused at the edge of their table, shifting his duty belt. The burger had to have been pressing into the walkie-talkie. "I might have an answer for that one."

"Really?"

"Have you been to the county historical society, south of here off I-55? They have a museum and more stuff than they could ever display. Whenever anybody has family junk they want to get rid of, personal pieces that wouldn't sell in a farm auction or estate sale, those people are happy to take it. They've got to have the most hazard-filled storage rooms in the state based on what they've collected. When my father-in-law moved into a nursing home, my wife donated a box of worn-out children's blocks, a photo from the 1902 Missouri Farmers Association meeting up in Columbia, and a beat-up cornet. They even came to pick it up."

"That's interesting. We'll see if they'll let us poke around a bit."

"I guarantee it'll thrill them to have someone come by." He pulled on his coat and adjusted the hat. "You two take care."

"Will do."

Jude lifted the mug but remembered to stop before he drank from it. "So, historical society?" Audie was on her phone, searching for the organization.

"They're closed for the day, but they have Saturday hours in the afternoon. One p.m. to four."

"Sounds like a plan." He twirled the cup, a few drops splattering onto the tabletop. "I don't know. Do you think Donnie Hickenbocker could be our killer?"

"He's such a hateful man, anything's possible. He's almost too obvious."

"But nobody mentions him except as the over-excitable preacher. If there was any hint of suspicion, wouldn't it have come out by now? It seems we're the only ones who think he's obvious, and that's just because you were smart enough to find those yearbook pics."

"Doesn't anybody remember he dated Angel Faust?"

"Maybe it was brief. Maybe no one paid any attention to him. He has a raging case of small-man syndrome." Jude ran his hand through his hair. "Maybe it was him, or one of the Bells. Or Tom Powers did it in the conservatory with a candlestick. In the meantime, can I interest you in an actual meal and coffee roasted more recently than Tuesday?"

"Sweetheart, I thought you'd never ask."

Chapter 35

On Saturday morning, Mozart's *Rondo Alla Turca* filled the camper at a volume where strange men hammering mysterious memos could be heard if need be. Audie tapped a short stack of papers on the kitchen table, evening the edges. Bob Laroque's updated tree slid into the binder's green folder, notes and to-do's nestled into the blue one. She grabbed the worn clipboard and fixed the remaining page to it. *What are the chances?* About a million to one. They'd need a rabbit's foot, a right-side-up penny, and the entire Blarney Stone to strike gold at the historical society. But the blank inventory sheet was coming along anyway.

After all, if the Cubs can win the World Series after 108 years, anything was possible.

From the marker board on the fridge, she plucked the pen and added laundry detergent to the shopping list. While morale on this job remained steady, supplies ran low. Stocking up at the next trading post—i.e., Walmart—might see them through to Thanksgiving.

Doubtful. Her personal camp cook couldn't get by on beans, hard tack, and lard. At least they were well-fed on the trail. Jude seemed to be fattening them for winter. She added warmer pj's to the list anyway.

Outside, the axe thwacked against an unsuspecting log, breaking it down to a usable size. At least this time, he wasn't blowing off steam from something stupid his wife had done. The woodpile needed to be burned or packed before they moved on, which had better be soon. They were going to get behind on the Barkley research if they didn't wrap up with Bob here pronto.

Jude came indoors late morning, cleaned up in the Jefferies Tube, and began whipping up an ad hoc brunch of waffles and grilled chicken. Take that, Cookie.

"Aren't those supposed to be fried?" The aroma of southern spices, rich and warm and wonderful, filled the marrow of her bones.

"You won't eat fried."

"True. And nobody should. Half this town's got coronary disease from Rick's cafe."

"Of all the gin joints in all the world."

"Exactly."

The sweet-savory combo soon appeared on plates and sooner vanished. She cleared the table while Jude packed their bag with the usual gear plus clipboard. They headed outside.

"Wow." The local population had sky-rocketed since yesterday afternoon. "When did this place get so trendy?"

"It's Spark in the Park tonight. Renarde's the new hot spot."

"Hot, it isn't." A gust of freezing air cut through them, and she pulled her coat tighter.

"Okay, not until the bonfire's lit, anyway."

The Jeep crawled around the camp loop. With this quantity of motorized behemoths, an unseen child darting onto the road was inevitable. Visitors at the Halloween shindig would outnumber townies by a factor of three, if license plates could be believed. "Illinois, Kentucky, even Iowa. This must be quite a party."

Forty-five minutes of winding road and an interstate later, Jude eased them in front of the Ste. Genevieve County Historical Society, a brick building on Pine Street in Gervaise. The east end of the structure bordered an antique shop and the west, a hair salon. Ghosts and pumpkins covered the salon's facade, with a mummy saying, "Witch cut is right for you? Our spirited stylists can help!"

The society building was two-stories tall. From the sidewalk, Audie could see storage tubs pressing into the upper windows. Her heart fluttered, but whether that was in anticipation or dread would've been difficult to say.

As they entered, a lone woman studied a glass-faced cabinet across the open room. Spinning around, hope sprung eternal, her face brightening in pleasant surprise.

"Welcome!" Her sensible shoes clomped on the original hardwood floor. "I'm Bonnie Steinem. Are you folks here to see the museum?"

The "museum" consisted of three walls of those encased exhibits, with tidy, organized, but crowded shelves in every one. Tented notecards sat amongst rusted tools, broken cookware, and ragged homemade dolls. In the display nearest to them, smaller items huddled together to make space for a dented cornet.

At least the musical career of the sheriff's father-in-law would live on.

Audie smiled and offered her hand to the woman. "My name is Audie West. This is my husband, Jude." Immediately, the melting. The funniest part was, he didn't understand it. *Oh love.* "We're genealogy researchers working on a project up in Renarde."

"I'm driving there later myself! The grandkids are big fans of the fire festival. We've been going since the first one could walk. But you were saying about research?"

"We were told old belongings that don't have a home occasionally find their way here. Do you keep any records of families who bring in donations?"

"Oh honey, do we have records." She led them to the counter at the center of the room and heaved a peeling, leather-bound ledger from beneath it.

Jude eyed the tome with abject terror. "Nothing computerized, I take it?"

"My daughter offered to scan some files for us, but she went and had baby number three and is a busy girl these days." She opened the book to the first page. "What name are we interested in?"

"Let's start with Laroque, or possibly Durand. The main people we're searching for died in the mid-to-late nineteenth century. The family lines were messy, with multiple remarriages and several children not making it to adulthood. We're unsure who may have ended up with their things, but I'd guess sentimental items would've been tossed within a few generations."

"We don't want to waste your time," Jude chimed in. "We can do the hunting and leave you to your other work."

The woman chuckled. "That's sweet. And hysterical. I'm ready to poke my eyes out with one of the antique forks. You two wander the exhibits. I'm a speedy reader, and I'll let you know if I find anything."

Audie thanked her and abandoned all hope. But they moved off to the adjacent case to wait. In the exhibit stood paintings of the early French settlements that gave the neighboring towns their names. The cabinets provided mini-history lessons as they showed off family heirlooms—broadly defined—corresponding to the period—also broadly defined. They made four circuits of the space, talking in hushed, museum tones. Of course, no one but Bonnie was in the room, and the tall, tin-covered ceilings amplified each syllable anyway. They'd begun the fifth round, wondering how much longer they could feign engrossment in things better sent to Harold Carver's backyard, when Bonnie yelped.

"Found one!"

At the counter, she pointed to an entry from 1936. "Durand. Didn't come across anything for Laroque. But a woman named Durand left some keepsakes behind when she passed in the 1860s, and they changed hands amongst nieces and nephews until the last relocated to California and couldn't take great-great-auntie's sundries with them."

It's an All Hallows miracle. Audie glanced around. Had they been looking at Elise's things and not realized? "Is anything on display?"

The woman squinted at the notes. "No, I don't think so."

And there went the miracle. "They weren't thrown away, were they?"

"Heavens, no. That's a mortal sin here."

"You have a list of what was left?"

"I can do better than that." She scrawled numbers on a pad to her left and tore off the sheet with gusto. "I have a box and shelf number. Whatever they donated is right upstairs."

Blarney Stone, I could kiss you.

Bonnie led the way, and they soon entered a time capsule of local days gone-by. The windows were indeed blocked, but each tub and carton was neatly stacked with a printed label affixed to the front. They seemed to be organized by era. Crossing straight to the middle of the south wall, Bonnie rechecked her note and tapped the wire rack just above her head.

"Honey, would you mind?" she asked Jude.

He reached for a tote marked A26, Shelf 5, and brought it down to the floor. Audie saw him wince but try to hide it. They needed to hire an official heavy-lifter. Perhaps Nathan, the pride of Renarde High, would be interested when his hall monitoring gig ran out.

Bonnie removed the lid, and the faintest aroma of burnt ash wafted into the room. The odor triggered something for the curator, and she faltered. "Goodness. Did you say there was a tie to the Laroques? Didn't they suffer some sort of tragedy? A drowned baby and a fire on one of those river islands?"

Jude rubbed absently at his shoulder. "You know about that?"

"I've got too many empty hours on my hands, so I read old papers." Her forehead wrinkled as she considered invisible stacks of newsprint she'd handled. "A lot of old papers."

"If these are Elise Durand's belongings—or rather, Elise Laroque's at the time—they may include things that survived the disaster."

"From the smell of it, I think you've hit pay dirt."

Audie knelt and withdrew the first items from the tote. "A pair of framed pince-nez eyeglasses." She set the delicate frames on the wood floor. Jude extracted the clipboard from the pack and started filling in the inventory list. "A linen handkerchief with the initials 'EP' embroidered on it."

"EP?"

"Husband Number Four was a Peterson."

"That's quite a monogram collection."

"Seems like she always reverted to Durand, though." That first love. Audie dug deeper. "A prayer booklet from 1861, the year Elise died." She hadn't even broken the book's spine.

"Probably some minister gave it to her as her health declined," Bonnie said. "Nothing like waiting until the last minute to save a soul."

Audie set it with the handkerchief and moved to the next piece. A sudden cold front moved in. "Oh no."

"What is it?" Jude blocked the overhead light as he peeked over his list.

"Two small gold lockets. Identical." She opened one, and a tiny curl of silky, blond hair dropped onto her lap. The lock in the second was chestnut, similar to her own. On the back of each heart, a name was engraved.

Eliot.

Emile.

The Durand boys.

"Elise had two sons with her first husband," she explained to Bonnie. "Both died before their second birthdays."

"That miserable woman." Bonnie absently fiddled with a bracelet. The lettered beads spelled out names, likely those of the grandchildren she'd be seeing shortly. "Then to have a third torn from her arms by the river?"

Not quite, Audie thought, but she kept her mouth shut and set the lockets aside. A knitted shawl emerged next, with beautiful rose-work edging. Below it was a metal case, the last of Elise's things.

She lifted out the case, maybe eight inches square. The smoke smelled strongest here, and patchy soot filled the ridges of her fingertips. The lock had long been broken, so she raised the lid, only to find another box within. *Are matryoshka boxes a thing? They're certainly not French.* This one was wooden and hand-crafted, but instead of a painted Russian doll, it held a pocket watch, a leather money bag, and a dull copper gunpowder flask.

"At my place, this stuff would clutter a kitchen at the end of the day," their docent sighed. "Either the man of the house was more particular about his necessities than mine or the woman of the house wanted to reclaim her cooking space."

"Would you call this a valet?" Jude studied it. "I may need one of these."

"If you find one, buy a second for my Nick. It's gorgeous, isn't it? And beautifully preserved. Wasn't Laroque a woodworker?"

"Yes." The miniature chest was a work of art. Pieces of inlaid wood varied in color from the different species Henri must've used. A repeating star pattern wrapped around the borders, and a fleur-de-lis graced the lid. "He lives up to his reputation."

The bells on the door downstairs jingled, and Bonnie excused herself. From the chatter, it sounded like a neighborly visit and not a historical one.

Jude crouched, taking the box in his hands and touching the stars. "Amazing. A master artisan constructs this in the 1830s or '40s. It survives a stormy inferno that kills its maker, remains with his widow until her death, then passes from relative to relative until no soul who ever knew him is still alive."

"Yet here we are, holding it. Like the smoke, Henri lingers on."

Jude took out the flask, following the contours of the hunting dog intricately embossed there. The spirit of Elise's second husband must've been released like a genie, shouting from the beyond all the regrets of a shortened life, because the next thing he said had nothing to do with Bob's ancestors. "Aud, I'm sorry I lost it yesterday about Kate."

That knot in her stomach reminded her it hadn't left. "I never should've started on that road without you."

"It's not like I was open to the ride." He studied the metal with such intensity, she did too. *West Genealogy—experts at avoiding eye contact for over ten years.* How could a simple accoutrement, critical to the survival of Henri's young family, be so elegant? The car keys and pocketknife resting on their own counter each night felt sorely plain. "And I think you were right."

She held her breath.

"At least, partially. I still don't want to peep in on her, even from a distance. That's not fair to her or to me. But I'm not against digging into my tree." He returned the flask and closed the valet. "We know my relations haven't been stalwarts of honesty. The lineage hanging in my father's office could be as much of a fraud as he is."

She reached over and brushed the ever-loose lock aside. His tan skin reddened. "That's a powerful decision, love. I'll love to help. But this time, you lead the way."

"Oh no!" Palms raised, facing her. "Not on your life. If we're going this route, it needs to be done right. That means you're the boss lady, as always." Up came the box again. *Well, the area* is *bereft of wood to split, and those hands can't be expected to occupy themselves.* This time, he traced the outline of the fleur-de-lis. At once, something cracked and popped. "For the love of—"

"Did it break?"

"I don't—it doesn't look like it." He turned it over. "Something sure gave way, though." He lifted the cover. Inside, a rectangular index-card-sized piece of wood had dropped open from the top. Hinged with precision on the interior of the cutout, the piece masqueraded as a solid portion of the lid when in place. Beige stationery, folded tightly, peeked from within. "Wow. Was Henri a spy? Maybe a Pinkerton?"

"They formed three years after his death, so no Pinkerton. But it's not every day we find secret papers. What are they?"

Jude unfolded the first with care reserved for newborns and laid it between them. A map had been hand drawn, marked with a cemetery and a church. In and around the graveyard, little cloud-like shapes resembled trees. Behind the church but beyond the graves, light pencil encircled a single tree. Was that a cross in the center? The layout was vague—could be one of a thousand churchyards they'd seen across the Midwest.

"Based on the landmarks, it's not the Renarde cemetery." Audie smoothed the paper while Jude reached back to the hinged panel. He removed the contents of a slit envelope and handed them to her.

"Great. Faded 1800s French. In cursive." *Note to self: add magnifying glass to the shopping list.*

"Can you read any of it?"

"Let's see. At least it isn't long. It's from Henri's sister, Josephine, the one who lived in St. Louis. She says she received his last letter." She shifted the sheet into a pocket of light from the window. "They're coming for Gareth as soon as possible, but the floods have delayed them."

"So they *planned* for the child to go to Josephine? And he's Gareth again? When is it dated?"

"April 23, 1847." Audie blinked, struggling to focus. "Wait. She borrowed a bassinet from a neighbor but hopes Henri can have the baby's clothes ready when they arrive, since they'll need to move quickly."

"The baby? Gareth—Henri Junior or whatever they were calling him—was over two by then."

"This is confusing. Josephine might mean baby as in toddler, but then a bassinet wouldn't be appropriate. He would've outgrown it by then. And it sounds like the pickup needed to be clandestine." *I've got to be messing up the transla—* "Oh dear Lord."

Jude leaned over to get a better view, though it would literally all be French to him. "What?"

"Just three sentences at the end. 'I pray the waters recede and Maurice and I arrive in time. If not, may God have mercy on our failings. Another tragedy would condemn us all.'" Audie looked up to Jude. He mirrored what she was feeling.

"So."

"Yeah. So."

"Another tragedy, she says. Two children? Henri Junior and Gareth are different kids?"

"One a baby, one a toddler? Could be. If so, where is Henri Junior? And why was baby Gareth going to St. Louis under cover of night? Which one, if either, was swept away by the Mississippi?"

"Who is the letter addressed to, both the Laroques?"

"No, only the brother." The mailing address was the mercantile store not in Renarde but in Lucius, on the Illinois side of the river. "Henri didn't include Elise in correspondence about removing their child from her keeping." The image of those two earlier baby gravestones in the Durand cemetery floated into mind.

But what did it all mean?

Jude whistled, long and low. "Holy Mother of God," he muttered, staring at the letter. "That was a prayer, not a curse, by the way."

Exactly.

CHAPTER 36

With the letter and map filed deep in their bag, Jude lifted Elise's tote to its home on Shelf 5. In his periphery, Audie frowned at the shoulder full of crackling scar tissue.

"I can't help it. I come with my own sound effects."

Minutes before four o'clock, they descended from the 1800s and found the museum's curator packing her purse.

"Thank you so much for your help, Bonnie. That was a gold mine."

A platinum mine? Texas tea? Definitely better than the yellow shiny stuff.

"My pleasure, dears. Maybe I'll see you at the Spark." She walked them to the exit and waved goodbye as she flipped the hanging sign to "Closed."

"I feel a little bad about taking the papers," Audie said.

"No one has known they were there since Henri hid them in 1847. They won't be missed now." At the Jeep, he opened the door for her. Nothing on the windshield today—surprising.

"And Bob should be able to claim the whole box anyway, as he's family."

"Right."

He climbed behind the wheel, but the ridges on her forehead stopped him from turning the key. She stared out the windshield, narrowed eyes peering into a space-time portal in the middle of Pine Street.

"Okay. What are you thinking?" He squinted in the same direction, but all he saw was a man emerging from a mom-and-pop grocery with an armful of fun-size candy bars.

Halloween. Almost forgot.

"Why were only her hands burned?"

He really ought to invest in a neck brace for wife-induced whiplash. "Gonna' need more, love."

The line at the bridge of her nose deepened to Grand Canyon level. "Remember the article about the fire on Chene Blanc? Elise's hands were burned, nothing else. And the injuries were mild enough to be healed by 1840s medicine. If the entire island and her house were ablaze, how did she only hurt her hands?

"I guess it's strange that her dress didn't catch fire, or that they didn't mention her suffering from the smoke. But I don't understand what that's telling you."

"I may be crazy." She slumped against the headrest. "I have a terrible story growing in my mind."

He let his hands fall from the wheel and focused on the logo covering the horn. Listening mode engaged, he said, "Let's hear it."

She opened her mouth but closed it before anything came out. A few quiet moments passed before another attempt. "All right. Elise lost her first two sons before their second birthdays. We found death certificates for them—whooping cough and pneumonia. Both were real killers in the 1800s."

"And today."

"Yes, and today. They die a year after each other. Then her

beloved husband, the one she chose first, is taken months later." Without looking at him, she reached for his hand.

The one she chose first.

Accurate words. Precise words. He could never be hurt by what they meant. For Elise, there would always be Philippe. For Audie, there would always be Oliver. He squeezed her thin fingers, and she resumed.

"Put yourself in her shoes. She had to remarry right away. No time to process or grieve. A widow without a family had little means of survival. She weds the next man available, Henri Laroque, and moves onto an isolated patch of island, cut off from life in town. Even if Henri was the most loving and attentive man in history, her mental state cannot be healthy after so much loss. The longer she's alone, missing those babes in her arms, the more it dissolves." Her voice developed a tremor. She cleared her throat.

"Henri Junior is born in 1845. What a blessing—another boy. All is well until he's approaching his second birthday, the age her first darling children died. And at this point, it's another winter, and she's due soon with Baby Number Two—or, Four, really—Gareth. Now take the isolation, the long nights, the harsh weather, and add unbridled grief, unresolved trauma, and pregnancy hormones."

"I see where you're going."

"It's possible, isn't it? So much anguish bombarding her at once? She can't bear it. She can't watch the child of her second choice live longer than those of the first. Henri comes home to a dead son and a hysterical wife. She says it was an accident. He believes her. How can he not?"

She turned to face him, and it took all he had to meet her there. He knew what he'd see, and it was as gutting as it was understandable. The gray eyes pleaded for him to say her story wasn't insane, that she wasn't unfairly projecting onto some other woman terrible deeds. That her own crushing grief could've reasonably led to feelings and actions—as unconscionable as they were—like the saga she spun if the variables had been shifted a single inch after Oliver had—

Well, after Oliver.

He nodded, afraid to say anything, to say the wrong thing. *Go on. It's okay. I've got you.*

I always will.

"And the map? The church and cemetery? I bet it's on the Illinois side of the river, probably near where Henri received his secret mail."

"What does it mean?"

"My guess is it's where Henri buried his firstborn."

"Oh Lord."

"If the toddler was killed before spring, which he likely was, the Laroques were unable to reach Renarde. They were cut off. But he could make it to Lucius."

"Why wouldn't he bury him on the island?"

"The river made the water table too high? Or he didn't want Elise to have a daily reminder of what had happened? Considering her mental state, they may have decided not to tell anyone about the death. They'd try to pass off Gareth as Henri—no one would've known she was pregnant going into the winter.

"Also, it would've been important to bury the child on or near sacred ground. I'm guessing the circled tree is the grave. He marked the map because the area might be a lot different with everything in bloom."

She let go of Jude's hand, hers drifting to her lap. "But I think Henri knew. He knew inside she wasn't well, that his son's death wasn't accidental. He pushed it away for a month or two after the second boy, Gareth, was born. But then he had to take action. He wrote to his sister, confided his fears in her, and asked her to save his child." She stopped. A tear slipped down her cheek.

He carried the thread for her, powerless to carry anything else. "Josephine whisks the baby away under cover of darkness. Elise wakes to find him gone. Henri tells her the truth and the remaining fraction of her sanity breaks. That night, as the storm hits, she lights up the forest and the house—"

"Burning only her hands as she kindles the flames," Audie added.

"—and attacks Henri. She had plenty of sharp implements from his woodworking, if not her own kitchen. She pushes him into the river, crosses to the shore herself, and tells the one story she can. Her child was ripped from her arms—which is true—and the Mississippi washed away her husband. Which is also true."

For a full minute, neither of them spoke.

"Wow."

"Yeah."

"You got all that from two hidden papers."

"Two papers plus records plus news items plus missing ancestors and changed names and baby ages that make no sense." She wiped at her cheeks with both palms. "I'm sorry. It's a whopper. I could be completely wrong."

He touched her arm again. "Sadly, Aud, you may be very right."

Four-thirty. The bonfire would wait for no man, and after the last few minutes, Jude could use the warmth. *How hot does it need to be to reach a numb and frozen soul?* He started the car and rolled away from the curb, but the tale lingered. He missed the first one-way street going in the direction they needed and had to continue another two blocks into residential Gervaise. At the corner house, trick-or-treaters raced up a sidewalk, plastic jack-o'-lanterns swinging like mad. He turned right, and the Jeep's headlights revealed a trio: pirate, princess, and ninja. The smallest of the three, the tiara-wearing royalty, seemed fiercer than the others combined.

As it is with every woman I know.

Half a mile later, he steered onto the ramp for the interstate, pointing the car toward Renarde.

"I wonder if all of Gervaise will be at the Cinders shindig."

"Even if they aren't, that fire looked big enough to feel from here." The words came out steady and even, but weighted down by a thousand anchors. "They had more wood than even you could split."

"I accept."

"That wasn't a challenge. I can't believe someone has more pent-up energy than—"

Her sentence broke off so abruptly that Jude swerved as he glanced over. The air horn of a semi-truck blasted past them on the left. "Aud?"

She'd gone rigid as a steel pipe, her focus once more fixed through the windshield. "I need to talk to Lionel."

"The guy from the hardware store?" *Seriously, woman. A neck brace.*

"And from the old baseball team."

"Why?" But he pressed harder on the gas pedal anyway.

"I've got a question that needs to be cleared up."

"Okay. Where do we go when we get into town? His shop?"

"No, it'll be after five by then. He'll be closed."

"Then we'll be able to find him at the festival. Sounds like it's the place to be."

"I'm afraid that may be too late."

CHAPTER 37

Four blocks off Main, Jude snagged the last open spot. The decked-out house had a "Witch Parking Only" sign hanging on their tree. *Tow me—it'd be the perfect end to this week.* Walkers traveled in caravans—bands of little ones tripping over superhero capes, bigger kids hauling pillowcases, parents trailing behind as visitors flocked toward the square. Everywhere, glow sticks bobbed and weaved between bushes and along sidewalks.

In the lead, Audie skirted zombies and squeaky red wagons. Jude hustled to keep pace. She wanted to speak with Lionel, yes. But getting sucked into the fun house around them was not an option.

He caught up as they broke into downtown and the traffic forced her to stop. Cars crawled as more people poured in ahead of the bonfire. She started left, stuttered right, then dove straight through between the vehicles. *Now who's Moses?* Pushing through the throng, they came to Spark central, food vendors and craft booths lining the perimeter of the park. At the third one, a familiar figure stood barbecuing brats.

"Lionel!" Audie shouted, but she had no chance against his teen helpers and the sizzling grill.

"Lionel!" Jude bellowed from somewhere near his spleen, and

the man looked their way. A complete rib cage and spinal column painted the black apron he wore. How festive, were it not for their unfortunate discoveries earlier in the week.

"Hey, you two! Glad you stuck around for the big event."

"Can we talk to you for a second?"

"Uh, sure." He passed off his tongs to a ponytailed girl wearing a cheerleading jacket. "Turn these, would you?" Her wide-eyed horror was not a good sign. Tonight's first batch of links was doomed.

Lionel ducked under the plastic flags roping off the rear of the booth and they joined him there, where it was nominally quieter.

"I'm sorry to bother you," Audie said, "but I've got two questions, and I'm hoping you can help."

He wiped grease off his hands and onto his apron. The skeleton became a homicide victim. "Shoot."

"What happened the night of the baseball state championship?"

He rolled with the randomness like a pro. "This past spring or a different one? Renarde's won state eight times in Class 2A ball."

"The year they won with you on the team. Your junior year."

"Way back then? Wait, how did you know I played?" But he decided it wasn't important enough to care—good, because explaining their yearbook snooping was going to come off as creepy at best—and moved on. "Sure. What a ride. Our roster was loaded with the area's best players that season, and we really came together in the playoffs." The nostalgic smile and distant gaze—in his mind, he gripped that trophy again for all it was worth. Seventeen in a small town, but king of the whole world.

"I'm guessing there was a big party afterward? To celebrate?"

"Boy, was there. But it was mostly just the team. We were up at Bluff Park, like usual. It was kind of a hangout. A few fellas had their girlfriends with them. A couple of siblings came, other friends. We had a lot of fun."

"Drinking?"

He shrugged. "Certain guys always took it too far, as you'd expect. People being people."

"Any fights?"

"Nah. We were too excited for that, even the drunk ones."

"So nothing out of the ordinary happened?" Every atom of Audie's being begged him to say the right thing, to confirm her hunch, whatever that was.

The hardware man saw her desperation and tried, scratching at his beard, eyes squinting through the haze of decades. "Not that I recall. Miss Audie, why are you asking about a teenage party from thirty years ago?"

"I—it seems I'm chasing wild geese." Once more, the anchors dropped to the seabed, and her shoulders sank with them.

"Well, that's okay. Anyway, you said two questions?"

"Oh right. The night of the first Cinders and Cider, you were part of the bonfire crew?"

"I worked it with some of the other boys from the ball team, yeah."

"You were there the entire time? Getting things ready?"

He blushed over a sly smile. "Well, not quite. I may have snuck off for a minute. There was a girl—Lisa Schroeder." He set aside the mental trophy, young love replacing it. "She'd been finishing parade floats, so we didn't have much chance to see each other that night."

"Who did that leave at the bonfire?"

"Now, I wasn't gone too long, you understand? I wouldn't make the others do my work."

"I know, Lionel. But who was there?"

"Ah, that would be..." He took off his hat. He must store forgotten details in his matted hair. "Rick Metcalfe and Brice. Brice Powers. He was chasing Rick around like a puppy that fall, after Tom went off to school and ever since Rick—" He snapped his fingers. "That's what happened at the state party! I'd left already, but I heard about it later. It was a big deal. First, Rick's truck wouldn't start when he was ready to leave. The boys had to call Travis Bell to come fix it."

"Hey, now." Jude flinched as a deep voice barked in his ear. Behind the neighboring tent, Travis Bell dumped a pan of hot grease into a five-gallon bucket. "Don't be dragging me into that mess, Graymeyer. I was down with the flu—whole dang town seemed to know it. When the call came in, Faye rang Hunter, sent him on out there. All Rick needed was a jump." Bell glared at his neighbor—*in booth and business... these two really needed more time apart*—and disappeared beneath a tarp flap.

Lionel pivoted back to the Wests, rolling his eyes. "I was about to get to that, if he'd let me finish. So, Rick fell in the dark or something while they were fooling around with his truck. That's when he tore his knee up." He grimaced. "Crazy. Hours earlier, he was the star of Missouri's sports world. Then he's injured, can't play his senior year, and loses his early scholarship to Mizzou."

"Thank you, Lionel," Audie said. "We'll let you get to your work."

"Sure thing." Lionel recovered his composure and was soon his jolly self once more. "Hey, you want a brat before you go? Rick's furnishing our booth's meat tonight."

"Later, thanks. We'll come back afterwhile, okay?

"See you then!" He ducked under the rope. From the other

side of the canopy, they heard an exclamation as he took in his grill's sorry state of affairs.

The Wests meandered along the line of booths, Audie's attention fixed to the ground in front of her feet.

Isn't the writing usually on the wall? "Your husband is thick, dear. Please tell me what you're thinking."

"I'm not sure myself. The pieces are there, but I can't put them together." They came to a break between the tents and got a good view of the log pile stacked like a tepee at the center of the square. "That is a lot of wood."

Then something sent her stumbling backward. Jude caught her just before the curb. "Audie!"

"The wood. The bonfire."

He set her on her feet. "A verb, sweetheart."

She swung around to him. "The photo of the baseball team—it was pointing us to the team *and* the bats. The blunt trauma to Hunter Kane's skull was from a baseball bat."

"How can you be so sure?"

"I'm not. But what else would a teenage boy have in his truck?"

"Tools? And Tom was barely a teen anymore. Do we even know if he had a truck?"

"Not Tom. He wasn't an athlete."

"Brice? You've got to be kidding."

"Brice, yes, but not only him."

I never did care for 20 Questions. "Help me here, will you?" He studied the stacked pyramid waiting to be lit. Other than a craving for s'mores, it gave him nothing.

"Think. The autumn after the championship, who was helping Brice get primed for the varsity team? Who was working with him on his swing and surely had a baseball bat in his truck? Who had been mysteriously injured six months earlier and lost his chance at a college scholarship on the same night Hunter Kane was called to give him a jump?"

"Holy cow."

"Right," Audie said. "Rick Metcalfe."

Chapter 38

Everyone's best guess was that Owen Carmichael was somewhere watching for the last of the trick-or-treaters and passing out candy. Terrific. In an open square of sidewalk at Main and Montgomery, Audie sighed in exasperation.

"It finally makes sense, and now we can't find the sheriff."

"Wouldn't say it's making all that much sense, but I'll believe you. Why don't you hang around Lionel's brat stand? I'll get over to the restaurant, see if I spot Rick."

"And do what? Confront him? That's an awful idea."

"But we ought to keep him in sight until we can locate Carmichael. Surely he'll show when the bonfire starts."

She shifted to read the clock atop an ornate green pole. "Ten minutes until it's lit." All five-foot-two of her bounced like an overcaffeinated marmoset. "Jude, what if Lionel tells Rick we were asking about him? They're going to meet each other at the booth."

"Another reason to keep track of him."

"Fine, but not by yourself. We'll go check the restaurant."

Would a small primate help in this situation? *Unclear.* "I spotted Missy Aikman selling pies for the library fund. Why don't you—"

"Why don't you stop treating me like a child?"

The flames from her marble eyes burned hotter than a blowtorch. His hands flew up, palms out. "Sorry!"

She backpedaled a pace, fire doused by shock at her own reaction. "No. I'm sorry." A breath, another, uneasy, unsure. "Look. I know I'm not altogether there, okay? I know I say things and do things I really shouldn't sometimes. You're only trying to help. But right now, Jude, I can't be shuffled off to a safe corner. Please."

Slowly, he lowered his arms. Harold Carver had nailed it—theirs was an interesting life. "Yep," he nodded. *Messy and complicated and interesting and right.* "Let's go."

Two blocks from the festivities, the herd thinned at last. A sign hung on the entrance to Metcalfe and Son's: "Closed for Cinders & Cider—come get your fix at the Brat Stand!" Audie gently pulled on the handle. Of course it didn't open. She cupped her hands at the glass—the dining room sat in darkness, but the window to the kitchen glowed yellow.

"Let's try the rear."

The narrow gap between the diner and the floral shop spit them into an alley containing the usual dumpsters and litter tumbleweeds. A rubber wedge propped open the door to Metcalfe's. *Is this smart? Absolutely not.* She darted to the dumpster closest to it anyway and crouched down.

"Can you see anything?" Beside her, Jude peeked around the metal edge.

"No. But I think I hear voices."

The hum of not-so-distant revelers masked the details. "Me too. At least two men."

"I can't understand a word." Bent low, he skirted the bin and broke to the right of the kitchen opening to kneel where the door would shield him. She followed. Here, the voices rang loud and clear.

"You have to come clean, Rick," the first man said. "It's long past time."

Rick Metcalfe snickered. "You're a fool, Baden."

Marshall? Jude's eyes needed to be pushed back into their sockets.

"Don't you understand? I *saw* you."

"You didn't see anything."

"No? You and Brice were at the bluff that night, swinging that bat around, laughing and carrying on while you waited for Hunter. Brice would've followed you anywhere. You took advantage of him."

"To do what?"

"To get rid of the kid who made you look like a dang fool in front of all your friends!"

Audie fell into Jude, and he scrambled to right them both before they knocked the door closed. Heat rose in her cheeks, and she mouthed *mea culpa*.

"I'm not the fool, Marshall. It was thirty years ago. You're imagining things that never happened." Movement from within the kitchen. "Get out of here. People are waiting for me."

"I know what I saw! I was in those woods. It was the only quiet place with all the Spark nonsense going on. I heard you talking about Hunter, and the more you talked, the worse it got. Brice started catching on. He kept saying you were just going to scare him, right? Chase him away from Cassie, right? When you quit answering, I think it dawned on the poor kid you wouldn't stop at scaring him."

A metal object scraped along another surface. "And you saw me do something?"

"No, Rick, or we wouldn't be having this conversation. Hunter pulled up in that junker of his. I wanted to warn him, but it was too late. And I was fourteen. Who was going to believe me? I ran to town, trying to figure what to do. With that dang festival going on, I couldn't find a single soul I was looking for. My parents weren't home, the police were leading the parade. By the time I came back through the square, you and Brice were at the bonfire with the rest of the jocks. I wasn't stepping anywhere near that."

"Like I said. You never saw anything."

"Which is why you need to come clean yourself. I can't go to the sheriff—heck, today I'd never be able to prove a thing. But other folks are getting close, Rick. Don't you want it off your chest? Don't you want to give Tom Powers peace about what happened to his kid sister?"

"I never laid a hand on Cassie. And you should've learned by now, Marshall, to let sleeping dogs lie."

A surprised gasp came from inside, followed by shuffling feet and a thump. Audie grabbed both of Jude's arms as he coiled to leap in. "Don't!" she hissed into his ear like a mad woman. "You don't know where he is. You're not armed."

He pushed off her hands, but didn't spring. He had to be calculating the defensive properties of his pocketknife. Something heavy opened—the freezer?—and something else dragged across the floor.

Lord, have mercy.

"We've got to get the sheriff," she whispered. But footsteps approached. Rick emerged, carrying a large, foil-covered pan and whistling. Inches from Jude's face, he kicked at the rubber stopper. If he glanced back, the Wests would be in full view. Audie held her breath.

Metcalfe never turned. He hung a right at the edge of the restaurant and headed in the direction of Main Street, hauling fresh supplies to the party. By the time Jude could move without attracting attention, the door had just closed. He grabbed the handle and braced a foot on the frame, but the industrial lock stood fast. Pain shot through his arm as he pounded a fist against the brick wall.

Audie was already sprinting down the alley. *Plan B.* They took a left at Montgomery to avoid running into Rick. But before they could reach the plaza, a wall of humanity blocked them like a rampart.

It was chaos. There had to be eight thousand people milling around, eating, drinking, calling to friends they hadn't seen since the last Spark. The town had more than quadrupled its size in a matter of hours. He dug for the phone in his jacket pocket—no signal. Of course. Audie was saying something, maybe something useful, maybe fun facts about the Rio Grande for all he could hear. He bent, and she yelled in his ear.

"There's probably an emergency tent. They might be able to break into the restaurant."

He straightened to his full height and wished it were higher. Scanning between moving shapes in the dimness, the names of distant booths were unreadable. Plus, the dancing glimmer from torches on the perimeter of the square cast crazy shadows on everything it touched. He clenched his teeth and grabbed Audie's hand, towing her into the pack. She was shaking already.

He had to get her out of there, but first, Marshall. And they needed to find the sheriff before Rick Metcalfe got away with murder.

Again.

An announcement boomed from unseen speakers, telling the

crowd to gather—the countdown was beginning. The horde swarmed around them, and Jude was a salmon swimming upstream as he fought for the path of least resistance. There wasn't one. They were pushed and carried along with the wave, straight toward the bonfire.

"Jude?"

Oh no.

Her tone had shifted, broken, from a single minute before. Another troupe of merrymakers smashed into them, and her fingers slid from his grasp.

"Audie!" The petite figure melted into the multitude. "For crying out loud, let me through!"

Everybody around him must've been a lumberjack—broad and tall and determined to be near the main event. The great horde slowed. They'd reached the edge of the central ring.

"Audie!" He no longer cared who got elbowed. He made it a few people deep when his name came from behind, maybe to the left? About-face and bearing toward the pyre once more, curses came at him with every step.

He hit the rope marking the safety zone as Sheriff Carmichael handed a lit torch to JB Pelton, dressed in his best uniform. Audie was nowhere to be seen.

"Would you do us the honors, Deputy?" Both were beaming, the love from the audience feeding the civic importance of the moment.

Jude's head swiveled like an angry owl, and at last, he caught sight of her. It was not a good look—ghostly pale, the amber cast distorting her delicate features.

Looming over her was Rick Metcalfe, a kitchen knife gripped in a shadow at her side.

Rick stared straight at him, ignoring the surrounding mass as his hand wrapped around Audie's upper arm. Cheers redoubled as the first licks of flame traveled heavenward along the logs. She stood rigid, frozen. But her eyes darted between the fire and Jude.

He turned and, for once, saw what she saw. At the base of the structure, the blaze roaring to life mere feet away, a baseball bat rested amongst the cords of wood.

Son of a biscuit.

The murder weapon.

He paused only long enough to glance back at her. In that instant, her expression transformed from reasonable anxiety considering the butcher knife to a level of horror he'd never seen.

But he bet Ollie had.

Just once.

She knew what he was going to do.

"No!"

He was already running. He threw off his jacket—*does leather melt? not the moment to find out*—and hurdled the rope into the circle. Through the laughter and applause came alarmed shouts. The sheriff's hulking form lumbered toward him, spewing expletives. Jude slid to the bonfire like it was home plate and reached for the bat. Hands grabbed his shoulders as his fingers brushed past it. *No!* He shook himself free, lunging forward again and gripping it, then falling back to watch the flaming wood tumble over and around him.

CHAPTER 39

His name scorched her throat as she screamed it. She crunched into Rick Metcalfe's shin with her heel, tearing her arm free and stumbling over the safety cord. The sheriff and deputy hauled something—someone—away from the collapse. Volunteer firefighters flung a blanket over the three and rushed to quench the inferno spreading far beyond its original footprint. One caught her sleeve.

"Ma'am, you can't—"

"That's my husband!" She wriggled out of a grip hampered by massive gloves.

Carmichael swatted red-orange embers off his coat as he struggled to his feet.

"It's Rick!" She spun him, dazed, toward the crowd. "He's got a knife."

Then her knees hit the bricks beside the motionless man she'd married.

How could all of time fly by at the speed of light and the sound of a thousand tornadoes then drop to absolute nothingness?

"Jude?" The pulse that had thundered in her ears disappeared in a vacuum and her soul went with it. She floated above the scene, seeing only her own silhouette and Jude's sprawled form.

Bloody.

Broken.

Not again. Please, God, not again.

She watched herself angle his face into the light, her unmarred hands obscene against his soot-covered skin. His eyelids didn't twitch. Blood from a gash on his forehead coursed in a river through the ash. How many times? How many times would she have to suffer the trial and finish alone, bereft? A shell with no heart?

Not again.

She couldn't do it again.

Most holy apostle, St. Jude, patron of lost causes, in our most desperate hour, pray for us, intercede on behalf of your servant and namesake…

"JB!" The bellow above her shattered the vacuum, and the universe rushed at her through a tunnel. Rick stood where she'd left him, stunned at the turn of events. Renarde's young deputy tackled him, and the knife clattered across the pavers as the surrounding crowd scattered from the danger zone. Like an expert rodeo roper, JB Pelton sat on the man's back and twisted his wrists tight behind him.

Then the face in her hands moved and whatever heart she had left exploded.

Jude folded in half, choking through polluted lungs. She lifted his head onto her lap, clearing his airway, cradling him and rocking them both to the internal drums pounding between her ears. The mob buzzed with confusion, somebody shouting to give the firefighters more space to work. Then a hulking shape loomed over them.

"Will someone please tell me what in blazes just happened?"

She couldn't stop rocking. Jude coughed hard, wheezing to bring in enough air.

Between fits, he rolled to his side and kissed her hand.

The pieces of shattered heart quivered.

Dear God.

For the communion of saints, in all times and places, we thank you, Lord.

She put her hand against his back as he strained to sit up. As soon as he was stable, she flung her arms around him, inhaling his sooty hair, feeling the smoke rattle through his body.

Thank you. Thank you a million times.

The shadow of a bat fell across them. The sheriff may as well have been talking to himself. "And why am I holding this?"

"I'm okay, love." The hoarse—but coherent—whisper in her ear overrode the drums, and the angry tribe in her skull softened. She couldn't tell who was shaking. It didn't matter.

An EMT appeared. More coughs twisted Jude onto himself, but he nodded to her to answer the lawman's hanging question. She shifted enough to be heard.

"Rick killed Hunter Kane with that bat thirty years ago."

Jude recoiled as the tech shone a penlight into his pupils, and she turned away too. The scene around them had broken like a mosaic, tiles no longer connected to the whole. The flaming tepee was a bird's nest of charred logs, but the fire was under control. County police, there to help with festival crowds, dragged Metcalfe to his feet. One of them picked up the knife and called to Carmichael.

"Is she hurt? This thing has blood on it!"

Oh no. "Marshall Baden!"

Jude waved off the EMT as he moved on to the growing goose

egg at his forehead. "Get to the diner! I promise not to go anywhere."

JB yelled for his fellow responders to follow him, and the crew took to the less-populated side street that would land them behind the restaurant.

When were we there? Minutes ago? Hours? Marshall. The saints couldn't decide who was best for the situation, so she prayed for intercession from all of them.

The county officers pushed the confused crowd further from the smoldering pile, away from Rick Metcalfe, away from the Wests. Red droplets continued down Jude's temple as Audie brushed the bangs from the knot. Starting there, she worked her way along his body, searching for more damage. His shirt was torn and burnt at his right forearm. Pink flesh with blackened edges showed through the tear.

"I really am okay, love." Lifting her worrying hands, he ducked to make her look at him. "A little singed. That's all." He kissed her wedding ring. "I promise."

To Carmichael, still standing with the bat, he said, "Thank you, Sheriff."

"You're a lucky fool, Mr. West."

From the darkness to their left, Tom Powers emerged. A step behind, Brice's sagging shoulders rivaled those of Atlas.

"Owen?" The eldest son of Alice and Gordon blinked at odd intervals, but his grim expression was otherwise resolved. "My brother has something to tell us."

CHAPTER 40

Brice Powers, paler and more miserable than any human had a right to be, sniffled. *And he hadn't had a flaming pile of logs land on him.* Jude tried to clear the dam of ashes from of his throat. It didn't work.

"I'm so sorry," was all Brice could get out at first. The man somehow withered into his sixteen-year-old self. "I never meant for it to happen."

A hint of morning glories softened the air's acrid smell. Still sitting on the pavers, Audie rested her cheek against Jude's shoulder. He wrapped one arm around her.

Tom did the same to his little brother. "Just tell the truth. God already knows."

But Brice slipped away, slumping onto a wrought iron bench and holding his head like it was a bowling ball. "Cassie shouldn't have been seeing that boy. Hunter was no good for her, but she wouldn't listen. So Rick had an idea. We could scare him off. It'd be easy, and Cass wouldn't need to be involved." His unsteady breath took in too much smoky air. In solidarity, Jude joined him in another round of coughing.

"The night of the festival," he resumed, turning away a water bottle from Tom, "when Lionel went to see his girlfriend, Rick and

I snuck off from the bonfire. I called the Bells, told Faye I had my dad's truck and it ran out of gas up at Bluff Park. We knew they'd send Hunter because Travis had the flu.

"Rick hid in the woods, and Hunter comes in his car with a can of gas. We'd parked the truck in the shadows, but when he realized whose it was, he tried to leave. There was bad blood between them. I should've realized."

"What was the bad blood?" An entire family of frogs had taken residence in Jude's throat. Audie patted his chest.

"One story at a time, okay?" Carmichael said. "Brice, go on."

"Rick steps from the woods." He closed his eyes, reliving the moment when hopes for a normal life had been mangled into a horror story. "He's got my baseball bat with him. He'd been working with me on my game, and it was in his truck. He starts hitting the ground, the trees, whatever he can find, bearing down on Hunter and laughing. Hunter is backpedaling like crazy, trying to get away, but with us on one side and the cliff right behind him?

"Cassie...Cass appeared out of nowhere. Maybe she'd been with Hunter when Faye called. She knew Dad didn't let me drive alone yet. She comes up silent as anything, like she always did when she ran. Rick catches a glimpse of movement and brings the bat around in self-defense. He didn't actually hit her. She... she..."

The dam of tears finally broke. His fingers wrapped around the seat of the bench like it was a bucking bronco, and he pushed out the words while he still could. "We were right at the edge of the bluff, no rail like they've got there now. She lost her footing and just... disappeared."

Tom sank down beside him. How his legs held him up that long was anybody's guess.

"I was screaming her name, but it was too late. She'd landed on the first ledge, about thirty feet down, staring straight through us to the sky. Then I realized Rick wasn't next to me, and I turned around to see him take a swing at Hunter's head. One hit, that's all it took. He dropped faster than a stone." Brice shuddered like the bat had struck him instead.

"And then?"

"Rick went cool as ice. He said if I didn't calm down and shut my mouth, he'd say I killed Hunter. It was my bat. I'd called the Bells, lied about the truck. It was my sister I wanted Hunter away from. In my mind, he made sense.

"Once I quit yelling, he got all nice again, told me it would be okay. He knew where we could put them, where they could rest. I wasn't thinking straight. I wasn't thinking at all. I'm still not sure how he got her up off that ledge, but he took care of everything. I opened the hatch to his truck, but that's about all I could manage. We drove down to the woods behind the cemetery. He found an unlocked window at the church office and lifted the keys to the Clayburn mausoleum. We thought they'd never open it; everyone knew the family had died off." Another deep shudder. "We laid them in there so carefully. He even said a prayer."

"What about Hunter's car?"

"We went back to the park to get it. I drove Rick's truck over to the old Steckman place down Highway Z, and he drove the car. There's a pond that didn't get used much. Rick let the car roll in. We waited until it sank. Hustled to the bonfire and made it a minute before Lionel."

His entire being laid bare with the tale finally told, Cassie's younger brother melted like an ice cream in July. "How could I leave her like that? How did I let everyone—Mom, Dad, you," he wagged his head at Tom, incapable of meeting his expression, "go on not knowing? But Rick, Rick always said it was for the best. We'd ruin our lives otherwise. I was sixteen. What did I know?"

When Audie spoke, several faces turned like they'd either forgotten she was there or assumed the delicate fairy in their midst was too traumatized to be paying attention. *Considering the last twenty minutes? Possible.* But not because his Tinkerbell was delicate.

People, if you only knew.

"Why didn't the Bells say something to the police about you calling them?"

By the look on his face, that detail had never crossed Brice's mind. The sheriff said, "From what I hear, they were lying low back then. Faye was on probation from the pill business, the shop was on the brink of bankruptcy. They weren't likely to volunteer for a chat with law enforcement."

"So when Dillon Clayburn, the returning vet, was going to be buried in the mausoleum?"

"Everything fell apart," Brice groaned. "I was ready to tell—I was!—but Rick had a plan. Another plan. And like an idiot, I just kept following." Through clenched teeth, he said, "I said I'd take care of Cassie. I had to wrap her in that blanket, because she was nothing but bones now."

"And Rick moved Hunter?"

He nodded in answer.

An ambulance screamed past on Main, lights flashing, bound for the interstate. *Oh man.* The newspaper editor was about to become front-page news. *Speed's good, right? They wouldn't be rushing if it was too late?*

The sheriff followed the vehicle as the siren faded. "What does Marshall Baden have to do with any of this?"

"He saw Brice and Rick at the bluff," Audie said. Jude rubbed at her arm. With no more fire nor adrenaline, October's chill stabbed at his bones. She had to be freezing. He'd give her his jacket if he knew where he'd thrown it. "Marshall heard their plan to scare Hunter but didn't stick around long enough to see what happened."

To carry that question for thirty years, to wonder if he could've made a difference… "This must've been the one story he wanted to tell his whole life. But he had to get it right or the town would never forgive him. He never had the proof."

"Until we started unearthing bodies."

"Was he your midnight creeper? The one leaving the anonymous notes?"

"Must be. And tonight, we heard him trying to talk Rick into owning up to the truth. That's when Rick attacked him."

Carmichael shook his head. "You two are darn lucky you're not dead."

Audie's entire frame—right down to her gossamer wings—shivered, and Jude twisted toward him with a glare. "That wasn't necessary."

"Sorry." He studied the baseball bat. "This is evidence, huh? That's why you dove in there like an idiot?"

"That's a bit harsh." But Jude's brain, lungs, and burnt arm sided with the lawman.

Brice sighed. "It was my bat, covered with both our fingerprints. Rick's insurance policy, I guess."

A week's worth of old secrets and collective trauma and questions and confusion and turmoil began to fall from Owen Carmichael's mouth in an exquisite series of summarizing curses.

Once, I would've appreciated that.

Instead, Jude cut him off, mid-blaspheming, before Audie had a chance to react. "Sheriff."

The big man stopped, exasperation nearly popping the shiny metal star off his coat. He looked down at them, then at the Powers boys, then at the remnants of Renarde's Thirty-first Annual Cinders and Cider Festival. "Fine," he said at last. "Have it your way. But if I bust open my spleen and die from holding all this in, I'm telling JB to arrest you both for manslaughter."

CHAPTER 41

In the emergency room of Trinity Regional Hospital, Audie sat in a visitor's chair that rocked whenever she blinked too hard. The doctor tore a last strip of adhesive tape, aligned it with the free edge of the gauze pad, and pressed it onto Jude's arm. He withdrew a pace, studying the result like Cezanne. *Patch Work—a Still Life.* At least it matched the head wound now.

"How's it feel?"

Jude flexed the limb, lean muscles rippling along his bare chest and bicep. "The burn or the bandage?"

"Either. The tape will hurt more than the burn when you have to change it."

"Great." He moved the arm some more, and Audie saw him bite back a wince. But the gauze stayed in place. "It's fine."

"Here's a prescription for antibiotic cream. You've got a second-degree burn, so keep it clean and covered. The bump on your head will go down in a day or two. No concussion. In the meantime, avoid bringing flaming pyres down onto yourself, yes?"

That had been difficult to explain. Yet the special breed that makes up an ER staff had pressed forward, unperturbed.

"Aye, aye, doc," he saluted. The man's white coat breezed

behind him as he disappeared out the door.

Still perched on the exam table, Jude turned, and those rich hazel eyes said he was bracing to rip off a whole different bandage.

"Aud, I'm really sorry."

The stupid chair made her seasick. She stood, stepping to the rear of the space and studying the informational posters hanging in the corner.

"Nope. It's my fault." Did that come out casual enough? Huh, based on these PSAs, the county had an intriguing combination of health concerns. "I spotted the bat in the flames, and I couldn't stop staring at the blasted thing. Like being hypnotized by a train wreck."

"A knife-wielding lunatic may have been influencing your thinking just then." In her peripheral vision, he brushed bangs away from the covered knot. Great—a better line of sight to stare holes of marrow-deep concern straight into her soul.

"Rick never scared me."

But a collapsing inferno, you in the middle?

This room needed windows; she couldn't breathe. She hadn't had a full breath in hours. She inspected the floor, her bag, anything but that tan skin and that black hair and those battered arms that would do anything—anything—for her.

Because he knew. Rick wasn't the problem.

History repeating itself was.

Jude hopped from the table. She only half-turned as he neared with his hands open to her. She shook her head; he didn't budge.

A man more stubborn than me—Dad would've been impressed. She finally allowed the embrace, and he folded her into his chest.

"Never again, boss," he whispered, still raspy. "I promise."

The endorphins took twice as long to kick in as they should have, what with a traffic jam of conflicting emotions blocking the way. But gradually, the night's horrors began to shuffle to their compartments, curtains closing, drawers shutting them out of sight for now. Her finger rose to trace the pointer of the compass tattooed on his shoulder, the first of his art. He smelled like smoke and antiseptic. But he was warm, and his heart beat beneath her ear. All the tension she'd been carrying dropped away the longer she listened.

"Hey, don't you two have a camper for that?" Owen Carmichael smirked in the doorway.

Jude didn't let her step away. "How's Marshall?"

"He's going to make it. I talked to the doc after his surgery. Had a lacerated intestine. Getting thrown in that freezer and slowing the blood loss saved his life."

"I think that was a happy accident."

"Ain't that the truth?" The sheriff adjusted his duty belt. "If I do this job for fifty years, I hope I never have another case like this. How did Rick and Brice hold onto that secret for all this time? And Cassie and Hunter, hidden right in the center of town? Makes me wonder what else is in those crypts."

"Not me. I'd like to go back to assuming all occupants are listed on the tombstones."

The sheriff's brow wrinkled. "Are you two okay? That arm going to be all right?"

Jude stretched out the limb, proving it still worked. "Just a flesh wound, as they say."

"We've done all the damage we can do here, and then some. We'll leave Renarde in your capable hands."

"Does that mean you solved your family-tree mystery?"

"As much as any puzzle so muddied by time can be." Bob was in for a thought-provoking conversation. "We'll give our client the hard facts, fleshed out with the most complete story those facts tell."

"It's a clumsy recipe." Of course her personal chef would go for the kitchen analogy. "Take every crumb of data and measure in a healthy dose of informed conjecture. Then stir in all knowledge of the human psyche."

"Sounds a little like my line of work." Carmichael scratched at his chin. "Also sounds like a perfect way for a couple of civilians to wind up in trouble if they get ahead of themselves."

Jude raised his hand, a Boy Scout again. "I solemnly swear we'll be on our best behavior, sir."

"I doubt that." He snapped his fingers. "I almost forgot. Now that he's residing in my jail cell with Angel Faust as a neighbor, Rick is sharing a few things."

"How helpful."

"The bad blood between him and Hunter? Rick and his buddies were alpha male jocks. They picked on anyone who wasn't, and Hunter Kane was a perfect target. The night of the state championship party, Rick's truck battery died. Hunter comes to give it a jump, but Rick and the crew are drunker than skunks. Rick gets to bullying him real bad and finally goes after him physically. Hunter, who's half his size, yanks open the pickup's door like a shield. The pride of Renarde High smacks into it hard and twists his knee, tearing his ACL. Boom—end of the line for his athletic career, hours after winning the big trophy."

"And so young and stupid becomes young and murderous."

"Yeah. Anyway, I'm serious about you two staying out of trouble, okay?" He departed into the hall, calling over his shoulder, "But whenever you happen to be passing through, stop by the station. Deputy Pelton could use the entertainment."

Jude's shirt hung beside a picture of lung damage caused by

smoking. *How fitting.* She helped him slip it on, examining the burnt oval in the fabric at his right forearm. "You're going to have a scar."

He shrugged and reached for the buttons. "Not my first."

"Will this be the beginning of more art?"

He cocked his head down at her. "I thought you said no more ink."

"I said you didn't *need* any more ink, not that you couldn't get more if you wanted it. I'm not your mother."

"Thank God for that." He poked at the hole, under which the bandage lay stark white. "Maybe it'll heal into something interesting. A Scooby-Doo face. Or demon eyes."

The dichotomy of my husband, ladies and gentlemen. "Try for a samurai mask. It'd suit you, my fearless warrior."

With his discharge papers in hand, she and the injured hero headed for the checkout desk. A wiry, black-clad child in the next room from theirs squirmed as a tech laid purple wrappings around a fresh leg cast. Batman may be down, but he was going in style. The waiting area held a solitary ten-year-old, playing on a tablet and still wearing her Wonder Woman costume over a heavy sweatshirt and tights. Baby brother's accident had not been an ideal ending for the Justice League's evening.

Jude signed a half-million forms at the counter, and they were free. Emerging into the autumn night, Audie pulled her coat tighter. Under a halogen lamp, he checked his watch.

"One a.m. Halloween is over."

"All Saints' Day."

"That's fitting for us, isn't it?"

"Because we're surrounded by dead people?"

"Yes." His laugh rang clear and bright and vibrant, and Audie said her thousandth prayer of thanksgiving since 6:30. "Also because we spend *our* life giving theirs back to the living."

"Such poetic waxing, Mr. West." She slipped her hand through the crook of his elbow. At least the leather jacket had escaped unscathed from the insanity. "I'm glad you see it like that, because tomorrow—later today, I guess—we move on."

"Great. Renarde has not been good for our insurance premiums."

"Let's hope Belsever is less painful."

"Is that a town or a surname?" He fished the keys from his jeans pocket.

"I can drive, you know."

"I'm not an invalid, you know." He unlocked the Jeep as they neared. It flashed its amber lights, happy to see them. "So, Belsever?"

"A town, about an hour from here. This is the vanishing third-great-granduncle we need to find so Janet Barkley can sell some old family property."

"Oh right. Well, this case gave us attempted vehicular homicide and a spectacular impression of the bonfire of the vanities. Janet's third-great-granduncle can't possibly top that." When she didn't answer, he slowed his stride. "Right?"

"Of course, dear," she said too fast.

But none of this week had been expected either, had it? A normal job to help a client had not only gone off the rails, but around, over, and through them.

No warning signal, no red-and-white crossing bar at the train tracks. Just an out-of-control engine barreling into them, leaving bits too small to grasp.

Clutching to each other.

Maybe if it had been the first train ever to run her down—

maybe that would be one thing. If it had caught only her and not the spouse now wondering what demons he needed to prepare for next, perhaps her gut wouldn't be knotting as badly as it was.

Maybe then she'd have hope of remembering how to sleep.

But in her mind, every piece of firewood collapsed onto him in an infinite loop, double-exposed against another reel seventeen years older.

One where she didn't walk out of the hospital to laughter and relief and plans for tomorrow.

Where the walk had been as a widow, not a wife.

I will not pass through those gates again.

He wouldn't be alone, donning armor, bracing for a fight. Things needed to change, starting with her.

Beside the Jeep, she waited while the knight she'd never expected to need opened her door as usual. She kissed his cheek before climbing into the cab.

I will not pass that way again.

She gave him her own patented smile. He saw through it, of course, but a girl can try.

"You're right, love. We'll be together. What can possibly go wrong?"

Dear Reader,

Thank you for coming along on this, the first of Jude and Audie West's adventures. To have their story enter the world means almost everything to me.

But you, my dear Reader, mean far more.

I am humbled that you gifted this story with some of your precious reading time. If you'd like to share your thoughts on the book with others, you can do so on Amazon. Your review is worth thousands of my words. I greatly appreciate your support.

To always be the first to know about upcoming books and other tidbits from me, please don't forget to sign up for my newsletter at www.LaurieAlberswerth.com. I look forward to sharing exploits with you, whether they are the Wests', my own, or those of the critters outside my office window.

Well, all but the deer. They ate my hyacinths. Until I receive a formal apology and reparations, we are not on speaking terms.

Your partner in all things murdery,

Laurie

This book is just the first of the mysteries
to plague poor Audie and Jude.
(It's their own fault for signing up
to live in a mystery series.)

Other works by Laurie Alberswerth will be
available soon. The series is best enjoyed
in the following order:

Bones & Bloodlines

Coming soon

Grain & Gravestones

Kin & Curses

Books 4 & 5: in the works!

Now that you've read *Bones & Bloodlines*, want to see how the Renarde in your head compares to the one in Laurie's? Head over to **www.LaurieAlberswerth.com** for a FREE download of the Wests' trusty binder!

About the Author

Laurie Alberswerth was certain "ENG" stood for English, not Engineering, when she checked the box for a college major. Funny story. Yet somehow, the writing bug survived four years of heat transfer and machine design, followed by a two-decade career as a Mechanical Stress Analyst.

That bug, like the cockroach, could survive a nuclear war.

A St. Louis native, the days and nights spent at Missouri state parks were fuel to the campfire when setting Jude and Audie West on their mystery-solving journey. And who knew the family-tree workbook purchased for her husband on their first anniversary (what else does one do for a "paper" gift?) would lead to so much time spent in libraries and courthouses, fighting with more microfilm than all the spies at MI6?

Laurie's own heritage—Lithuanian, Slovakian, and German—is a source of deep-rooted traditions and soul-satisfying (if not heart-healthy) food. She may or may not have two great-great-grandmothers who may or may not have independently hidden the body of a husband in the dirt floor of a basement.

But it's okay. They were bad guys.

Made in the USA
Monee, IL
30 September 2023